T0150072

PENGUIN BOOKS

LIES THAT BLIND

Elizabeth Smith Alexander was born in St Andrews, Scotland in 1954, although her family moved to England a few years later. Her earliest memories include producing a newspaper with the John Bull printing set she was given one Christmas. She wrote and directed her first play, Osiris, at age 16, performed to an audience of parents, teachers, and pupils by the Lower Fifth Drama Society at her school in Bolton, Lancashire. Early on in her writing career, Liz wrote several short stories featuring 'The Dover Street Sleuth', Dixon Hawke for a D.C. Thomson newspaper in Scotland. Several of her (undoubtedly cringe-worthy) teenage poems were published in *An Anthology of Verse*.

Liz combined several decades as a freelance journalist writing for UK magazines and newspapers ranging from British Airway's *Business Life* and the *Daily Mail*, to *Marie Claire* and *Supply Chain Management* magazine, with a brief stint as a presenter/reporter for various radio stations and television channels, including the BBC. In 2001 she moved to the United States where she earned her master's degree and PhD in educational psychology from The University of Texas at Austin.

She has written and co-authored 17 internationally published, award-winning non-fiction books that have been translated into more than 20 languages.

In 2017, Liz relocated to Malaysia. She lives in Tanjung Bungah, Pulau Pinang where she was inspired to embark on one of the few forms of writing left for her to tackle: the novel.

Lies That Blind

A Novel of
Late 18ᵗʰ Century Penang

Inspired by True Events

E.S. Alexander

PENGUIN BOOKS

An imprint of Penguin Random House

PENGUIN BOOKS

USA | Canada | UK | Ireland | Australia
New Zealand | India | South Africa | China | Southeast Asia

Penguin Books is part of the Penguin Random House group of companies
whose addresses can be found at global.penguinrandomhouse.com

Published by Penguin Random House SEA Pte Ltd
9, Changi South Street 3, Level 08-01,
Singapore 486361

First published in Penguin Books by Penguin Random House SEA 2021

This is a work of fiction. Names, characters, places and incidents are either the
product of the author's imagination or are used fictitiously, and any resemblance
to any actual person, living or dead, events or locales is entirely coincidental.

ISBN 9789814954426

Typeset in Adobe Garamond Pro by MAP Systems, Bangalore, India

www.penguin.sg

Extract from a letter written by Captain Francis Light (1740-1794) to his friend George Doughty, received in England on 24 December 1793, ten months before Light's death:

*'History shows no examples of the
first adventurers making fortunes,
It is sufficient that hereafter they are spoken of.'*

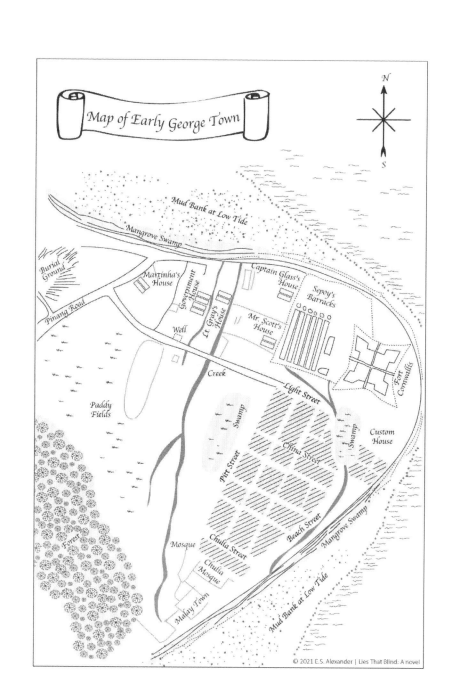

Map of Early George Town

N

S

Mud Bank at Low Tide

Mangrove Swamp

Burial Ground

Martinha's House

Captain Glass's House

Government House

Sepoy's Barracks

Pinang Road

Lt Gray's House

Mr. Scott's House

Well

Fort Cornwallis

Creek

Light Street

Paddy Fields

Swamp

Custom House

Pitt Street

China Street

Swamp

Beach Street

Mangrove Swamp

Forest

Chulia Street

Mosque

Chulia Mosque

Malay Town

Mud Bank at Low Tide

© 2021 E.S. Alexander | Lies That Blind: A novel

Contents

Chapter 1

Eclipsed

I always imagined that Dalrymple, in a previous life, had been an overseer during the construction of the Cheops pyramid. Every day he peered down on us from his elevated perch, his gaze like a lighthouse beacon. Yet it was not the whip we feared from him, but something more pernicious. We, the junior writers under his authority, would frequently jolt awake in the small hours, drenched in sweat. Not from fever, although disease was ever-present, but from nightmares of having made the slightest error in our work; then we would know the sting of his opprobrium. After two years of longing to be anywhere but here, doing anything but this, I thought I had become inured to the undertow of despair that had shipwrecked my soul. What I had not imagined was what would happen when Father made his biennial visit to check on his Indian investments which, as his only son and heir, included me.

I squinted at the pile of papers that continued to menace me: records of opium trades and intelligence extracted from the captains' logs, all of it feeding the voracious maw of my employer, the East India Company. My eyes blurred, not only from being mired in this dust moted monotony, but because of the fledgling tears that bubbled up from a deep well of frustration. Two nights ago, just before he departed for London, Father had made it clear how he intended my life to unfold. When banished here two years ago at the age of seventeen, I had believed that with enough administrative experience I would return to England to join the family firm. Now, Father had other ideas.

At first, I had half-listened to his usual complaints: I had been *such* a disappointment to him and Mother, although thank God I had *some* brains so was not the *complete* imbecile he had once feared. Father had heard—through the grapevines binding Calcutta to London— that I had not applied myself sufficiently and Dalrymple had gleefully confirmed that, once Father arrived here. Which was *unacceptable*, given the considerable trouble and expense to which Father had gone to secure this much-coveted appointment for me.

I only became suspicious as he rambled on about how, after forty years of service, the company would pay me three-quarters of my salary in retirement and full pay if I completed half a century's toil. Of course, such pensions represented no great generosity on John Company's part since over half the people who worked for them in India died long before that many years could be accumulated. If they did not perish from cholera, dysentery, or any number of other fevers common to the region, I was convinced boredom swept most clerks like me to an early grave. I had never intended to stay here *that long*.

When Father mentioned his good friend, Warren Hastings, I naively thought he merely intended to discuss the man's impeachment trial taking place in the House of Commons, during which Mr Edmund Burke had needed four whole days of oration to cover all the charges of corruption and mismanagement being levelled against the former Governor-General.

That would have been the perfect opportunity to voice my concerns about the house of cards I believed would soon teeter due to John Company officials' misguided policies that had had disastrous consequences: the famine that had caused ten million Indians to die from starvation; the subsequent loss of tax revenues; the precipitous fall in the value of stock that had led to uncertainty over whether the exorbitant government loan the company had received would ever be repaid, or if it would go bankrupt. It had been for these and other reasons that the Honourable Company's ambitions had needed to be reined in and why, when Lord Charles Cornwallis succeeded Warren Hastings as Governor-General, he did so as the representative of His Majesty, subject to Parliamentary discretion, *not* the East India Company's Board of Directors in London as had been the case with his predecessor. A state of affairs that sorely aggrieved Father, who had spent considerable sums of money underwriting all those pocket borough seats for his cronies who, as Members of Parliament, had been bought to help him unshackle the restraints the government now imposed upon his golden goose, the EIC.

We never got to talk about any of this, however. Father brought up Hastings only to point out that he had begun his career as a humble clerk in Calcutta. Hence, the Honourable Percival Lloyd—recipient of considerable dividends, which were dependant on the EIC's unhindered success—wanted to know: How did I, James Lloyd, Esquire, plan to emulate Hastings' steady rise and one day become Governor-General of India myself?

By the age of 25, Warren Hastings had come to the attention of the infamous Robert Clive. A year later he was made an ambassador of sorts in Bengal's capital, Murshidabad. Three years after that, he had earned a seat on the Calcutta Council. My father, as much as he loved his friends, never let anything get in the way of his fierce ambition. He wanted to see me achieve an even quicker trajectory so this dilly-dallying had darned well better stop! I had six months in which to pull myself together and start impressing those who mattered the most; Dalrymple would be a good start. Father's 'or else' hung between us like a miscreant dropped from the scaffold but not yet dead.

I snapped back to the present when my right wrist began to cramp. Yet I dared not rest and risk Dalrymple berate me yet again for laziness. I moved my hand by rote so that our cruel overseer would think that I was working, although my mind remained rooted in the past.

A cheeky young kitchen maid had once been employed at our Buckinghamshire manor house around the time that Mother's

German-designed stove had been newly installed. While berating the girl for her indolence in not maintaining the object's once-gleaming exterior, my mother had suggested she apply more 'elbow grease'. To this, the foolish servant had replied that if elbow grease was going to make her job easier, why didn't the mistress give her the money to buy some? A good beating later, the girl was dismissed and shown the door. As a child, I had also misunderstood my mother's meaning, for this was not some miracle substance that could be purchased but what my father now demanded of me until my dying day: hard labour. But with pen and ink rather than a scrubbing brush.

I should have told the old man that I considered my work to be the most soulless, dismal activity outside the trials of Sisyphus. Yet, had I done so, his already low opinion of me would have sunk ever deeper and his financial support disappeared as quickly as that kitchen girl's position. Father's final words ignited the guilt which he, more than anyone else, knew how to stoke: His health was not good—his *blasted gout* had been playing up again, among his many other ailments— and he wished to be convinced that I was not *totally* worthless, before he passed away and left his fortune to me. I knew I would die here before that happened—if not from fever or melancholia, then by my own hand.

Dalrymple's voice disrupted these dark thoughts when he announced the break for lunch, his final words drowned out by a near-deafening scrape of chair legs against the wooden floor. Someone would have needed to shout 'Fire!' to have cleared the room as quickly. I followed the throng, casting my eyes about for a companion with whom I might share the outstanding *burra-khana* that awaited us in the dining hall. Then I saw him in the corridor and my spirits lifted, as if hoisted up to the crow's nest of a ship after months of being imprisoned in the cargo hold. I relished not only this two-hour respite from slavery, but the excellent conversation I might have with a man whose life had always been far more interesting than my own, and from whom I might seek solace.

The illustrious company surgeon and botanist, Dr William Roxburgh, had appeared like a wish-fulfilling genie.

Chapter 2

Illumined

We entered the dining hall bustling with company officials and the white-attired, voluptuously moustached Bengalis who attended to our every need. Even Lord Cornwallis' reputation as a man determined to root out wastefulness had not put an end to the extravagance of company mealtimes. It would have required the quelling of a small revolution, more successfully than he had managed in the American colonies, for the new Governor-General to achieve such a victory. Not least because the delicacies freely offered were as fine as anything King George might have tasted. Tired of thinking, I told Roxburgh to go ahead and order meals for the both of us while I settled myself in my chair and tried to look cheerful.

'We have much tae tittle tattle aboot,' announced Roxburgh after he had selected a platter of lamb, breasts of peacock, and cumin-infused rice, to be followed by Persian delicacies. 'But first, young Jim, let's whet oor whiskers wi' a glass or two of India's finest arrack.' Since I had no whiskers to whet—my inability to sprout facial hair being a great embarrassment at the age of nineteen—I thought this a strange expression.

Arrack, to me, was anything but a fine drink—being liquor fermented from the juice of coconut palm—and too strong a spirit for my constitution. I had often been accused of being a belligerent drunk, using alcohol to fire up the confidence that enables the unsayable to be said. The taste of arrack, which I did not like, made it easy enough to resist any such temptation on this occasion. But given my relief at being with someone as admired across all three company presidencies as Dr William Roxburgh, I agreed to partake of half a glass.

When our food arrived, we lapsed into silence for a while. The only sound between us occurred when my friend asked me to pass him more meat. I remembered that, the last I had seen of him, Roxburgh was being sent to Samulcottah, a small garrison town to the north of Madras, to oversee the company's botanic gardens. As I moved my food around my plate, tasting very little of it, I asked Roxburgh how he was enjoying his new position. Between mouthfuls, he told me that he had petitioned his benefactor, Madras' most well-connected and influential independent trader, Andrew Ross, to help him lease land in Coranda to develop an experimental farm on which to grow vegetables and grains. Such production, Roxburgh said, would help to sustain the poor, who were in constant need of food, as well as allow him to conduct further experiments on commercially useful crops. It delighted me to hear that my friend planned to do more than simply make more money for men already wealthy beyond the desires of Croesus.

As our attendants descended once more on our table to remove the empty dishes, Roxburgh sat back in his chair with hands resting on a stomach more pronounced than what I remembered from the last time I had seen him and asked, 'And what of yersel', young Jim? Ye dinnae look sae happy, I have tae say.' Although I had thought we had concluded the main course, my friend snapped his fingers and requested the waiter to bring a clean plate and another serving of breast of peacock. Upon its prompt arrival he insisted that I alone devour it. 'You're looking awfy thin tae me.' I smiled at my recollection of our first meeting, when Roxburgh's strong Ayrshire accent, together with his tendency to pepper speech with Scottish phrases as incomprehensible as Chinese, had befuddled me.

William Roxburgh and I had become acquainted not long after my arrival in Calcutta. Looking for something interesting to distract myself during an especially dreary week, I had slipped into a talk he had been giving to the factors and learned why this Scottish surgeon concerned himself with seeds and soils rather than torn skin and sutures. Roxburgh's time at Edinburgh University had led him to discover the many ways in which agricultural production could be increased. Now a botanist of repute, Roxburgh advised the company on how to successfully identify different qualities of cotton, dyes, and spices, so that it might extract the greatest profit from each trade. My friend had soon come to the attention of Andrew Ross, who enthusiastically took Roxburgh under his wing.

While I half-heartedly ate the peacock breast, I related to Roxburgh most of the conversation—although, more accurately, Father's monologue—that had arrested me the previous evening. The only part I chose to omit was how my parents expected me to become Governor-General of India one day; the audaciousness of that idea embarrassed me.

'So, climbing up the greasy pole of John Company hierarchy disnae sound as if it suits ye, Jimmy. What fires up yer passion, then?' my friend asked as he crunched his way through a bowl of pistachios.

As breathless as a besotted suitor I gushed, 'I desire to be a journalist, having long admired James Boswell whose *The Journal of a Tour to the Hebrides with Samuel Johnson* has been published to great acclaim. I purchased a copy before leaving London and it is very much the kind of intimate conversation with a subject of great interest that I would like to write.' I glanced shyly at my friend, who had a strange look on his face. 'What is it?'

Roxburgh continued to stare at me as if puzzled by my admission.

'Did I say something wrong?' I asked.

My friend lubricated his larynx with more arrack before speaking. 'I dinnae know much aboot Boswell's work—although his private life disnae impress me and he comes across as a very gossipy, indiscreet sort—but I gather many of today's *journalists* are dubious fellows.'

'Really? What makes you say that?'

'The last time I was in London a friend of mine invited me tae lunch at The Turks Head Inn in Soho. Those in the literary establishment know it simply as The Club. One of the guests in attendance was a gentleman called Mr John Nichols.'

'I have heard of him,' I interjected. 'He is the editor of the prestigious *The Gentleman's Magazine,* a man much admired in literary circles.'

'Aye, well,' began Roxburgh. 'Mr Nichols told this rather amusing story pertaining to the Americans' General George Washington. He had earlier been at pains tae point out how many blackguard writers loiter around coffee shops and alehouses picking up pieces of tittle-tattle that they present in a credible way to a gullible public. The ease of which is all the greater when tales originate from abroad. That acclaimed editor had, surprisingly, very little good tae say about most men who pursue journalism so ye might not wish tae risk yer reputation by entering such a murky occupation, young Jim.'

My curiosity piqued as to what gossip might have been shared about General Washington, I ignored Roxburgh's disdain for journalism and asked, 'What prompted such a conversation about the Americans' Commander-in-Chief?'

My Scottish companion leaned closer. 'One young chappie recently presented the editor with a story that Mr Nichols described as mere propaganda, not journalism, with his article being full of half-truths and outright deceptions.'

'What does that mean, "propaganda"?' I asked.

'Aye, I had not heard that word before myself, but Mr Nicols explained it as a means of propagating an overly favourable impression of one's subject without any attempt at balance or truth. He drew oor attention to an essay written some thirty years ago by Dr Johnson entitled *Of the Duty of a Journalist,* in which the great man pointed oot the importance of establishing facts before—as he put it, "slaughtering armies without battles, and conquering countries without invasions".'

My friend shook his head and chuckled, then warmed his throat with another swig of arrack. 'But let me test *you* as Mr Nichols did oor party that day.'

Convinced I could best any challenge, I said confidently, 'Go ahead.'

'There appeared an article in the April 1783 issue of the *Rambler's Magazine* entitled "A remarkable discovery; or, Mrs General

Washington, displayed in proper articles", the writer claiming that the former Commander-in-Chief of the Continental Army, George Washington, was really a woman. The accompanying illustration showed Washington attired in a dress,' began Roxburgh. 'This assertion was apparently supported by an admission made by General Washington's late wife, Martha, and reported in the *Pennsylvania Gazette* some months earlier.'

My face must have given away my shock at this revelation, but Roxburgh only smiled and carried on.

'Let us further examine the veracity of that report,' he began. 'According to Mr Nichols, a copy of the *Whitehall Evening Post* of the 25th January 1783, reported that Mrs Martha Washington, before dying, confessed to her chaplain that she had long known of her husband's true sex but had agreed to the deception because of "motives of the most refined friendship". The writer mentioned having gathered this information from the *Dublin Register* which, in turn, received the news from an issue of the aforementioned *Pennsylvania Gazette* printed on 11th November the previous year. What, then, would be your verdict on General Washington's true nature, young Jim?' my friend asked.

I admitted that as improbable as it seemed there appeared to be considerable proof, since three separate newspapers had reported the story, that the former leader of the Continental Army was indeed a woman in disguise. The written word, so confidently presented, was surely sacrosanct. And how many times had we heard stories of women disguising themselves as men to enjoy the freedom of adventure? Women like Hannah Snell, who had later made her name and a living on the stage, recounting the years she had pretended to be a soldier then sailing to Mauritius as a marine with Admiral Boscawen's fleet, never once discovered.

'Then you are convinced?'

With a hesitant nod, suspecting a trick, I mumbled, 'Yes.'

'Yet the story about General Washington being a woman is false,' declared Roxburgh, rather too smugly for my liking. 'For Mrs Martha Washington still lives and never made such pronouncements. According to Mr Nichols, the *Pennsylvania Gazette* appeared on November 6th and 13th that year, not November 11th, and there is no such publication as the *Dublin Register*.'

I slumped back in my chair, annoyed at not having asserted my misgivings no matter how many newspapers had repeated this untrue tale.

'Most journalists today appear tae be an unscrupulous lot who would sell their grandmothers for a juicy story and I am surprised you, young Jim, would wish to be counted among them,' said Roxburgh, wiping his mouth and throwing the cotton napkin on the table, as if in disgust. Roxburgh's frequent use of the word 'young' in front of my name sounded condemnatory.

'But surely one should not judge a group based on few bad characters?' I said, my voiced raised such that several nearby diners turned to look at us. My cheeks aflame, perhaps because of the arrack I had been sipping, I nevertheless lowered my tone. 'Is there not merit in infiltrating such an occupation as journalism in order to improve the quality of the stories being written?'

I worried that my friend now thought less of me, not least when he paused, looked up to the heavens as if in prayer and said, '*Sepius nefas, numquam in nuto.*'

I reached into my store of rusty, schoolboy Latin for the translation: *Often mistaken, never in doubt.*

'But yours is a fair rebuttal,' conceded Roxburgh in response to my blushes. 'Except, young Jim, ye appear to be ignoring the reality of your circumstances.'

My illustrious friend then moved on from the subject of journalism, presumably to spare me further discomfort. I half-listened as he related some of the changes that Lord Cornwallis had implemented to the workings of the EIC but snapped back to attention when he asked if I had maintained my interest in the history of the Mughal Empire.

'Yes,' I responded, somewhat petulantly. 'For India's former rulers at least had the humanity to protect the people here against the famines that have long been their common experience.'

Perhaps aware of my sour mood, Roxburgh leaned across the table and gave me a kindly smile. Whether he saw himself in the role of a caring father or an older brother—neither of which I had experienced—he said, 'Allow me to explain what I meant earlier because I do have your best interests at heart, Jim, even if what I said appeared condemnatory.'

I mumbled my assent.

'Answer me this: Are you a man of independent means who can carve his own path without the support of others, namely yer faither?'

'No.'

'Have you come to the attention of a wealthy benefactor, as has been my case with Mr Andrew Ross?'

'No.'

'Do you have an established body of work—a written portfolio, perhaps—with which tae attract such a benefactor?'

I slumped in my chair like a sagging pudding that had been removed too early from the oven. 'No.'

My Scottish friend sighed and looked at me with pity. 'In that case, yer options appear limited at the moment, dear Jim. As fer me, I have been able tae progress mah own interests through the magnanimity of someone with deeper pockets by demonstrating to Mr Ross how we might *both* profit from my ideas. Why else would he underwrite my experimental farm unless he could see significant advantage tae him and his business?'

I shrugged my shoulders, accepting the truth of this. 'So, where does that leave me?' I asked, forlornly.

Roxburgh extended an arm across the table and patted me on the hand in the manner of a father who, having refused the wishes of a young boy, now felt bad about it. 'I would advise ye to wait a few more years and heed your faither's advice. Make influential connections here, then look for ways in which tae find financial support for your writing aspirations. Perhaps someone ye meet will wish their biography tae be written.' He raised his glass as if toasting that thought. 'Maybe Lord Cornwallis whose unfortunate reputation has followed him from America will wish his story tae be cast in a more favourable light. He might welcome some positive propaganda.' At this, my friend gave a hearty laugh.

'But that could take years.' The whining in my voice appalled me.

'Have ye heard the expression the Buddhists espouse: 'The Middle Way'?'

'Yes,' I said.

'Well, that's what I urge ye to discover, young Jim. Be practical. There is no need to give up on yer dream of writing, but neither should ye overindulge yer fantasies by believing you can make a living from it given the present reality. D'ye understand what ahm saying?'

I did, of course. But I did not like it one little bit. He was telling me to be content where I was, toiling at work I hated, in a place from which I wished to escape every day. For someone whom I had imagined would cheer me up, Roxburgh's lecture only served to plunge me into a deeper melancholy.

'One further point to think on,' said my friend, rising from the table with an almost inaudible groan. 'It is easy enough to say you desire to be this or that in life, but a wise man first discovers what a particular position or role might entail beyond what he imagines it to be. Indeed, what it might require him to become.'

Thanking Roxburgh for his counsel and bidding him farewell, I dawdled back to the writers' room. As soon as this workday was over, I determined to drown myself in beer.

Chapter 3

Casting Light

'Drownin' yer sorrows, laddie?'

I raised my eyes from the bottom of the cloudy mug of Burton Ale I was cradling in this back-alley alehouse and looked up at the burly country trader—a man who had been entertaining a group of fellow seafarers for most of the evening, during which each seafarer had tried to out-boast the other with claims of profits and profiteering. This Scotsman sounded as if he had been away from his homeland for a greater number of years than Dr Roxburgh and was more easily understandable. Now seated alone he rose up and advanced towards me like a charging bull.

Eager to escape, I tried to wrestle myself free from the bench that had numbed my buttocks for too many hours. Like a shadow against a dark alley, the Scotsman loomed over me and placed a meaty hand on my shoulder. Forcing me back into my seat, he growled, 'Here, stay a while,' obviously expecting no argument. 'I've a mind for some company now that my friends have buggered off.' He thrust out his hand and introduced himself as Captain James Scott.

'Jim Lloyd,' I muttered in response.

Adorned like a native of Malaya, the captain wore a high-necked silk shirt and matching loose trousers over which was tied a knee-length sarong that held his *keris,* a wavy edged, curved dagger that could have sliced my belly open like a sacrificial lamb. His appearance was all the more unusual given the man's pale, freckled complexion, blue eyes, and the unruly mop of strawberry-blond hair that had come adrift from its black ribbon mooring and framed his liquor-worn face in wispy fronds. Earlier in the evening, I had seen the disdainful looks he had drawn from the East India Company officials seated nearby, who, like most who shared my employ, believed fervently in the superiority of white men and detested when their countrymen dressed like 'degenerate natives'. I had heard frequent complaints that these private traders were men of low morals who engaged in numerous malpractices. That did not stop my employer from benefiting from them as stalking horses, letting these men take the initial risks to find new markets that John Company would later swoop in and control once the trade proved viable.

My new drinking companion, I soon learned, was captain of *The Prince,* a 250-lasten ship with sixty crew and six cannons that sailed a circuitous route from Bengal down to the Coromandel Coast, over to Acheh and Junk Ceylon, through the Straits of Malacca and then up the eastern side of the Malay peninsula to Trengganu. Along the way, Scott said, he would typically convey piece goods and opium from India, trading them for tin and pepper and anything else with which he could make a sizeable profit. Occasionally, he told me, he even made his way to Canton.

I must have temporarily dozed off as he rambled on, only coming to when I heard him utter the phrase, 'those monopolizing Dutch bastards', and realised he had been talking about the loss of Tanjung Pinang, a vital trading port on Banten, an island to the south of Singapura, to the Hollanders in 1784. Our long-time enemies had left the British traders with nothing to buy, complained Scott, forcing him and his business partner to sail haphazardly around the Straits in search of new trading opportunities.

Concerned that my lack of interest might appear rude to a man I did not wish to get on the wrong side of, I asked, 'And did you find any?'

'Aye, we did that,' slurred Scott who, having already finished his drink, signalled for another. I shook my head at his silent question and raised my mug to show that it was still half full.

'But you're no seafaring lad, by the looks of ye,' proclaimed Scott. 'D'ye work for John Company?'

'Two years already, yet a lifetime still ahead,' I groaned, at which dismal recollection I downed the rest of my ale as if taking part in an East End drinking contest. After belching as delicately as I could, I added, 'As a junior writer.'

Scott shrugged away that uninteresting morsel then glugged down the frothy contents that only moments earlier had been placed in front of him. Slapping his left hand so hard on the table that our mugs appeared to jump in fright, he called out for two more. Then, turning back to me, he claimed that I had missed a great opportunity not to take to the seas as he had done from the age of seven when he had joined the Royal Navy.

As if this piece of information reminded him that he had been at sea for almost twice as long as I had been alive and could regale me all night with his many adventures, Scott chuckled and said, 'There was this one time while sailing in the Straits of Malacca that my ship was seized by the Hollanders who accused me of gunrunning and selling powder to the Selangor Malays, because Malacca's bastard Dutch governor had forbidden them to trade with the British.'

'And were you?' I asked, wide-eyed. 'Gunrunning?' I sat up straight in my seat to try and ease the pain in my back then, giving up at the effort, leaned forward again.

Scott looked at me as if I were a lunatic. 'Of course!' he guffawed. 'There's a hefty profit to be made buying condemned muskets from company stores and selling them to whichever local chiefs are currently at war with the Dutch. Good business for Francis and me and happy natives.' Scott barely took a breath before continuing, 'Now, as you can see for yersel', I'm not a man to scare easily but will admit to shitting myself that my captors were going to transport me to Batavia. Ye've no doubt heard the rumours about the VOC prison there?'

I shook my head, at which point the room began to lurch as if his stories had transported me on to his ship.

'That hell-hole is so overcrowded and disease-ridden my chances of heavenly judgment would have been greater than living to be tried by a Dutch court. Ye know what they do to their prisoners, Jim?'

Scott lowered his voice, prompting me to lean further over the table to better hear him, uncomfortably aware of the spilled stale beer that now seeped into my shirt.

The captain took out his keris and sweeping it unnervingly close to my nose given his inebriated state whispered, 'They employ Japanese mercenaries who can free a man's head from his neck with a single stroke. Otherwise, a prisoner might be broken on the wheel, hanged, scourged, and branded with the mark of the VOC, or at the very least whipped to within an inch of his life.'

'But you escaped,' I said, and in my mind's eye I saw myself at Scott's side as we battled our way out of the Dutch East India Company's Batavia headquarters, a sword in one hand and a musket in the other.

'Not exactly,' admitted Scott. 'The swine clapped me in irons in their guardroom at Malacca and fined me two thousand silver dollars for sailing in Dutch waters without a passport. But the charges of gunrunning were dropped, thanks to the intervention of a Dutch trading acquaintance of ours named Reinaert. So, I suppose not all of those bastards are bad.'

I lifted my mug and found to my surprise that it was empty, although I could not remember drinking the contents. 'Where will you venture to next?' I asked, wondering if I would ever see my bed this side of midnight.

'I sail to Puloo Penang the day after tomorrow, to meet with my business partner and check on my interests there,' my companion said, then went into a long explanation of the godowns he owned on the island, the additional land he might commandeer in readiness for the establishment of a village he intended to name James Town, and various other business activities that I gathered included banking and moneylending. 'Anna birthed a wee bastard last May and is hankering for me to come back to see the lad.'

'Ah,' I said, not sure how else to respond.

Silence enveloped us like fog rolling off the River Thames. Too much alcohol had befuddled my brain; it was time for me to leave. Once again, I attempted to rise but my companion leaned over, slapped me on both shoulders and almost winded me. 'It was my idea originally, to settle Penang.'

'That's one of the islands off the western coast of the Malay peninsula, isn't it?' I said. 'Looks a little like a sea-basking turtle on the map?'

'Aye. The Honourable Company needed a safe haven for their ships sailing from India to China and back, as well as a port for straits traders. I persuaded the powers-that-be that Penang would fit the bill and now Light and I—that's my business partner I mentioned earlier, Captain Francis Light—have pretty much got everything sewn up.'

'Sewn up? What does that mean?'

'It's a canny arrangement, I have to admit. Francis administers the island and I make the money. Scott & Company. Since Light, my *sleeping partner*—', at this James Scott made a great show of winking at me, '—holds sway over everything that goes on there without undue interference from government and its restrictive regulations, it wisnae long before we became the wealthiest trading house in Penang.'

I felt inclined to say that this sounded like an abuse of Captain Light's position as well as a conflict of interest but did not wish to provoke the big man seated opposite me. Then again, achieving such uncommon prosperity in the shortest amount of time had long been the reason why opportunists were drawn to the East. Especially those lacking in wits or talents. As Father had been fond of saying, 'A moderate share of attention and your being not quite an idiot are ample qualities for the attainment of riches in India.' I imagined the same applied on the island of Penang.

Nevertheless, James Scott did seem a clever and calculating sort of fellow. 'Did you not wish to govern Penang yourself given that *you* had first seen its value?' I asked.

'Ach no!' my drinking companion exclaimed, sending a fine spray of ale in my direction that I casually wiped off my cheeks with the back of my hand. 'I want to enjoy life, not give myself ulcers dealing with all that politicking. The correspondence Francis gets from the Sultan of Queda, the island's owner, wid drown ye sooner than a squall in the ocean. Seems to me it's worse than a jail term to be stuck behind a desk dealing with all that bloody paperwork and handling complaints from men too inept to manage their affairs properly.'

'But it suits your friend, Captain Light?'

Scott looked at me strangely and it was only later, reflecting on our conversation, that I determined he may have been debating whether or not to take me into his confidence concerning the steadfast ambitions of his business partner, Francis Light.

Chapter 4

Ignited

Although I had asked Scott to tell me more about his fellow country trader and business partner, I had no real interest in the answer. I merely hoped my companion would tire of telling stories and allow me to leave. My mother used to complain that my 'infernal questioning was enough to test the patience of a saint,' so I peppered Scott with those.

'Francis has always hankered after making his mark to ensure the name *Light* matters,' confided Scott.

'Why does he think otherwise?'

'Because it comes from his servant-girl mother not his country gentleman father, who of course could never marry. Although Francis was baptised, William Negus never gave his son his name.' Scott shook his head and went on, 'There is a lament we heard from a Dutchman in Batavia that Francis has never forgotten: 'One can have dinner with a man tonight and be present at his funeral tomorrow; the day after tomorrow it will be auction day for his goods, and two days later he will be forgotten'.'

'Your friend fears being forgotten?' At this I could not help but consider the men whom history remembers most for their infamous deeds, like the rapacious activities of 'Lord Vulture' Robert Clive. Perhaps one day, too, Charles Cornwallis, unless he was to make a resounding success of his time as Governor-General of India since many still thought of him as the man who had lost us the American colonies. Surely there were times when anonymity might be preferable to that kind of remembrance.

Yet this was not a topic to be debated with James Scott. The floodgates opened as he poured out the most intimate details of his friend's life. They had met as midshipmen on *HMS Arrogant* in 1761 while taking part in convoy duties between Portsmouth and Gibraltar to protect British trading ships from the marauding French. After the two were laid off in '63, they went their separate ways but stayed in touch. Light, six years older, sailed to India as a 'volunteer,' which indicated that he had high expectations of finding employment soon after arrival. That proved to be the case when he was taken on by a prestigious Madras trading firm, became their agent, and was sent to Acheh in northern Sumatra to cofound a factory on their behalf. But after some 'unfortunate dealings,' according to Scott, Light left to forge his own path. The two men later reconnected in Junk Ceylon, and by 1771 had set up in business together.

My interest piqued, I tentatively approached Scott's earlier hint. By now, the germ of an idea had taken root in my mind but shrivelled to nothing when I tried to cultivate it. 'Which firm did Light leave, and why?'

'Jourdain, Sulivan, & De Souza,' answered Scott, addressing only the first part of my question.

'Prestigious indeed,' I said, recalling that one of those partners, Laurence Sulivan, had risen from director to become Chairman of the East India Company across three terms.

Scott moved his upturned hands in a way that suggested weighing scales. 'Whether Francis left of his own accord or was pushed out after the failed Jiwa-Monckton affair is anyone's guess; he prefers not to speak of those days. But as I told him, it was better that a man such as he, who is more of the world than most Englishmen and can see a future scene of wealth and population under a jungle, should carve his own destiny.'

'Something unfortunate happened in Acheh?' I probed.

'Not directly. While there, Francis' reputation for business acumen and profitable deals came to the attention of Sultan Jiwa of Queda,' replied Scott.

I listened carefully to the unfolding story of how Light had tried to interest Jourdain & Co. in Sultan Jiwa's offer of a license to trade in Queda and the island of Penang, as well as to share in his monopolies in exchange for offensive military assistance. The sultan wanted help to reclaim plundered property and ships that a band of Bugis mercenaries had made off with after sacking the sultan's capital, Alor Setar. But despite repeated entreaties by Light to take advantage of this opportunity, his employers never responded to his letters.

I had been about to ask why Light would think an association of independent merchants with no military force of its own would wish to get embroiled in fights with piratical fiends, even if they could be convinced that an alliance with the Sultan of Queda would benefit their trade, when Scott continued. 'Undeterred, Francis approached Warren Hastings directly who at that time was the Governor of Madras. My friend sweetened the pot by telling him he sold opium to the Malays for eight hundred Spanish Dollars per chest. After which the Madras Council took the bait.' Scott chuckled and shook his head.

'Why is that amusing?' I said.

'Because, Jim, never in former years had opium been sold there for more than three hundred dollars.'

Emboldened by the ale that seemed to have replaced all other fluids in my body I said, 'So, your friend lied.'

Again, Scott mimicked a pair of scales with his hands. 'Francis will exaggerate a little if he thinks it will achieve a desired outcome.'

'Do I gather the negotiations with Sultan Jiwa did not end well?'

For the next half-hour I listened as Scott pored over the details. The aforementioned 'Monckton,' I learned, was the Honourable Edward Monckton, the EIC man whom the Company had chosen to lead the mission, even though he was a too young and inexperienced negotiator, according to Scott. It had angered both the Scotsman and his business partner that Light had not been chosen to represent the Company when dealing with Sultan Jiwa. That suggested to me—although, of course, I said nothing—that Calcutta did not trust Francis Light to handle the matter alone.

When the affair floundered, as both Scott and Light had known it would, blame for the failure was not levelled by the Madras Council at the negotiating nabob, Monckton, however, but at the feet of Francis Light. Here the Scotsman took a deep breath as if girding himself before reciting part of the related company note he appeared to know word for word: '*The persons employed by the concerned in that trade have, as it now appears, misled them by making specious representations in order to continue themselves in an employ lucrative in all probabilities to themselves, although ruinous to their employers.*' Scott slapped his hand across the table as if it were a serving wench's backside and grimaced at me.

I thought I now better understood Light's resentment at not having a name that would inure him against such an indictment. Light the country trader might have had a local reputation, achievements, and wealth far greater than that of the Honourable Edward Monckton, but as a mere country trader he was always going to be the scapegoat for the failed affair, irrespective of the lies he had told to instigate it.

As if readying himself for sleep, my companion slumped forwards on to the bench and cradled his arms over the sodden wood. His face darkened, as if the merriment of moments ago had been blighted by troubling thoughts. There is nothing worse than being in the company of a maudlin drunk. As much as I had been entertained by Scott's tales, it was time for me to find the bed I sorely craved. After rising only slightly, I reluctantly lowered myself again when I heard the Scotsman mumble, 'Be careful what ye wish for, lest it come true. Isn't that the saying?'

'Yes,' I replied, wondering what nuggets were to come from that.

'Aye, well, Francis gets to be called Superintendent of Penang, so I imagine he's happy enough, but my friend's got his self into a hell of a mess because of it.' James Scott looked intently at me with bloodshot eyes. 'Ye know, John Company only pays him a thousand rupees a month from which he has to cover many of the settlement's expenses. In order to smooth things over with the sultan while they wait for Bengal to confirm the terms of their agreement, my friend gave Sultan Abdullah—Jiwa's son and heir—some of his own arms and ammunition. For which he has never been compensated. It's a good thing Francis has got me to look after our financial investments. But he sorely needs an assistant otherwise he is likely to work his self into an early grave.'

'Well, I am sure he will find a suitable person soon,' I said. 'But I must get to bed, Captain Scott, otherwise I will be no good for work in the morning.' Once again I made an abortive attempt to rise, like an impeded jack-in-the-box.

As if in a world of his own, which did not surprise me given the barrel of ale the man must have drunk during the evening, Scott murmured, 'Light desires his name to be in the history books. And what a story that would be, if only he could find not only an assistant, but a suitable chronicler.'

I froze, like a marionette bent at the knees, then sat back down. Could this be the 'middle way' my wise friend, Dr Roxburgh, had urged me to find? To become the paid assistant of the new Superintendent of Penang while also honing my skills as his biographer?

My desire for sleep evaporated like a puddle in the Bengal heat. I remained with James Scott for a further two hours.

Chapter 5

False Impressions

Fort William, Calcutta, 19 December 1788.

Dearest Father,

I trust this letter finds you safely returned to London and the loving bosom of family. May the many complaints you have so stoically endured these past years be soon satisfactorily attended to by your physicians. We all desire that you live a long and healthy life.

Father, no sooner had your ship sailed back to England than I chanced upon a wealthy country trader named James Scott who informed me that his business partner, Captain Francis Light, needs an assistant on an island he is superintending on behalf of the Honourable Company, named Penang.

You may already be aware that Captain Light, representing company interests, took possession of this strategically-important trading post in August of '86. He is both highly thought of and influential. While Sir John Macpherson was acting Governor-General, he described Captain Light as 'a man of excellent character and good information who stands in the highest esteem with the Malay, Siamese, and Pegu chiefs.' That is proven by the fact that the good captain was conferred a title of nobility, 'Dewa Raja', by a Malay potentate some years ago.

From everything I have heard of him, Captain Light is a man of great merit. Acting as his assistant will afford me the opportunity to learn new skills and demonstrate my talents within a thriving trading settlement where I can really make my mark, rather than sitting in Calcutta mindlessly making copies of company minutes and records. I am convinced that under the good captain's tutelage I will be a greater asset to the Honourable Company and to you than remaining in my current position. For I do believe I have certain aptitudes that have not been allowed to flourish in the restricted environment of Fort William.

Sadly, I do not have time to wait for this letter to reach you and to receive your response before setting sail for Penang but have acted according to the motto on Mother's clan crest: *Audentes Fortuna Iuvat.* Fortune will surely favour this bold move, and I trust that I will receive your blessing for pursuing it.

Be sure to tell Laura that I will write to her once I am ensconced in my new position. Her parents' desire that she become the wife of a nabob in India is understandable, but I think it will better suit all our needs if I take advantage of this new experience and see where it leads.

In the meantime, given the three hundred rupees I will receive as a monthly salary and the likelihood that my expenses will be minimal in Penang, I do not need to drain your resources any further, at least for the time being.

Once I am settled on the island and have other good news to share, I will write again with the address at which you can reach me. In the meantime, please extend my loving thoughts to Mother and my two sisters, whom I trust are all in fine spirits.

Your loving son,
James

***

Satisfied with my letter, I decided to leave it until the next day before I ventured down to the harbour to find a Navy or company mail boat that carried missives from Calcutta to London. It would likely take at least six months for this letter to reach my father, assuming the ship made it safely around the Cape of Good Hope and did not meet any enemy vessels. Father's response to me, assuming he wrote back immediately, would arrive an additional eight or nine months after that, since Penang was further from England than India. I therefore had more than a year before Father's lambasting letter arrived, ordering me back to Calcutta or London and berating me for having defied his orders. In the meantime I would have acquired the skills, reputation, and hopefully enough money from trades to establish my independence. The book I planned to publish about Captain Light would pave the way for my freedom.

I chortled to myself as I imagined the glorious future ahead of me: Pats on my back from admiring peers; the cheers of an enraptured public at my book recitals; the sumptuous smell of baked hams and venison wafting from the tables of the high-ranking ladies and gentlemen in London who would seek me out as an amusing dinner companion; the lightning bolt thrill of seeing my name in print. The sight of which, I knew already, I would never tire.

All this, thanks to that chance encounter with James Scott who had, as promised, delivered my letter of introduction to his friend and business partner when he returned to Penang.

The day after our meeting in that alehouse, I had gathered my plumbago pencil and an old, torn sheet of laid paper on which I had, at first, intended to make notes about my achievements in Calcutta. But my hand had hovered, motionless, like a suspended piece of marble. Since I *had* no achievements to boast of, how could I commend myself to Penang's superintendent so that he would appoint me as his assistant?

After many fruitless minutes it occurred to me that it would be best to concentrate less on the administrative side of my future duties since I was, after all, employed by John Company as a writer and that should speak for itself. I needed to concentrate on convincing Captain Light that I would be his ideal chronicler. I wracked my brains and jotted down all the articles, poems, and letters to editors that I had prematurely penned in my youth and sent to the most prestigious magazines in England and Scotland. There was no need to mention that all of them had been rejected and therefore never appeared in print; it was the effort that counted.

Still frustrated by the dearth of worthy accomplishments that might impress Captain Light, I recalled what James Scott had said about the man: '*Francis will exaggerate a little if he thinks it will achieve a desired outcome*'. I adopted a similar tactic in order to be successful with *my* desired intention. Like the readers duped by those newspaper stories concerning General George Washington, how likely was it that Light would discover the truth?

Screwing up the old notepaper I had been scribbling on, I jettisoned it into the waste basket with triumphal flair. Then, gathering up a sheet of the finest vellum and allowing my imagination full rein, I began to write.

Within a few weeks I had received Captain Light's confirmation of my appointment as his formal assistant and informal chronicler. Fabricating my accomplishments had done the trick. I was about to welcome in the New Year in a new role at an exciting, exotic location. I could scarcely wait for life to become more uplifting so that I could demonstrate my worth not only to Father and my prospective employer, but to myself—in the profession of *my* choice.

Chapter 6

Light and Shade

George Town, Penang. Wednesday, 7 January 1789.

For weeks I had imagined Francis Light as a Zeus-like figure, so gods and divinity were on my mind when I finally met the man. But as with most things I discovered about Penang, I was mistaken. Or perhaps not, for were not the Greek gods created in order to mirror back to us our human failings?

As our rowboat approached the shoreline, ready to deposit me on to the huge granite boulders that formed a barrier between the sea and the slightly elevated town, I could see that James Scott dwarfed his older, more careworn companion. This only reinforced my conviction that I had arrived not a moment too soon. The overwhelming administrative responsibilities of this island appeared to have taken their toll on my new employer, along with the intermittent fevers that Scott had told me his friend suffered from since settling here.

I scrambled over the slippery rocks, less adept at walking than a newly hatched duckling as I had not yet found my land legs, and finally fronted the two country traders. James Scott barely concealed his mirth at my awkward arrival before introducing me to his long-time friend. Light was of average height and build, with thinning, light-brown hair that framed a face whose lines could have doubled as a map. Yet his handshake was strong and vigorous. When he spoke, I detected the faint Suffolk brogue that betrayed his birthplace.

Both men were conventionally dressed in their blue captain's jackets. But it became evident within minutes of my arrival, with Scott fidgeting and running two fingers between his skin and neckerchief like a man trying to ease himself free from a hangman's noose, that the Scotsman desired to take off. I presumed to go back to donning the native attire he had told me he preferred to wear and perhaps cavort with his multiple mistresses.

'Well, I'll leave you two to get acquainted,' announced Scott as he squeezed Light's shoulder then held his hand out to me. '*Selamat datang ke Puloo Pinang,* my young friend. Welcome to your new home.'

'It's Prince of Wales Island now,' shouted Light to his friend's departing back. James Scott merely waved in acknowledgment without turning around.

Immediately my new employer announced, 'Let's get you settled into your lodgings. We can talk along the way. Jim, is it? Or do you prefer James?'

'Jim, sir. And I should call you—?'

'Captain Light.'

I nodded, aware of a faint disappointment.

Light began to walk off in a southerly direction. He informed me over his shoulder that I could take the rest of the day to settle in but should present myself at Fort Cornwallis the next morning at ten o'clock, when I would begin my work. I picked up my two bags, grateful that most of my belongings would follow later in the chest I had arranged to be shipped here from Calcutta, and ran after him. Then the superintendent stopped, as if to give me more of an opportunity to soak in the grandly named edifice he had just mentioned: Fort Cornwallis. I turned my head to the left, in the direction of Light's gaze, and noticed the flagstaff some two hundred strides from where we stood.

'I scarcely arrived here when I received intelligence that the Dutch fleet was at Selangor,' said Light, nodding towards the fort. 'The Dutch are much aggrieved at our possessing this island and I thought it probable they would procure some bandits to cut off our supplies or attack us. Since I had only one hundred undisciplined men and a few Europeans, I thought it expedient to erect that small fort to save us from any sudden night attack. And I was right to do so because before we could get up any defence, we had visitors of all kinds: some for curiosity, some for gain, and some for plunder.'

Light chattered on about the unique shape of his stockade and used words like nibongs, bastions, and gabions. He pointed out the various platforms laden with nine pounders he had purchased from Captain Scott, with obvious pride as to the assured security of George Town. He concluded his description of the town's defence with a story of how, upon arrival and dismayed by the group of lazy, undisciplined sepoys he had been lumbered with, he had filled one of his ship's cannons with silver coin and blasted that bounty into the jungle so that his men would clear the area he had designated for the construction of the fort with greater speed and zest. Then, as if I might not have heard him the first time, Light said, 'I certainly did blast those silver dollars into the jungle. Yes, that got those lazy sepoys moving for a change.'

Only later, when I had the opportunity to more objectively appraise Fort Cornwallis did I come to realise that Captain Francis Light had a gift concealed beneath his plain appearance. The ancient Greeks had a word for this: *kharisma*. In Light's case it was the power to make you see something through his eyes while suppressing what you would otherwise observe on your own. He appeared neither a man like my father who bullied you into submitting to their will, nor an obvious charmer who could sell magic elixirs to the gullible—or so I thought at the time. But he certainly wielded a natural power of persuasion, a kind of magnetism like the lodestone used to facilitate safe passage for the earliest sea explorers, that convinced you it was safe to follow where he led. At the time I could sense Francis Light harboured a steely determination to ensure Penang's success, which boosted my resolve to serve him well. Having burned my bridges in Calcutta, I had to.

Seemingly invigorated by his storytelling and my approval of his ingenuity, Light took off again. He spoke about the increasing number of vessels anchored in the harbour that now arrived at Penang to trade in preference to Dutch-held Malacca, and the ports of Queda.

'Is that because Penang is a free port where no duties and taxes are imposed?' I said.

'Exactly,' replied Light. One of my roles, he went on, would be to take charge of the shipping lists. I should itemise the date of each ship's arrival, whether one of John Company's vessels stopping here to re-victual before sailing on to China or Macau, or the small Malay prahus that sailed the regional routes. Light rattled off the nature of goods that I should also note for our records: Pepper and betelnuts from Acheh; opium from Bengal; cloth from the Coromandel Coast; aromatic woods, elephant tusks, gold dust, tin, and rice from the Malay peninsula, and so on.

'We still rely on our neighbours in Queda for provisions such as rice, and India for poultry and cattle,' explained Light as he scurried along, sprightlier than I might have expected from a man of his advancing years; I estimated his age to be close to fifty. 'This island had largely been uninhabited jungle and I took the initiative of allowing settlers to take whatever land they could clear in order that we might eventually cultivate pepper, nutmeg, and cloves, among other valuable commodities. While Penang produces very little at the moment, our reputation is growing as an entrepôt for the exchange of goods mainly from the Coromandel Coast and eastern ports of India, as well as the likes of Mergui, Pegu, and Junk Ceylon.

'Only fifty-four vessels arrived here the year I took possession of this island, but we now see upwards of five hundred annually, a ten-fold increase. I knew this place had huge potential.'

I shifted my bags—becoming heavier by the minute—from one hand to the next and asked the question I had been formulating in my mind as I looked around. 'If Penang does not collect duties and taxes from the ships arriving here and I assume settlers pay nothing for the land you wish them to clear and cultivate, how do you finance public works?'

'All in good time, Jim. All in good time,' answered Light.

Very little in the way of public works were apparent to me. The only two thoroughfares I could see that might loosely be called roads—but in truth were little more than rutted footpaths—was one that ran parallel to the shoreline, named Light Street, and another at right angles to that which appeared to hug the island's northernmost tip for some distance, called Beach Street. I imagined everything underfoot became a quagmire during the rains, which I heard fell heavy at certain times of year. Rudimentary drains had been dug by a group of slaves shipped in from Bencoolen two years earlier, Light informed me, although most of them had proven to be too old and infirm for such service. I was used to a certain stench that permeated Calcutta but here it was overpowering as only poorly drained swamp land can be. There was another pungent smell, as if this place was harbouring a sulphurous stash of rotten eggs. I looked with longing at the hinterland where distant, verdantly clad hills promised cooler temperatures and fresher, cleaner air.

As if reading my mind or perhaps my uncomfortable expression, Light explained, 'Although I believe the man on the spot knows best in all cases, I have refrained for as long as possible making any additional works, buildings, or improvements in expectation of directions from the Honourable Board. But as you can see, George Town, which I named in honour of our king—' Light paused so I could take in the rows of basic timber houses with woven palm fronds for roofs, '—offers sufficient dwellings for the inhabitants to live and work at the moment. The brick kilns I established near the harbour have allowed us to erect more secure godowns and the Customs House you might have seen earlier. God help us were there to be a fire and all our goods be lost.'

We walked on. All manner of people strode past us, from pig-tailed Chinese to bare-chested Chulias in their gleaming white dhotis, each rubbing shoulders with men who could have hailed from Borneo, Sumatra, or Siam. Some nodded to acknowledge Penang's superintendent, others stopped to shake his hand and exchange a few words. I saw only the occasional European: pale-haired Danes or Swedes, swarthy-skinned Spaniards and Portuguese.

From time to time. Light would draw me closer and mutter some new intelligence about the local inhabitants, telling me that he had become familiar not just with the language of the Malays but also their manners. He could instantly identify where a man hailed from based on his looks and behaviours: The peaceful, highly religious men from Trengganu who liked to study, trade, and earn a living from their artisanship without having to serve a grasping chief or raja, but would defraud you without a second thought; the fleshy, big boned natives of Kelantan who were hard-working and strong yet the most dreadful pick-pockets and thieves; the good-natured men of Pahang who nevertheless seemed to prefer fighting to work.

As if this litany of miscreants was a reminder, Light paused under an overhanging veranda to loosen his neckerchief and said, 'Maintaining law and order would be a bigger problem here had I not understood that you cannot subject this great diversity of inhabitants, who differ in religion, languages, and customs, to one form of government. Very few of the people residing in Penang, except the Chulias from southern India, have ever been acquainted with European laws but were brought up under their own feudal systems and customs. They are also jealous of one another and would not kindly submit a complaint or crime to the decision of a single administrator.'

'How then have you resolved the challenge of maintaining law and order?' I asked.

'By allowing the headmen of the various nations, each of whom lives in their separate areas on this island, to be responsible for administering justice according to their traditions. The garrison captain, whom you will meet in due course, lays down the law for the sepoys under his charge, while I only get involved in capital crimes or those directly involving non-military Europeans.'

'Has that been something you have had to contend with much these past three years?'

Light shrugged. 'We are beset by the usual riots.' He paused. 'Two Siamese were recently discovered with their throats cut and no perpetrator yet found. And there appears to be an unusually high spate of suicides lately, particularly among the Chinese. There is so much unrest we must always remain vigilant. This is not Calcutta, Jim.'

'I see,' was all I managed to say, since I had not expected Penang to be quite so primitive.

Light continued, 'But political relations are made needlessly difficult when a governor remains ignorant of the manners and customs of the people he has been charged with overseeing. That is why it will be important for you to quickly understand the differences among the people who compose our society, in order to best assist me.'

'Yes, sir, I understand,' I said, eager to impress my new employer with my command of some of the Indian languages I had learned while in Bengal, along with the little Malay I had taught myself while waiting to sail to Penang. But I never got the chance as Light announced that we had arrived at my lodgings and he would speak first with the Chinese owner, a relative of their headman or 'Kapitan China', Koh Lay Huan, whom Light said should be held in the highest regard as one of the earliest settlers and a successful merchant. My face sank in disappointment, but I said nothing. I had not expected to lodge with Captain Light, of course, nor did I wish to stay in the barracks with a bunch of unruly sepoys, but I would not have chosen to live among the Chinese whose language I did not know and who, from my experience of the ones who lived among us in Calcutta, were rather too fond of setting off firecrackers for no good reason, and whose constant burning of incense I did not like.

'Take this,' said Light. 'I drew this rudimentary map so you can study the layout. Given George Town's size I doubt very much you will get lost because I cleverly laid out the town in this rectangular block pattern, as you can see.' He tapped a finger at the appropriate place on the map to show a series of neat, right-angled walkways, then disappeared around a corner where I heard the knocking of knuckles on wood, some brisk chatter, followed swiftly by the closing of a door.

Light reappeared, scowling. 'It seems word did not get passed to the right people after all. I suggest you wait here, Jim, while I seek out the Chinese towkay to resolve this.'

'Captain Light?' I said, before he had a chance to stride off. 'Might it be possible to lodge with the Malays since the Chinese landlord appears not to be expecting me?'

Light looked startled. 'Whyever would you wish to do that?'

I shuffled my feet and looked down with some embarrassment. 'After arriving in India, I became fascinated by the history of the

Mughal Empire, whose bloodline I have come to learn goes back to Jenghiz Khan.'

'Malays are not related to the Mughals,' snapped Light.

'Yes, sir, I am aware of that. But both groups are Mohammedans and I wish to understand that religion and culture better. I had hoped that residing here would afford me such an opportunity as well as help to improve my Malay. Not least since we will presumably be in constant communication with the Sultan of Queda and his *wakils*.'

Light made a scoffing sound and pointed out that there was a difference between the language written and spoken in the court and that used by the *rakyat*. I replied that knowing everyday Malay would surely still give me an advantage with Penang's local population.

'You do realize you are asking to reside among pirates, Jim,' barked Light.

'I did not think that would be the case,' I responded with more of an edge to my voice than I had intended. Why was this so difficult for him to understand?

'Then allow me to offer some background that will change your mind.' Light sighed. 'The Malays may be divided into two orders: those who are inoffensive and easily ruled but capable of no great exertion beyond planting paddy, sugar cane, and a few fruit trees for which no great labour is required. Then there are those who skulk in rivers and bays in their prahus, watching for the unwary trader whose goods they plunder. Addicted to smoking opium, gaming, and other vices, they spend their whole time in sloth and indolence, only rousing themselves when an opportunity presents itself to rob and assassinate with abandon.' Light barely took a breath before continuing. 'The feudal government of the Malays encourages these pirates, since every chief is desirous of procuring these desperate fellows to bring him plunder and execute his revengeful purposes.'

Like a court prosecutor confident that his summation would return a guilty verdict, Captain Light looked at me, but obviously did not expect my particular reply. 'I am still interested to live among the

Malays, sir, if the additional distance to their township would not cause you too much extra exertion.'

Light's face appeared to darken as if a rain cloud had singled him out. His eyes narrowed and his voice seemed to chill the surrounding air. 'I am already beset by three sets of antagonists: Sultan Abdullah of Queda grows increasingly impatient over the treaty we had expected would be ratified by London and Bengal by now; Lord Cornwallis, whose notorious parsimony prevents me from investing in further benefits to this new settlement and appears ignorant of the fact that a rising settlement cannot be expected to yield much profit, *and* for some inexplicable reason thinks the Andamans would fit the company's purposes better than Penang; and our European enemies, not least the Dutch, who eye my success here with increasing jealousy and hatred.

'I should not venture to trust myself alone with the Malays, on account of their treacherous nature. But I am beleaguered enough without battling you over where you choose to lodge. Should you decide to ignore my expert opinion, that is up to you. Just be sure you are prompt at Fort Cornwallis tomorrow morning.' And with that, Francis Light turned on his heels and hurried off, presumably back to his office at the fort where James Scott told me he also resided.

Had it not been for my surprise at Light's explosive reaction to my genuinely well-meaning request I might have bolted after him to say I would lodge with the Chinese after all. But I became as rooted to the spot as a tree. I imagined the captain was tired and had not wished to walk further on to Malay Town so watched him grow more minuscule with each lengthening stride.

Disappointed at this inauspicious start to my employment, I determined to apply myself with the utmost energy and diligence so that I might demonstrate my value to Penang's superintendent the very next day. I truly desired to be helpful to Captain Light but should never forget that he needed me just as much as I needed him. After all, I had just freed myself from the yoke of one oppressor who sought to constrain my personal liberty, I did not need to substitute Father with Captain Francis Light.

With that thought, I turned heel myself and made towards Malay Town, confident that I had sufficient language to make myself understood and enough money to pay for a bed and food. As I grew closer to the *kampong*, past a smattering of fierce-looking Armenians, I began to doubt the wisdom of my stubbornness. If Light was right about the Malays, that they were treacherous men, I might end up like those two dead Siamese or at best dossing in the street for the evening, scuttling back to Light tomorrow with my tail between my legs.

Chapter 7

Unburdened

George Town, Puloo Pinang.
Sunday, 15 February 1789.

My dearest Laura:

I trust this letter finds you well and in good spirits. Please extend my kind regards to your parents who may now be feeling less well-disposed towards me.

Father has no doubt conveyed the news to your family that I have left the Honourable Company's service in Bengal, assuming the letter I wrote him last December reached London safely. If that was not the case then this latest development will be sadly yours to share!

Please know that I seized the opportunity to become the assistant to Captain Francis Light on the Malay island of Penang in order to gain the experience I have long felt was unavailable to me as a junior writer in Calcutta, as well as perhaps to make a considerable income from trades here and write the *magnus opus* from which I hope eventually to carve my long-desired writing career.

I trust you can find it in your heart to wait another few years before we are reunited so that I can set this new direction for my life. I assure you it will be more glorious to align yourself with a famous writer than an anonymous company clerk. After three years apart already—which dragged for me because of the nature of my work, yet I trust sped by for you with all your social engagements—two or three more years should not feel very long before we are together again.

In the meantime, allow me to paint a picture of my new life, from which you will see that Penang is nothing like Calcutta. My new employer is a harsh taskmaster and I have barely had a day to myself in the six weeks since I arrived. I was promised Sundays off but that has not transpired thus far, although I intend to take this up with Captain Light as soon as our relationship is on a sounder footing, which is not the case at the moment.

But I digress…

Penang is, in some regards, quite beautiful, a pearl or *mutiara* as the natives call it rising up from an azure sea. Yet other than the land that has been cleared for the settlement, named George Town in honour of His Majesty and protected—for want of a better word—by a crumbling stockade called Fort Cornwallis, the rest of the island is dense jungle.

There are no seasons in Penang. Here, you don't expect to gather posies of bluebells during springtime; lazily rub ears of sun-burnished summer wheat; smell pies baked with apples picked in autumn; or hear snow melt on rooftops and drip icily on to the streets at Christmastime. There are only the monsoon winds that bring less rain or more rain. The heat is relentless, although thankfully not as punishing as in India.

I am told the island runs sixteen miles from north to south and is some eight miles wide. In the centre lies a ridge of hills, one of which rises two and a half thousand feet above sea level and offers air that is more pleasant to breathe than that endured on the plains. One day, soon, I hope to climb it.

Upwards of a thousand souls have settled on the island since Captain Light arrived: Chulias from south India; Chinese; Achehnese; Arabs; Burmans; Siamese; all, of course, in addition to the local Malays. However, the lawlessness here is like the jungle, with relentless, destructive actions going on largely unchecked. The inhabitants regularly fall prey to riots, robberies, and assaults. Settlers complain that their homes are broken into if a member of their family is not on guard at all times. While such events bedevil the Honourable Company's presidencies in Bombay, Calcutta, and Madras, at least there one feels the safe hand of the British judiciary. Here, there is no legally constituted court or anything beyond a small civil force that attempts to check the European seamen who come ashore to abuse the locals and cause mayhem through their excessive drinking. Captain Light asked Bengal for help to create a judiciary but was told to manage things himself the best he could. That appears to be Lord Cornwallis' attitude towards Penang; it is almost as if the Governor-General is vying to ensure Captain Light's experiment fails.

The lack of laws advantages some, however. This island is ruled by traders for traders, mainly English and Scottish men who set their own rules. Since each of these wealthy individuals is vital to Penang's success, Light chooses to play no role in the mercantile activities of any but his own firm, Scott & Company.

Regarding my day to day living, I have found a *makcik,* a kindly, older woman, who takes care of me within the Malay kampong or village. While the local people have a reputation as cutthroat pirates, I consider this to be an outrageous slander. Everyone has been very kind to me and I would grow fat from makcik's cooking were it not for the extra distance I must walk every morning and evening to and from the fort. Since contradicting the captain's wishes regarding my lodgings on the first day I arrived, Light has never once asked me how I am being accommodated. I would have thought my desire to live among the Malays would please him, since he has assimilated himself to their dress, manners, and way of life, as have I—an admission that I hope does not shock you! But since my original refusal to bend to his will, my employer has treated me quite off-handed. This attitude befuddled me until I came across the copy of a note that Captain Scott had written congratulating John Company on their selection of Light as Penang's superintendent. In part, it read: *'Let therefore no alteration deprive him at least during (Penang's) infancy of the sole directing power…A contrary behaviour will dampen his ardour and render him indifferent to the success of measures he does not continue to direct.'*

From this insight, I now have a better measure of Captain Light; regarding the events he is not in direct control of, he could not care less. That, sadly, includes my welfare. Every day I work myself to near exhaustion in an effort to impress him, but to no avail. I am determined to step up my efforts and look forward to a day when the administration of Penang might be set aside for a few hours, so I can show off my skills as his chronicler. Surely then Captain Light will bring me into his confidence. But all of this is to be kept between us. Please do not breathe a word of these difficulties to my father, to whom I will only furnish positive news.

That is all I have to share for now, dear one. I hope I do not sound too dispirited. My sincere intention is to make a success of this opportunity to the extent I am able.

Please write back soon to assure me that my change of circumstances has not been met with a change of heart in you.

I am,
With much love,
Your ardent admirer,
James

Chapter 8

Means and Ends

Fort Cornwallis, George Town. Monday, 2 March 1789.

I waited for what I hoped was an opportune moment, having been too nervous to raise the matter earlier. Captain Light and I were in our usual lair at the fort, seated across from each other, our desks almost touching in the cramped space of his office. I could only see my employer from the shoulders upwards due to the mountain of material erected like a fortress between us, the pages of account books and ledgers curled like autumn leaves from constant fingering.

'Captain Light?'

The superintendent had been staring into thin air for some time. He looked over at me with that mixed expression I had come to know well: part distracted part annoyed at having been roused from his distraction.

'Yes, what is it, Jim?'

I stood up carefully so as not to disturb the sheaves of documents I was about to file. 'I—I thought you might like to read this. I am not sure what to call it. A 'vignette' seems most appropriate. It is a story I have been working on since my arrival, based on a brief tale that Captain Scott told me when we first met.'

'What tale?' Light asked, suspiciously. 'You did this in your own time, I hope.'

What time might that be? I was tempted to retort, but merely said, 'Of course,' recalling the late evenings I had squinted in the light of a candle stub to perfect this work before daring to show it to him.

'If you have a moment to read it,' I said, handing over the few sheets of paper. 'Please.'

With a deep sigh Light accepted them.

After several minutes, but without shifting his eyes from my writing, Light said, 'My school friend was called James, not John.'

'Ah,' I said, picking up a pencil to note the corrections I would later make.

'And the correct name of my alma mater was Woodbridge Free School.'

I scribbled accordingly. For several terrifying minutes my gaze never left Light's face, only relaxing when I saw him smile twice and heard him chuckle.

'This is a fine story from my childhood, Jim,' said Light, handing the papers back to me. 'Well done.'

I blushed at this first praise from my employer. 'But it is only a partial work, captain, missing certain colour and authenticity due to the fact that the information came second-hand, not from you.' I waited for Light to respond. When he did not reply I added, 'I had hoped we might begin my chronicling activities soon.'

'I have no time for ancient history at the moment, Jim,' said Light, glancing at the paperwork that threatened to swamp us both.

I plunged on. 'But might you have time to help me understand something that has puzzled me since my arrival? It is, I assure you, relevant to my role as your assistant in addition to perhaps helping me chronicle certain matters that can be expanded upon later.'

'And what might that be?'

'I understood from Captain Scott that the previous sultan of Queda, Sultan Muhammad Jiwa Zainal Adilin Mu'adzam Shah the Second—' I paused, hoping for some approval of my correct pronunciation but when none was forthcoming continued, '—the current sultan's late father, had conferred a title of Malay nobility on you: Dewa Raja, which I understand means God King.'

Light's eyes glinted with interest. As my father had long impressed upon me, there is no topic of greater fascination to a man than himself. Now that I had my employer's attention, I could build on it. 'But in the interim, your relationship with that royal house appears to have soured.'

As evidence, I held up a letter from Sultan Abdullah, unearthed from those that the Malay raja sent over on an almost daily basis. 'As one example, this missive mentions the rumour that the sultan had instructed a man named Cik Long Ismail to kill you. While the Malay king refutes this, writing that he would have no cause to encourage such a heinous act, it does raise the question as to why this slander arose in the first place. For, continuing on—' I glanced once more at the letter and hoped I had translated it accurately from my still rudimentary Malay '—Sultan Abdullah writes that *you* wished to take possession of Penang in the first place, suggesting that your original request on behalf of the Governor-General, to set up a transit for repair work on British war ships, is not the real truth and he wishes to meet with you to discuss this matter. The sultan also hopes to speak with you about how to prevent further spread of this rumour of an assassin that he feels is tarnishing his reputation.' I paused to breathe.

Captain Light rose so suddenly from his desk I feared I had angered him.

'Come,' he said, beckoning me to follow. 'I think we both need to get out of this prison. You want the truth of the matter? Then let me offer it to you. Yes, let me give you the whole, unvarnished truth.'

And with that we both strode into the sunshine.

We sat on the harbour wall looking out at the bay at vessels of all sizes. The most distantly anchored was an East Indiaman of perhaps fourteen hundred tons, carved from Indian teak, that would sail on to China or Macau; then nearer, a half-dozen five-hundred-ton ships owned by independent traders like James Scott; while closest to the shore were the numerous thirty-ton Malay prahus that had arrived in great numbers at Penang. The harbour bustled with men of all sizes and hues, carrying goods they had purchased back to their ships, or heaving huge chests from their cargo holds in anticipation of profitable transactions. Despite the hustle and bustle and noise, I relished the peace from no longer being screamed at by paperwork.

'What precisely is it you wish to know concerning my relationship with the Queda ruler?' said Light at length.

'I thought you might begin by relating how you came to negotiate with Sultan Abdullah for the ceding of Penang to the East India Company,' I said. 'Captain Scott has already appraised me of the two previous times you were unsuccessful in finalising negotiations for similar settlements in the region.'

'Has he now,' Light murmured. 'He told you about the Jiwa-Monckton travesty, and about my dispute with the Siamese in Junk Ceylon?'

'Yes.'

'Then where do you wish to begin?'

'Am I correct in thinking that some seven years ago, because of our wars with France and Holland, and the skirmishes with the Mysore warlord, Haider Ali, the Honourable Company was interested in finding a safe harbour to victual and refit its ships somewhere further east than Madras? And that the sultan of Queda's offer of settling Penang was therefore aired once again?'

'You have that largely correct.'

'My understanding is that Sultan Abdullah originally sent you to Bengal as his wakil to help secure an annual payment of thirty thousand Spanish Dollars in exchange for ceding Penang to the Honourable Company? Is that also correct?'

'Scotty has kept you very well informed of past matters concerning these affairs,' said Light in what sounded like an aggrieved tone.

I leapt to the Scotsman's defence. 'I beg your pardon, Captain Light. I wanted to be sure that I did not waste your time by failing to do my homework with respect to chronicling your story.' I thought back to Dr Johnson's essay, a copy of which William Roxburgh had procured for me before I left Calcutta, not least the paragraph that read: *'A journalist is an historian, not indeed of the highest class, nor of the number of those whose works bestow immortality upon others or themselves; yet, like other historians, he distributes for a time reputation or infamy, regulates the opinion of the week, raises hopes and terrors, inflames or allays the violence of the people. He ought therefore to consider himself as subject at least to the first law of history, the obligation to tell truth.'*[1]

'I apologise if I have caused offence with my clumsy attempt at diligence,' I concluded, and must have looked suitably contrite as this appeared to do the trick.

Light waved his hand at me and said, 'No matter.'

'Then perhaps you might continue the story from there?' I prompted.

Light cleared his throat, stared out to sea, and began. 'The amount of money Sultan Abdullah originally asked for, as yearly compensation for the loss of his monopolies, was extortionate. His father had admitted some years earlier that he never received more than ten thousand Spanish Dollars a year for the same. I wrote to Acting Governor-General Macpherson to advise him to offer no more than that sum and, in exchange for the payment of troops and stores lent to the sultan by the Honourable Company, to also request that Sultan Abdullah make over a portion of land opposite Penang.'

The comment was out of my mouth before I could stop it. 'But were you not in Bengal as the representative of the sultan, not to help John Company best him?'

Light seemed to find the shock in my voice amusing. 'You have much to learn about the art of conducting business, Jim,' he said, once he had composed himself. 'Do you understand what is meant by a stalking horse?'

'Such as when the company uses country traders to minimise their risks in new markets?'

'To conceal the company's true intentions, certainly, not only from the local chiefs but oftentimes their own agents. You might say that was my role during these initial negotiations. I wanted to keep my options open.

'Now don't look so shocked. We're talking about a transaction here. It was business, nothing personal.'

Perhaps, I thought, but it was certainly personal *for you*. Light must have wanted to appear as if he was looking after the interests of both parties in order to better secure his own desired outcome of governing. To 'hedge his bets,' as I had heard many a Bengal trader say.

'Presumably Sultan Abdullah accepted the offer of ten thousand Spanish Dollars a year for Penang?' I said.

'Well, there was something more vital to him than that, as it had been for his father: military protection. Come, let's walk a while,' said Light, groaning slightly as he rubbed legs that presumably had stiffened from too much recent sitting.

We headed away from the fort and took a turn down China Street where artisans worked in the narrow shops beneath their lodgings.

'You see, Jim, Sultan Abdullah's sole purpose for responding positively to the Honourable Company's renewed interest in Penang has always been to ensure his enemies would become Britain's enemies, should he ever be attacked.'

'But did you not write to the Supreme Council early in '86 to say you had been granted the island of Penang in exchange for 'some small restrictions'? I believe I saw a copy of that letter to Bengal while filing your papers.'

I turned my head and saw Light shrug as if that was of no importance. 'I considered I need not trouble the Council with matters that might never come to a head. Abdullah is always looking nervously to the north, feeling safe only when his greatest foe, Siam, is at war with its sworn enemy, the equally capricious Burmans. This Queda sultan has never been popular, for reasons we can discuss another time, and my concern on behalf of Bengal was that he would foment trouble within his own country because of some long-standing feud, and then expect us to come in and clean up his mess.'

'Then how was the treaty drawn up to everyone's satisfaction?'

Light stopped to talk to a Chinaman about repairs to the rotting fort that the superintendent had commissioned, after which he nodded to me that we should walk on.

'You know what it's like dealing with these bureaucrats in Bengal, Jim. All they needed to do was send a few troops and guns to Queda to show their good intentions, from which Siam would get the message whether true or not that we would come to Queda's aid if needed. The Siamese are not so brave as to take on the might of the British military.'

'But the matter of the sultan's compensation?'

'Deflected by acting Governor-General Macpherson who wrote to Sultan Abdullah to say this had to be consented to by the Board of the Honourable Company in London, and King George. Sir John ordered a ship of war for the defence of Penang and protection of the Queda coast so that the sultan would believe his stipulations concerning military assistance would be fully met at some time in the future.'

'But they have not.'

'Not yet, no. Which is why the sultan is growing increasingly impatient with me.'

Two and a half years after Light had hoisted the British flag on Penang soil, I could well understand the sultan's frustration at having no ratified treaty.

'But, at the time, the sultan must have been satisfied enough to allow you to land here,' I surmised.

Light shrugged. 'Around the 8th of July, I think it was, I arrived at the *Balai Besar* where Sultan Abdullah holds audiences and met with him and the *Laksamana*, the admiral of his fleet. They read the translation of acting Governor-General Macpherson's letter, which stated that he had deferred entering a treaty with the sultan until an answer on the matters of compensation and defence was received from Europe. Abdullah then tried to tell me that it was needless for me to go to Penang and incur the expense of setting up a trading settlement as it might prove to be fruitless.'

'What did you say to that?' I thought again about the two occasions in the previous fifteen years when Captain Light's plans to secure himself a governorship had been scuppered.

'I answered that the greater expense had already been incurred and it would make little difference whether I remained at Queda or went to Penang.

'The Laksamana then desired to know if the Honourable Company would pay the king thirty thousand Spanish Dollars a year for the trade, and if not then how much would they be willing to pay. I told him I could not take it upon myself to declare what the Honourable Company would pay but that I was certain they would not allow the king to be a sufferer by their settling in his country. Indeed, I stressed he would not suffer in the slightest but gain much from the arrangement.'

So, Light had claimed ignorance to Sultan Abdullah about his annual compensation, even though *he* had advised the company to offer only ten thousand Spanish Dollars.

Light continued, 'The Laksamana also asked, in case the Honourable Company's letter should not be agreeable to the king, whether I would return to Bengal quietly and without enmity. To this I made no answer but withdrew to my boat, under the pretence of receiving some refreshment.'

Pretence! Captain Light had just admitted that he had lied to get out of a sticky situation. But instead of concerning myself with his deception, I delighted in the fact that my employer was being open and honest with me. A sign, I hoped, that our relationship was much improved.

'What is he like, Sultan Abdullah?' I asked as we strolled along.

'He is a weak man, too fond of money, very lax in the execution of the laws, not so much as a principle of clemency as timidity. His income consists in monopolizing likewise a good deal in presents and fines.

'If the king approves of the sum, he signs the paper—unless another person comes with a greater sum. He receives a small duty for every plough and on the sale of cattle and slaves. The rakyat are obliged to cultivate his lands and defend his country at their own charge. As I said earlier, not a popular ruler.'

'But matters must have been resolved sufficiently, now that you landed here.'

'We arrived at Tanjong Penaigre mid-July that year, yes.'

By now, we had almost concluded our circuitous route and had arrived at the top of Beach Street. We stood under a thatch of palm trees and gazed out at the translucent water that lapped nearby. The mangrove swamp at the edge of the shoreline gave off the whiff of sulphur that I had detected on my first day, and I sighed at the thought of re-entering the equally stinking fort.

'We'll leave that story for another time, Jim. There is someone I am due to meet at the Customs House and will leave you to return to Fort Cornwallis and conclude your work for the day.'

Thinking that Captain Light sought to end our conversation, I began to walk away. He called after me. 'Remind me the next time we speak to discuss Niccolò Machiavelli. Have you heard of him?'

I had not taken more than a few steps and turned back. 'The 16th century Italian diplomat?'

'And political genius,' added Light. 'Perhaps you are familiar with his work, *The Prince*?'

I replied that while I had heard of Machiavelli's book, I had not yet had the chance to read it.

'You should,' said Light. 'I will loan my copy to you. In the meantime, there is a line from *The Prince* you might wish to reflect on: 'For although the act condemns the doer, the end may justify him.' Until tomorrow, then.'

And with that message ringing in my ears, Francis Light strode off. He had just made clear to me that his possession of Penang justified the deceptive means by which he had achieved it. I could not argue with that, having taken the same approach when gilding the lily about my administrative and chronicling abilities to him. Only when I was in Captain Light's employ could I demonstrate my value. In order to make a success of Penang, Light—the aspiring governor—first had to secure it.

However, he had undertaken more than some well-meaning exaggeration. Considerable double-dealing and deceit had taken place, at least from what the captain had freely admitted, during and after his negotiations with Sultan Abdullah on behalf of the EIC. I wondered, aside from the ethical considerations, whether Light's possession of Penang, for which the Honourable Company had paid nothing so far for its lease, was even legal. Only much later, once Light had loaned me his copy of Machiavelli's *The Prince* did I come across another quotation that seemed an equally apt fit to these circumstances: 'He who deceives will always find someone who will let himself be deceived'.

I determined that Light's manner of conducting these transactions was not my concern. I seemed to have broken through what had once been a frozen ocean between us and all that mattered to me was to maintain a steady passage towards our mutual success. As Penang prospered, surely the island's owner would see that our triumph was also to his advantage and the sultan would be unwise to take any precipitous action that might scupper us. Because, from the way Light had described Sultan Abdullah, money was all that really mattered to him.

Chapter 9

Awestruck

George Town, Penang. Sunday, 12 April 1789.

Shortly after that conversation, Captain Light announced I had been working like a Trojan and should now take Sundays and alternate Saturdays off. There were so many things I could have done to amuse myself but I did not know where was safe to venture in Penang and there was little enjoyment in having adventures on my own. So, on this particular morning, I wandered through the familiar Chinese quarter looking for the cake seller whose *kuih* I had become partial to.

From a nearby back alley, I heard what sounded like the primeval screams of a tormented beast. I was reminded of the two murdered Siamese whose killer was yet to be apprehended and turned a corner to escape possible danger. I almost fell into the arms of a Hollander whom I had seen in the distance from time to time but, given his countrymen's reputation, had always given a wide berth. This morning he looked somewhat dishevelled, with his golden-brown hair worn loose about his shoulders, yet encased in the great black overcoat I had always seen him wear. I could feel his breath rising to meet my face and gazed down into eyes as gloriously indigo as the cloths coveted by fashionable ladies in London. This fellow was breathtakingly handsome.

Without a word, he grasped my left elbow and pivoted us towards the esplanade. As we rushed away from the scene of—I imagined—some new treachery, I gasped, 'What happened?'

'Just another suicide,' scoffed my companion between laboured breaths, then added, 'What a caterwauling, eh?'

I learned from him that a young Chinese widow had eaten an excess of opium the night before, not out of mourning for her dead husband but because of cruel treatment by her mother-in-law who had just discovered the body.

'Still,' I argued, 'she must have loved her daughter-in-law very much to be so grief-stricken at her death.'

My companion's laughter erupted like a clap of thunder; his head tilted so far back that from my side view as we sped along I could see his prominent Adam's apple protrude over his necktie. 'Those weren't wails of grief,' he seemed to mock, 'but of fear. The older woman worries she'll be accused of the girl's murder, if not directly then by abetting the suicide through incessant cruelty.' Stopping by the communal well he thrust out his hand to formally introduce himself as Pieter Reinaert, a name that sparked a dim recollection but when or for what I could not remember.

'Ah, so you are Light's new assistant,' Reinaert said, in response to my name.

'And chronicler,' I answered.

'And outsider,' the Dutchman added, slapping me on the back. 'Like me. Welcome to Penang, the home to outcasts, refugees, and their fevered dreams.'

Rather than be offended by his last comment, I thought it insightful. While I had never thought of myself as an outsider, the fact that I sought to carve my own destiny beyond society's expected, dutiful role of eldest son and heir surely made me at least unconventional? A thought of which I approved.

Facing Pieter Reinaert now, I could see that his outcast status was much worse than mine could ever be, for it seemed as if God had been undecided as to the nature of this man. With the lower half of his face masked he might have made the ladies swoon on the highways and byways, given those staggeringly blue eyes fanned by outrageously long lashes. But from the nose down his face ushered in a different story: that of the 'Devil's bite'.

I have never been inclined to believe, unlike the less well-educated, that this impairment of the upper lip indicated that carnal relations had taken place between a woman and the Devil, resulting in the birth of such a malformed child. Nevertheless, I found myself turning away out of embarrassment and gazed into the gaping maw of the well, thinking I might use this opportunity to quickly freshen up. But what I saw appeared much more alarming than an unhappy facial deformity. As I stared back at Reinaert he said, 'Worry not, my friend. That's not blood you see, but water tinted red by the roots of the penaga tree.'

I nodded and mumbled, 'Thank the Lord, for I have had some trouble sleeping since hearing about all the crimes and misdemeanours that take place on this island.'

'Me too,' answered my companion.

Neither of us said anything for several seconds as Pieter dangled a hand into the water and I stared into the middle distance. Then, knowing there were murderers still on the loose and with that Chinese woman's screams still ringing in my ears, I broke the silence with, 'I have come to realise this is not a safe place.'

Reinaert gestured towards the fort that sagged some distance to the east from where we loitered. 'But do we not have Fort Cornwallis over there to protect us?' he said, in a manner replete with sarcasm. 'Although Captain Light does have a gift for exaggeration. He once boasted that the small trading post he had established in Queda was his 'fort'. Yet I heard one of your nabobs describe it as 'the ruins of a thin wall built on a bog without any foundation'.' We laughed in unison at that pitiful description.

'Fort Cornwallis certainly doesn't live up to the symbol of protection and strength Light claims his English occupation represents,' the Dutchman said. Then, as if aware he might have sounded too critical of my employer, he quickly added, 'No island is easy to defend and Penang is no exception. But it was with undue haste that Light ordered his men to clear the land and build that barricade, oblivious to the fact that its position is less than ideal. Two or three gunships could easily anchor themselves within pistol shot and drive the artillery away, minimising its value for the island's defence.'

Unencumbered by Light's kharisma, I looked anew at Fort Cornwallis: a primitive, too-small stockade that lay so low on the sandy beach that it would indeed be of little use repelling any invaders. The structure hardly deserved the title of fort, being neither well-fortified nor strategically positioned even to my inexperienced eyes. That pitiful assembly of decomposing tree trunks seemed to cower as if ashamed of its existence, despite the grand name with which the fort had been endowed.

Working alongside Light at the fort, I had become well aware of platforms so decayed I was surprised they were capable of bearing even the lightest and feeblest of cannons. Once loaded with powder and set alight those guns might end up not just crashing on to the floor below, maiming our soldiers, but rolling out into the sea. I thought of the parable of the wise and foolish builders; Francis Light had not only established his fort on sand, but his town on a swamp.

As if I had shared these thoughts out loud, a sense of guilt impelled me to praise my employer's ingenuity. 'I heard that soon after his arrival Captain Light filled one of his ship's cannons with silver coin and blasted that bounty into the jungle so that his men would cut down the trees and foliage at a much faster rate.'

Reinaert chortled as if this was the most amusing thing he had ever heard and said, 'Captain Light does tell a tall tale. Neither I nor anyone else, including those sepoys, has ever laid sight on that silver.' Then, with a slap to my shoulder, he added, 'Come, friend! Join me for breakfast. It's not often I come across someone who interests me. And I've never met a chronicler. Who are you Jim Lloyd, and what do you seek in Penang?'

Only later did I realise that those were questions I should have asked the Dutchman. But at this point I regarded him as a useful source of information about Francis Light and the early days of Penang so that in writing my chronicle of the man and his achievements I might avoid charges of writing untruths and propaganda.

Chapter 10

Strange Sensations

Over idli sambar, poori, and uttapam—washed down with milky tea—Pieter Reinaert and I talked over and between each other, occasionally moving to remain protected by the shade of the attap-covered dwellings on Malabar Street.

Pieter, six years my senior, described a life that closely paralleled my own. He, too, had been banished to the East—at ten years of age in his case—by a Calvinist father who was intolerant of his youngest child's disfigurement. He had ended up in Sumatra, where he had clawed his way up to become a successful merchant, the owner of a trading ship named *Fame*. Despite his diminutive size, I was left with the distinct impression that Pieter Reinaert was a man who knew how to look after himself and, given his friendly manner towards me, would not deny me protection should the need arise. I sank contentedly into the lisping quality of my new friend's Dutch accent.

For the first time in months, I felt truly seen, despite the fact that my relationship with Captain Light was already much improved. Sitting here with this intriguing Hollander, something I had long suppressed surfaced. I was desperate for companionship with someone closer to my age, to whom, when necessary, I might occasionally complain and confide. Since arriving in Penang, I had felt strangely lonely, belonging neither to Light's world of trade nor that of the Malays where I lodged in the kampong.

'You are likely tight for money, given the pittance Light pays you. I will give you a loan to tide you over while staying here,' Pieter declared.

I had heard that the Dutch were direct in their speech, but that offer still shocked me. Taking my cue from his forthrightness, I replied that I had sufficient savings and, in any case, managed quite comfortably on the three hundred rupees Captain Light paid me every month.

'I can still help you,' said my new companion, after finally accepting my many refusals of his offer of an interest-free loan. He then shared vague details of an upcoming trade he was about to initiate that would net me a healthy profit with no need to put in any money up front. This was more than Light or even James Scott, now sailed away on some trading mission or other, had offered to do for me. I thought of the day when I might return to England with sufficient wealth to carve an independent life for myself as a journalist and thanked my new Dutch friend. 'I would be most grateful to take advantage of any such trade but insist that I pay my fair share up front,' I told him.

'Perhaps,' he said. 'But come, I have to conduct some business on my ship. Walk with me.'

We left our sauce-smeared banana leaves on the ground and headed towards the harbour, at one point passing a group of Indian convicts, men and women transported from the Honourable Company's penal colony in the Andamans. I remarked that while working in Fort Cornwallis I had come across two Bengali murderers and thought their confinement by the Indian sepoys overseeing them to be very lax. Perhaps *they* had slaughtered those two Siamese?

Pieter merely shrugged and we left the implications unsaid.

Soon we reached the harbour, whose chaos made further conversation a challenge. I ignored the hubbub going on around us, anxious to know how soon I might see my new friend again. I moved closer and asked if he would be at Light's dinner to be held some two weeks hence, in honour of a brace of English ladies—a Miss Anna Davis and a Mrs Beal—who, I had been told, were stopping off here on their way to Macau where they were to reunite with the married lady's husband.

Pieter smiled, sad or sarcastic I could not tell because of his deformed lip. 'I am never invited to Light's parties,' he said so quietly that I needed to lean in further to hear him and caught a whiff of some Persian pomade atop another scent, as if he had spent the morning scouring rusty nails.

'Is that because you are Dutch?' I asked.

He laughed. 'This animosity between our two countries is purely political, and, at least for now, we have our joint hatred of the French in common. Here in Penang, in order to belong, you don't have to swear allegiance to the same king or even worship the same deity; you only need to submit to the power of profit. But to answer your question directly, I am not invited to Light's gatherings because his live-in lover, Martinha Rozells, hates me.'

'What? Captain Light has a woman here?' I spluttered in amazement. He had never mentioned such a liaison to me.

'Not just any woman, a wife of sorts. If you can call her such, given that she's not the kind of wife Light's employers would approve of, being half Siamese, half Portuguese, *and* a Catholic. I gather she is in Queda at the moment, visiting her sister Yeen, and has taken his two children with her.'

Stunned that Light, with whom I thought I had established a connection, had not mentioned a family, I felt momentarily befuddled. With a desire to show support to my new friend, I reached out to grasp Pieter's hand. I let it drop almost immediately when I saw from his eyes that he had felt it too. A jolt akin to what would one day be called Galvanic current after its inventor, Luigi Galvani. A spark of some strange electricity that passed between our fingers that surprised and embarrassed us both.

All thoughts of Light's family arrangement gone from my mind, I opened and closed my mouth soundlessly like a beached fish. What could I say about what had just happened? Pieter Reinaert, on the other hand, narrowed his eyes, bid me a gruff 'good day' and strode off, shielding his eyes from the blazing noon-day sun. His oversized black coat billowed behind him like the wings of a gigantic jackdaw.

Dismay enveloped me like a shroud. I trusted that I would see Pieter again, this being a small island, but a sense of desperation set in as he disappeared among the harbour crowds. What if his business required him to raise anchor and sail away—for weeks, perhaps months? It shocked me to realise how bereft I had felt since arriving in Penang. I had no friends here, only passing acquaintances. I could not help but replay Pieter's growling farewell, like the condemnation of a hanging judge, in my head.

A sense of wretchedness set in. Life here was no more satisfying than it had been in Calcutta. Each day consisted of work, work, and more work. I had not written a word about the life of Francis Light other than the vignette I had shown him, created largely from my own imagination. I barely had time to get to know my neighbours in the Malay kampong, let alone discover more about their lives and history.

I turned away from the harbour towards the Chinese quarter, determined to gorge myself with kuih should I ever find that darned cake seller again. As I wandered along the miserable pathways, I considered what Pieter had said about Martinha Rozells hating him. Being part-Portuguese, Light's wife perhaps harboured an intense hatred of Hollanders, their long-time enemies. But she had no right to dismiss so thoughtlessly a fellow European, given how few of us lived here.

My mind chattered away, unbidden, like an imbecile too long confined in Bedlam. Would Pieter remember what he had said about that trading opportunity? Should I wait a day and then try and find him to confirm my interest and discover what financial investment I need to make? That might give me an excuse to see him again, or would he think me too forward for doing so? What had he meant by 'good day'? Would he wish to be my friend after what had just happened? What was the cause of that strange sensation?

Later, feeling devoid of purpose and having given up trying to find the absent kuih-seller, I considered that I had made a monumental mistake coming to Penang. What *really* was I doing here? To what end?

Chapter 11

Shedding Light

Light's ship, the Speedwell. 16 April 1789.

The *Speedwell* rocked us gently, like babies. We were docked at the mouth of the Kuala Muda river on the Queda coast, hoping to hear from the sultan soon. The ship's swaying movement, along with the incessant waiting, lulled me into a desire to sink my head on to Light's desk in his captain's quarters so I might catch up on some much-needed sleep, for night was rarely a time of rest and quiet.

In the Malay kampong it was common for me to bolt upright in the early hours of the morning, unnerved by the grunts of wild boars in search of food. The macaques—a monkey with an aggressive nature—would rustle the bushes near the *rumah* where I lodged, and I was constantly worried that I would wake up to find one on my chest, ready to sink its fangs into my face or neck. One evening, I had been especially unnerved by a constant scratching at the attap roof, convinced that marauding pirates planned to slice me open and steal my meagre possessions. In the morning, I was assured by makcik that it was merely a civet I had heard and there was little chance it could burrow through and attack me in my sleep. One of the men who overheard our conversation remarked that should pirates decide to come and kill me, they would use the door and not the roof.

Everyone within earshot found that hugely amusing and I made a weak attempt to join in their laughter.

As the *Speedwell* creaked and groaned as only anchored ships can, I longed to be back on land. I sighed deeply, wondering when we might be granted the requested audience with Sultan Abdullah or his Laksamana at Alor Setar. As Light had explained to me earlier, they were the only people allowed a monopoly on buying and selling opium in Queda. One or the other would purchase opium from the Honourable Company or its agents then sell it on at a profit. But today, the sultan was to receive a large quantity of this desired commodity from Light for free. He had sent ahead several large chests of opium and five thousand Spanish Dollars as a gesture of appeasement to the sultan, while both men waited with increasing impatience for an official agreement of their treaty to come from London. The letter from Light which had been sent with these gifts pre-emptively offered Sultan Abdullah ten thousand Spanish Dollars annually for eight years, or four thousand yearly if the sultan would agree to an indefinite period in which the East India Company could occupy the island.

I had been told by my employer that accompanying him on this trip was part of my tutelage concerning the Malay court. As we languished in the captain's quarters of my employer's ship, I learned from Light—over the many hours we sat waiting to disembark— that Sultan Abdullah was not only a ruler in the manner of our earlier medieval kings, and hence a law unto himself, but the principal trader, banker, and advancer of capital in his country. It did not do for any of his chiefs to become richer and potentially more powerful than the king, otherwise retribution would be swift and cruel. I wondered if this was not part of Sultan Abdullah's issue with Captain Light, in terms of the increasing wealth now being channelled through Penang in preference to Queda's ports, where the sultan imposed a ten per cent duty on every activity that took place. Minor chiefs, I discovered, set up unofficial customs-houses that allowed them to enjoy a life of ease and prosperity, far removed from those subjected to their outrageous taxes.

Light told me stories of the many corrupt practices common to the judicial system on the mainland: 'There was once a judge who became incensed at two small children fighting over marbles too close to the royal precincts and accused them of the crime of *lèse-majesté*,' he related. 'The judge decided the offence warranted a fine of two hundred and fifty silver dollars. Who do you think was made to pay?'

'The parents of the children, equally?' I suggested with a shrug.

'Wrong!' said Light, as if delighting in my incorrect answer. 'The judge fined a distant cousin of the youngest boy.'

'But why make an innocent person pay if they had nothing to do with the crime?'

'Because the cousin had just concluded a profitable deal and acquired a large sum of money. Rather than try to get blood out of a stone, as would have been the case with the poor parents of the children involved, here was an opportunity for the judge to get his hands on a guaranteed windfall.'

Then Light asked me if I was familiar with the hierarchy of a Malay court, and I told him I was not.

'The sultan sits at the pinnacle, along with the members of his family. Under them are the *Bendahara* or Prime Minister; the Laksamana I've already mentioned; the *Temenggung,* whose responsibility it is to look after the safety of the monarch and ensure public peace; and the *Bendahari* or head of the sultan's treasury. Below that tier are the titled nobility, and under them the *Shahbandar* or harbourmaster.'

'I assume there is a base to this extensive pyramid?' I asked.

'Yes, the *orang merdeheka* or free rakyat, and below them the *orang hamba* or slaves.'

Instructing me in this way appeared to maintain Light's high spirits. He was obviously used to being kept waiting by Eastern potentates and did not see this delay as representing any ill-will on the part of the sultan, or an ominous portent. Yet I knew that if I asked him whether there was a chance we might disembark soon he would snap at me again—like an irritated father whose child keeps asking when a coach journey might be over.

The last time I mentioned how long we had been kept waiting, Light answered with a Malay saying: '*Masuk kandang kambing mengembek, masuk kandang kerbau menguak*'. Then he added, 'But you may be more familiar with, 'When you go to Rome, do as the Romans do in order not to give or receive offence'.' He shrugged. 'After several years in Bengal, you must be aware that time takes on a different meaning in the East. An Indian might arrange to meet you at two o'clock and perhaps show up at four, if indeed he does at all.'

Light rose from his chair, walked around the captain's desk and, with two strides, reached the dressing table next to his bed. Above that were several shelves that boasted a standing army of bottles. 'Rum? Port? I also have a very palatable Madeira,' he called out. I began to feel immensely grateful to the sultan. As tedious as this waiting was, requiring me to quell my excitement at the prospect of visiting a royal palace, it afforded Light and me the opportunity to forge a closer connection. 'A little wine, thank you,' I said.

Returning with two glasses of Madeira, Light handed one to me and sank back into his chair. 'This is almost the exact location where my three ships were anchored before sailing to Penang in mid-July of 1786,' he mused.

'Ah,' I said. 'That is where our story left off the last time. Did the sultan relent and allow you to sail to Penang, based on the letter you both signed? The one that was to remain in force until the official agreement arrived from London?'

Light grimaced. 'I suppose you might describe the ensuing events as fortuitous, even if the manner was unexpected.'

'How do you mean?'

Light told me he had been pondering his next move, concerned that Sultan Abdullah was losing patience with the EIC and looking to form an alliance with the Dutch, when his officers reported that a flotilla of small boats carrying many Eurasian families was headed their way. Upon reaching Light's ships, the passengers claimed that had they remained in Queda, they would have been massacred, and they warned Light that all three of his ships were about to be attacked by the same mob of Malays.

'Why would they do that?' I asked, confused. 'And would the Malays really dare attack you?'

Light shrugged. 'I couldn't risk finding out. After all, something similar had happened years earlier off the coast of the Lancavy Islands.'

'The archipelago to the north of Penang?'

'Yes. Bugis pirates massacred the captains and crew of several of our vessels, including one called the *Friendship.* I was inclined to believe the news, not least because it was conveyed by a French Catholic padre named Arnaud-Antoine Garnault of the Société des Missions Etrangères. I was not at all keen on the man, who was too fond of involving himself in Malay politics for my liking, but I did not expect the missionary to lie outright.'

'So, what did you do?' Suddenly, my thoughts of bed and sleep were gone. I extracted my notebook and plumbago pencil and began to take notes.

'The die was cast; what *could* I do? For among Garnault's flock were the woman I co-habit with, and my two children, Sarah, and William who was just three months old. It seemed to me I must take command of the situation. What is that saying, 'Possession is nine points of the law?' I couldn't accommodate all the people on our three ships but gave the order to raise anchor so we could escort them safely to Penang.'

I ignored the question I should have asked next: What would cause the Malays to want to massacre Catholic Eurasians? But more important to me was wanting to know more about his wife, Martinha Rozells, and how they met. When I mentioned her name, Light waved away the possibility of an answer by saying that several copies of a book written by his former second-in-command and recently published in London would arrive in a week or so. I could discover what I needed to know about her from that.

He seemed more interested in burning off his repressed energy by railing against the sultan, his 'quondam friend,' in less than flattering terms. This was in addition to our masters in Bengal and London, who Light believed were foolish and should leave local matters to those with on-the-spot experience.

'The Honourable Company's Bencoolen factory, which proved to be an unprofitable disaster as it was situated on the wrong side of Sumatra for traders sailing the Malacca Straits, was set up as a collection station for pepper that was shipped from the spice islands to be conveyed to London. At one point, the directors wrote to their local agent advising him that since the British public much preferred white pepper to the black variety, the growers should concentrate only on cultivating the former.'

'But—' I began, to which Light waved his hand at me and spoke more quickly in order to complete his anecdote before I could say more.

'Those ignoramuses in London had to be tutored by their Bencoolen representatives that there is only one vine producing peppercorns and whether that commodity goes to market as black or white pepper depends entirely on how it is handled.'

'How did London respond to being told that?' I asked.

'Not well,' replied Light with a grin. 'You see what I have to put up with? Then there is Sultan Abdullah who, when the Burmans invaded Siam in early 1786, foolishly sent arms to Ava whilst at the same time writing letters of loyalty to the Siamese king.'

'Playing both sides,' I said, not daring to add that this was exactly what Light himself had done when negotiating between the sultan and acting Director-General Macpherson.

'Which did not work in Abdullah's favour because when the Siamese expelled the Burmans from their country and discovered what their southern vassal had done, they threatened to punish Queda in retribution for siding with their enemy.' Light took a long drink of wine and added, 'You have to know what you are doing to successfully play one hand against another.' Then he raised his glass, as if toasting his superior abilities in that regard.

At that moment, one of Light's crew knocked on the cabin door and, upon being invited in, entered the room and handed Light a letter, which he immediately ripped open and read.

'Blast the man!' exclaimed Light, throwing the parchment to the floor.

I picked it up but could not read the Jawi script.

'The sultan refuses to see me.'

'Perhaps at a more convenient time?' I suggested.

'He has rejected the offer I made him. Although he kept the opium, he has returned the silver.'

I heard Light mumble, 'This is not good,' as he darted out of his quarters. Next, he was barking orders up on deck. Unable to know what to do, I waited for him to return. When he did, Light looked dejected. 'The winds are not in our favour, in more ways than one. We are stuck here a while yet.'

Thinking that a change of subject from the sultan and Penang might take his mind off things I said, 'Machiavelli. You said to remind you to discuss him. I am anxious to hear more.'

'Not now, Jim,' he snapped, and that was the last word out of his mouth to me until we reached Penang many hours later.

As George Town came into view, I could see Fort Cornwallis not only as a sorry excuse for a stockade but also as a metaphor. For it highlighted the tenuous hold that Light and the EIC had on the island itself. Sultan Abdullah had exerted his authority in the matter of Penang's ownership by refusing Light an audience. Would he press his advantage as he had barely seven months after Light's arrival, when the sultan had cut off food supplies coming from Queda, until assured that he would receive the desired military protection? Might the sultan escalate matters beyond another embargo? Penang's garrison of four hundred men was insufficient to defend us from a Malay attack.

From fearing night ambushes by all manner of vicious animals— whether wild boars, monkeys, or pirates—my concern switched from danger to my person to how Light could defend the one thousand souls in Penang should the aggrieved sultan choose to reclaim his island by force.

I desperately wanted to find Pieter so we might devise a plan to assist Light out of this impasse. With my employer descended into melancholy and James Scott still abroad I needed someone with a knowledge of all parties to help me further demonstrate my worth.

What I did not yet realise was that an ineffable menace lay masked, controlled and concealed, like a cobra in a basket of eggs, much closer to home than Queda.

Chapter 12

Ill-considered

Government House, Penang. 7.30 p.m. Thursday, 23 April 1789.

'Why, Mr Lloyd, you seem quite out of sorts. Are you unwell?' the woman seated to my right at Light's dinner table whispered in my ear.

I turned to the pigeon-chested matron and lied. I told her I had merely been deep in thought about the many interesting conversations going on around us. Yet, for the past two days, I had become as riddled with resentment as a beggar with fleas. I tried not to scratch at the irritation caused by Light's callous disregard for *my* needs but was largely unsuccessful. Some part of me knew I needed to be careful not to make my discontent so apparent on my face, but I snubbed that inner warning.

We were interrupted by a small boy who burst into the room in advance of a female slave and ran directly to his father. His halo of black curls, pale skin, and large, expressive eyes soon had the visiting women clucking and cooing.

'Everyone?' intoned our host, clapping his hands to encourage quiet. We were instantly hushed. I watched as Light slipped the boy a pastry with a conspiratorial wink. The superintendent had spared no expense in laying out the finest dinner for his guests, with beef, turtle, poultry, all manner of fish and seafood, pastries, fruits, and other desserts heaped upon the table. Most of it imported, of course. There were also copious bottles of wines and spirits that I had been imbibing liberally in a failed attempt to cheer myself up.

'Everyone, this is my son, William Julian Light,' intoned our host. Light seemed to be in finer spirits than I had seen him since returning from Queda; showing off to strangers suited him. 'William, would you like to say hello to our guests before you return to your own home and bed?'

The boy in the cream cotton nightgown nodded solemnly as if accepting permission from the captain to inspect the troops. Pushed forward gently by his father, William slowly walked the length of the room and back.

'Lieutenant and Mrs Gray you know, of course, as they are our neighbours,' began Light, nodding to where the officer in question sat to the left of Martinha Rozells, with his wife seated directly opposite him. 'That gentleman seated across from me is Captain John Glass, the commander of our garrison, and alongside him is Captain Robert Hamilton, his second-in-command. Next to Captain Hamilton sits Miss Anna Davis from England, who is briefly visiting with her friend Mrs Beal, seated over on the other side. They are on their way to Macau to reconnect with Mrs Beal's husband.'

The boy shook hands with the men and bowed in a most charming manner to the English ladies who giggled as they ruffled the boy's hair, which he obviously did not like, and commented to his parents what a good-looking son they had. I smiled wryly, wondering what was really going on in the heads of Miss Davis and Mrs Beal about the boy's pale complexion, given the earlier mumbled conversation I had heard between them.

I had been admiring a framed sketch drawn by Elisha Trapaud whose newly arrived book was the cause of my disgruntlement. The illustration depicted the 'christening ceremony' that had taken place almost three years earlier, after Light had determined that Penang should be known as Prince of Wales Island. Only a few feet away from where I stood, Miss Davis had expressed to her travelling companion her shock at finding that there was only one white woman—her long-time friend, Mrs Gray—on the entire island and that a gentleman such as Captain Light had 'kept this Malay woman, whom he has lived with for almost twenty years,' in preference to the suitable marriage that was 'a great pity he did not make,' even though he was 'of plain appearance.' Since I was eavesdropping, pretending to be engrossed in Trapaud's illustration, I could not correct the younger of the two females; Miss Rozells, an exotic-looking lady with a serene, oval face, and almond eyes, was part-Portuguese, part-Siamese, not Malay.

Studying their host's live-in partner from a distance, the two women then opined in hushed tones how Martinha Rozells, perhaps no more than six years older than the two of them, must have been pretty in her day. Since neither of these pratepies was a great beauty, I found myself wanting to leap to the defence of our hostess, thinking her very fine in her full, chintz petticoat and green and white striped laced bodice, fastened at the wrists with gold buttons, her raven hair held up with a silver pin like a silken crown. At least, I did before reminding myself that I should not like her any more than I did the duplicitous Captain Light. Or was I being unfair to my employer? Perhaps the false information published in Trapaud's book had not come from Light at all but from the imagination of his former second-in-command who had been looking to curry favour?

I snapped out of these thoughts when I heard Light introduce the man seated to his right, Dr Johann Gerhard Koenig, the Danish botanist, 'who has kindly brought with him some strawberry plants that we shall grow on the Suffolk Estate, William. By which, everyone, I refer to the small garden house I have built three miles southwest of George Town.' Light turned to smile at his son. 'You and your sister will enjoy eating strawberries next year, William, I am quite sure of that.'

The gathering laughed as the boy jumped up and down in apparent glee, although I noticed that Martinha, on Light's left, had not uttered a word all evening except to instruct her slaves in their own language and maintained a somewhat vacant, Mona Lisa-like smile throughout. I wondered as to the whereabouts of William's older sister, Sarah.

'And last, but certainly not least, that gentleman seated between Mrs Gray and Mrs Beal is Mr James Lloyd from London, my new assistant. We must be extra nice to him, William, so he doesn't leave us in the lurch.'

Your new assistant? What happened to being your chronicler? I silently seethed. I thought once more of Trapaud's book—more a pamphlet, really, given that it was just forty-two pages long—and gritted my teeth. Light's son, perhaps no more than three or four years old, stood before me with the quizzical expression of a much older child. He bowed with solemn grace and held out his small hand. For a moment, I was confused, not sure how he expected me to shake it while it contained the pastry his father had earlier given him.

'For you,' said the boy, thrusting the sweet treat towards me.

Perhaps it was the wine, but my eyes misted over as I croaked, 'Thank you, William.' A cloak of despair enveloped me; how I had longed for a brother rather than my two vain and vacuous older sisters, with whom I had never been able to establish any affinity. But more than that, with his black hair, dark eyes, and uncommonly good manners, William Light reminded me of myself at his age. I would have snatched him up and hugged him had he not turned heel and ran back to his mother, who scooped him up into her arms and kissed him on the forehead before whispering something that caused him to nod his head and rub his eyes. Turning to Light, who handed him a fresh pastry, the boy obediently shook his father's hand then left the room with the slave.

'Goodnight, William,' Light called out. 'Sleep tight, my boy.' For all his reticence about mentioning his family to me, it seemed Captain Light was immensely fond of his son.

'The next generation of your business,' said Captain Hamilton, whose arm rested along the back of Miss Davis' chair, which appeared to cause her some distress since he had been intent on commandeering the only single lady in the room all evening.

'Oh, I believe my son is destined for far greater things than trade,' answered Light.

'I am sure the boy will make you proud in years to come, Governor Light,' opined Mrs Beal, an honorific that our host chose not to correct, even though *Governor* was a considerable elevation from the position of superintendent he actually held. It was also how Elisha Trapaud had described Captain Light in his dratted book.

Upon receiving the expected copies, Light had handed me this thin work entitled, *A Short Account of the Prince of Wales's Island, or Pulo Peenang, in the East Indies, given to Captain Light by the King of Queda.*

After reading it, I felt sorely aggrieved and cheated. What was the use of chronicling Light's story when such a book had already been written? Why had Light kept its existence a secret until now? More egregiously, why was Light so effusive in his praise of Trapaud's work when it was, to use the London editor's expression, blatant propaganda? Even the title was inaccurate, for this island had not been *given* to Captain Light at all but leased. Trapaud had also included a detailed description of a Malay wedding, inferring that this was the actual ceremony Light and Miss Rozells had gone through to cement their union. Only towards the close of the book did the author admit that this was not the case since, of course, he had not known Light in 1772 when that union had taken place.

Most incriminating of all in my eyes was the fact that Trapaud referred to Miss Rozells as a Malay princess, even going so far as to write—with 'certainty no less'—that 'the island of Pulo Peenang was given with her in dowry', and that Captain Light accepted it in the name of his Britannic Majesty for the use of the English East India Company. What poppycock!

Had the deceptive Elisha Trapaud never considered why a Mohammedan king would exalt a Catholic half-caste by designating her a princess of his court? Or whether it would be accepted practice, even in this foreign land, for a benefactor to offer land as dowry and then expect to be paid thirty thousand Spanish Dollars annually for its lease?

A dilettante like Trapaud—author, sketcher, and amateur actor, so I later learned—might have been wiser to stick to engineering in Madras and left the writing of a more truthful book, one that Dr Samuel Johnson would have approved of, to me.

But beyond my annoyance that Trapaud had published this propaganda about Light, something else bothered me. I had not been able to locate Pieter since returning from Queda. His ship had sailed and no one seemed to have any idea when the *Fame* and its captain might return. This only reminded me that I was captive to the same administrative tedium I had been slave to in Calcutta. Pieter and James Scott were men who set their own schedules and controlled their own destinies, whereas I felt under-appreciated and superfluous to needs, despite what Light had said earlier to his son.

By now the others around the dinner table had resorted back to their individual conversations. The company officers were intent on debating rumours that Lord Cornwallis was looking for any excuse to pull the plug on Penang, preferring the Andamans as a naval port. Mrs Beal shared several 'scandalous' stories about Governor-General Cornwallis that were quite untrue, as she announced to the other ladies, but that did not stop her from spreading them all the same. Only Martinha Rozells and I remained silent.

Everything on the table appeared to be cast in a ghostly shadow as I reached tentatively for a half-filled bottle to replenish my glass. At the head of the table there appeared to be a mild disagreement between Light and Dr Koenig.

'But there is considerable advantage to being of mixed race, sir,' boomed the Danish botanist nodding towards Miss Rozells, 'since it affords one the understanding needed to adapt to different groups and circumstances. I would humbly suggest you do your wife a disservice by waving off her proposal without giving it full consideration. She is like the chameleon whose eyes have the ability to move this way and the opposite simultaneously.'

As Dr Koenig began to do strange things with his eyes, I turned to Mrs Gray and whispered, 'What is he talking about?' To my horror, my words sounded slurred and I quickly placed my wine glass back on the table. Seeming not to have noticed my inebriation, the matron related that Captain Light had dismissed an earlier suggestion by Miss Rozells that might help reduce the lawlessness on the island. She had advised *'Governor* Light' to encourage more single men to marry local women, since the Manchu government had forbidden their people to leave China and many Indian men here were similarly unattached, leaving them with too much time on their hands. Time which they then used to engage in drinking, gambling, and other unsavoury outlets, not the least of which was opium smoking.

Miss Davis, wide-eyed, asked our host if there was much crime on the island in a manner that suggested she rather hoped that there was, presumably only when she and her companion were safely gone to Macau.

'It is a challenge, dear lady,' opined Light. 'Not only do crimes and licentiousness go on within our fledgling community, but the vast majority of them are committed by the Malays. That piratical bunch would cut your throat in a heartbeat and are only too content to remain in jail for months on end. We provide them free food and lodgings and they sleep undisturbed for as long as they care to with no distress to them, it appears, for their loss of liberty.'

'The current arrangement merely plays into the hands of those lazy curs,' added Hamilton, a man whose resting expression would give anyone the impression that he had a particular talent for sniffing out rotten eggs.

Light pointed out how the Council in Bengal had consistently refused his requests for a judiciary to help maintain law and order. During a pause in his address, a strange desire to support the silent Miss Rozells prompted me to speak up. 'I have heard of a similar proposal to your wife's advanced by Lord Cornwallis, concerning the current parlous situation in Bengal,' I said, with the good sense given the mixed company not to go into any vulgar details as to why such measures were needed. 'Dr Koenig's analogy seems very apt and Miss Rozells' ability to see things from a different perspective should surely be encouraged. If Penang is to represent something more than a place of commerce, Captain Light, and you desire to encourage people to live here and not only visit to trade, it surely needs more families.'

'Are you speaking from personal experience, *Master* Lloyd?' said Hamilton, which prompted some of the others to laugh, albeit as if embarrassed at his impudence.

Before I could reply, Captain Glass, who had apparently noticed that Hamilton had been pestering Miss Davis all evening, piped up.

'Maybe you should go easier on the wine, old boy. It seems as if you are too sloshed to see the signals.'

Unfortunately, so was I. With no thought as to the consequences, I blurted out, 'I am surprised our host does not provide his guests with a 'Negus', for that would surely keep Captain Hamilton's passions in check.'

Every eye in the room turned to me and my face burned as if I had sat too close to a furnace. My God! Had I just said the name Negus out loud?

Chapter 13

Dim Views

The room took on the ambiance of a museum filled with marble statues. Everyone looked at me, expecting more to be said. Summoning Dutch courage, I stammered on. 'Has no one heard of that drink? I did, quite recently, when informed of it by Captain Light's business partner, James Scott.' Even though my eyes were cast down, as if tasked with examining the warp and weft of my breeches, I could feel Light's eyes boring into the crown of my head. I looked up, took a deep breath, and gazed around the gathered company.

Mrs Beal spoke up. 'Whatever is a 'Negus'?'

I relayed what Scott had told me, intelligence so freely related by him that surely there was no harm repeating it. 'It is a diluted concoction of warm, sugared wine invented, if that is the correct word, by a former Member of Parliament for Ipswich, Colonel Francis Negus. Apparently, he had been intent on helping his friends stay sober so that they would be less inclined to challenge one another to duels during their heated political discussions.'

'A Member of Parliament, you say?' interjected Lieutenant Gray.

'What a grand idea,' enthused his wife, who looked askance at her listing husband.

'Or the actions of a skinflint. Sounds more like an excuse to water down the wine to me,' growled Hamilton, whose gaze I deliberately avoided, even though I could feel his scowl never leave my face.

The man's disdain and earlier rudeness fuelled my desire to further show off my private knowledge. 'Dead these past fifty years, but when alive a gentleman of considerable achievement in high circles,' I countered, speaking slowly to avoid slurring my words. 'Master of the late King's buckhounds; Ranger of Swinley Chase; Lieutenant of Windsor Forest. Colonel Negus married into the illustrious and wealthy Churchill family and so was hardly in need of diluting his guests' drinks for pecuniary reasons.' Despite my flaming cheeks, I warmed to being the centre of attention, in addition to besting this ignorant company officer to whom I had taken an instant dislike. But then I went too far. 'You might think twice about insulting Colonel Negus, Hamilton, since he is the paternal grandfather of our host, Captain Light.'

'Is that true?' exclaimed Mrs Beal, clapping her hands like an excited child at the prospect of yet more gossip.

The next few seconds seemed to stretch like a morning yawn. When Light spoke up it was in a manner that seemed to chill the balmy air. 'Yes, Mrs Beal, James is correct. I am the natural son of William Negus of Melton who, while educated at court, chose a more private life as a country gentleman. He died some years ago, but I am aware of Colonel Negus' connection to the drink you mention.' Light paused, then added more graciously than I might have done in his place, 'I thank you for reminding me of it, James. I shall be sure to have some 'Negus' on hand next time Hamilton comes to dinner.'

Other than the captain in question, the other guests indicated their approval of Light's intention with a nervous, embarrassed laughter; no one had missed the fact that Francis Light did not share his father's surname. I had now done something far worse than wear my earlier annoyance and frustration on my face. I had informed everyone in the room of Light's illegitimacy.

'What some men will do to be remembered,' joked John Glass, raising his wine to Light.

'What it is to have a name with social clout,' answered Light, adding *soto voce*, 'And how minor the achievements of already lofty men need to be.'

So, James Scott had been correct. Being denied the name of Negus had aggrieved Light for all these years. A name that would have opened doors for him, including at the court of King George, a benefit Light's natural father had chosen to eschew. Living with the name of his mother had indeed fuelled the superintendent's dogged ambitions for the name Light to be remembered in the history books.

While desperately wishing to avoid Light's gaze, I caught sight of Martinha, who raised a finely arched eyebrow at me—not in a way that seemed accusatory but rather amused. Locking her eyes on to mine, she reached over and placed a hand on her husband's, who was now engaged in deep conversation with Dr Koenig. I grimaced at her in the manner of a child found raiding the pantry at midnight, then turned away when I felt Mrs Beal's finger tap my shoulder. Had I heard about the scandal surrounding the elopement of Lord Cornwallis' daughter—Lady Mary—with a young guard's captain named Mark Singleton, whom Lady Mary Lindsay had described to Lady Campbell as a bad business for both, and had reportedly made the new Governor-General apoplectic with rage when he received news of it? I replied—in a manner I hoped would convey that I had no interest in any further details about the sorry affair—that other than Lord Cornwallis, I did not know the names of these other people.

Mrs Beal looked affronted at finding that her tittle-tattle had reached indifferent ears. 'Do *you* have a sweetheart at home?' she probed.

'No,' I lied, solely concerned about the effect my indiscreet sharing of his family history had had on Light and how it might affect our tenuous relationship going forward.

Giving up on me, Mrs Beal turned her head away and began to engage Captain Glass. Over the clattering of cutlery on plates, I could hear the occasional whisper as Hamilton continued his fruitless attentions towards Miss Davis. Several slaves entered and after receiving brief instructions from Martinha, began to clear away the dishes. Someone suggested repairing to the veranda to take in the night air and play a round or two of cards. I wanted to speak up and warn the company about doing that but felt I had drawn enough attention to myself for one evening.

Some weeks earlier, I had felt a series of pinpricks on my skin, as if some small devil was poking me with a trident. Alarmed, I had noticed several ugly red weals that had erupted almost immediately on my hands and arms. Upon seeing me scratch so vigorously that I drew blood, a young Malay—whom I knew only as Awang—ran after me holding a piece of what he called *lidah buaya* growing abundantly nearby. I recognised it as aloe vera. Placing the gelatinous part of this thick, bright green plant on my skin had an immediate cooling effect and I no longer felt the need to abrade myself.

'*Kubur orang putih*,' said Awang with a look of sympathy as he loped off. Only later, when I learned why the villagers gave Penang the nickname 'White Man's Grave', did I understand what he meant.

'We know to live far from the swampland where Chief Light built his houses and *gudang*,' one elderly Malay explained. 'We sweep our village at evening time and burn leaves and branches wet from the afternoon rains. Chinese people burn incense sticks and Indians shut their doors and windows at night.'

My expression must have shown that I did not understand his point. The older man had sighed and continued. 'White people ignore the pools of water under their houses. They sit on their verandas to play card games, enjoy wines late at night, and later sleep with their doors open. We know not to do this because of fever—'

'Caused by stagnant water and damp rot,' I interrupted with sudden insight. Ever since, I had been determined to stay clear of the putrid, standing water and stinking open drains where the biting insects that afflicted me appeared to breed. I had no intention of becoming one of the souls over-populating the island's Protestant cemetery.

My unspoken protestations at the dinner table were not needed, however. No sooner did the sound of chairs scraping on wood subside and the party begin to break into different factions than Dr Koenig, who stood nearest the shutters, said, 'What is that?'

'Quiet!' yelled Light to the slaves clearing away the remains of our meal, who immediately stood still as rocks as if struck by Medusa's gaze.

We heard the peal of bells as if being called to church. Then a voice, faint at first but gathering closer, shouted, 'Fire!'

Light immediately ordered Hamilton to accompany Miss Davis, Mrs Beal, and Dr Koenig back to their ship. Lieutenant Gray was to return his wife to her own house, then the two officers were to join him and Captain Glass at the source of the blaze. Their panic was palpable and for good reason. George Town's homes were all made of wood. Only ten buildings were constructed of brick. Worse still, the roofs of all the dwellings were of highly flammable attap. One lick of flame from an overturned oil lamp, and it would not take long for the entire town to be destroyed. That would also mean the loss of highly valuable goods stored in the harbour's godowns and would detrimentally impact the financial stability of the fledgling settlement.

Up to this point it was as if I were invisible. Sensing an opportunity to get to know Light's wife better and ingratiate myself to her in the hope of securing an ally, I called out to Light, 'Allow me to take Miss Rozells home to William. If the fire gets out of hand and comes too close to her property, I will make sure they both get to safe, higher ground.'

'Do that,' said Light just before he exited. Over his shoulder he added, 'You and I will speak further, James, when I return.'

Chapter 14

Ablaze with Admiration

Standing alone on the veranda of Martinha's bungalow while she checked on William, I looked beyond the molasses darkness that enveloped our immediate surroundings to a sight similar to what must have filled the inhabitants of London with dread in 1666. The great swathe of the night sky in the distance had turned a blistering orange, licked from beneath by white-hot flames as plumes of dense smoke enclosed the hellish tableau. I trusted that Dr Koenig and the two Englishwomen were now safely sheltered on their ship, the *General Coote,* yet worried for the many hundreds of inhabitants and visitors whose lives and livelihoods were at risk. What irony to live on an island surrounded by water and watch fire consume everything you own in the world.

I did not hear her sidle up next to me and was startled like a nervous colt when Martinha Rozells uttered the words 'Jalan Malabar' in my ear. She could see that the blaze raged most intensely in the Indian quarter, where the Chulias lived, as I had earlier. Concerned that she was afraid the fire would reach us despite the distance, I sucked an index finger and held it out beyond the wooden platform. The breeze blew away from us. '*Kita selamat,*' I said, resisting the urge to squeeze her arm in reassurance. We are safe.

Turning away from that dreadful scene, we stepped into the main room. The interior of her home was graced with panelling that afforded very little privacy as it divided the space into smaller areas. This was a simple square-built wooden structure, albeit more sizeable than the ones in the Malay kampong. I blushed to recall how I had earlier stumbled my way up the steep wooden steps that led to her door and determined never to drink alcohol to that extent again, if at all.

Martinha surprised me by sitting on the floor and gestured that I join her. She offered me a tin mug of water which I gratefully glugged down, then held out to receive more. We did this several times to help slake my alcoholic thirst. Sated at last, I noticed she had also brought in an oblong piece of wood and a silk bag that rattled as if full of beads or small coins. I recognised the board immediately as part of a game I had watched men play in the kampong. The board had sixteen holes carved into it: two larger ones at the ends and seven smaller ones on each side. Martinha opened the cloth bag and out spilled an array of tiny shells.

I explained in Malay that while I was quite proud of my improved language skills, having practised with the locals these past few months, I was not yet proficient.

She replied in perfect and only slightly accented English, 'Then why don't we converse in your language?' Before I could respond, mouth agape, she added, 'Forgive me, Mr Lloyd. Or may I call you James?'

'James. Or Jim, whichever you prefer,' I said.

'There is a game Francis and I play to amuse ourselves from time to time, James. Perhaps you think it cruel?'

'What game is that?' I stammered.

'To leave people with the impression that I speak no English. I am not around the officers much so even they do not suspect. But I was educated at a convent school in Madras. I am quite fluent in English, French, Siamese, Portuguese, as well as a little Spanish.'

As if anticipating my next thought, the lady continued, 'I knew immediately from their expressions as well as their reference to the 'black girls' that attended them what those two Englishwomen thought of me. It amused me to play along with their assumptions and act the ignorant native.'

I lowered my gaze, guilty of having believed those assumptions myself. 'Yet throughout the night you appeared to be—'

'Bored. It is easy to feign a vacant expression when you hear the same superficial mutterings again and again. Although I will admit I found you to be refreshingly candid. I think, if you will forgive my presumption, that we shall get along very well indeed.'

'I was insufferably impertinent at tonight's dinner,' I mumbled, eyes still downcast.

Martinha leaned across and patted my hand. 'Don't worry. What is illegitimacy these days, given the number of bastards around? Some of them born, like that dreadful Hamilton, *within* wedlock.' She tittered quite delightfully, holding her fan over her mouth, and I think it was at that moment that I became infatuated with Light's wife.

She added wistfully, 'Francis does not always heed my suggestions, but he trusts me when it comes to judging people. I like you, James. You need not concern yourself with my husband dismissing you while that remains the case.'

Placing the wooden board between us and scattering the shells across the floor, she went on, 'Let us spend this time playing a game of our own so as not to distress ourselves about events we cannot do anything about.'

I told her this sounded like a wonderful idea, grateful for understanding from a charming potential ally.

'Let us see how good you are at playing *congkak*,' said Martinha.

I followed her lead and picked up a handful of shells, placing seven of them in each of the small holes on my side of the board and leaving the larger hole—the 'house'—empty.

Martinha began her demonstration of the game, although I was somewhat familiar with the strategy required. She removed all the shells from one of the holes and moving clockwise around the board deposited one each into the next seven hollows, including her house. Watching her was mesmerising, a welcome relief from dark thoughts. When it came to my turn I tried to remember what I needed to do. She swatted my hand playfully with her fan when I either dropped one of my shells into her house—a wrong move—or thought my turn was over prematurely. My heart lurched every time at her touch.

The more I got the hang of congkak, the faster she played and I tried to follow suit, making many mistakes and laughing at the fun we were having. She told me she had taught the game to her children to help them learn to count. There were ninety-eight shells in play and whoever earned the most would be declared the winner. Before long there were no more shells in any of the small cavities, just the larger houses at each end of the wooden board.

'Let's count them together in Malay so you can practice your numbers,' she suggested. We chanted in unison, at the end of which Martinha looked at me with mock humility and declared herself, rightly, the winner.

'Again?' she asked and I nodded, immediately regretting moving my head so vigorously.

As we played one game after another and my confidence grew, although not my ability to best her, Martinha and I began to converse more. Midway through our third game, my opponent having won the previous two, I felt bold enough to ask, 'Before tonight, I had wondered how to address a Malay princess.'

Martinha's dark, almond eyes looked quizzical. I pressed ahead, recklessly. 'You are a Malay princess are you not?'

She fanned away that idea with the hand not clutching a palm full of small shells and laughed. 'Goodness, no. Wherever did you get that idea?'

From the duplicitous Elisha Trapaud, I almost blurted out.

Before I could reply Martinha said, 'My father came from Portugal and married my mother, who was Siamese. He worked as a laksamana for Sultan Jiwa's small fleet of prahus. So, I grew up as part of the royal court, where everyone is encouraged to think of themselves as one big family. A pleasant illusion.

'But I only ever existed on the periphery of the court. It was always clear to me from an early age, not least being a Eurasian Christian, that I did not truly belong in that world. Nor, frankly, did I wish to.'

She smiled a little sadly I thought then said, 'But let's not stand on ceremony, James. You need not call me princess, just Martinha.'

She told me that she and her sister, Yeen, had been well treated by Sultan Jiwa, who had arranged for Martinha to be sent to India to be educated. We briefly reminisced about India. She asked me about my time working for the East India Company, and I could not help but bemoan the outrageous conditions in which the Indian people had been plunged since that trading company had established its rule there. How ravaged that once-proud nation had become at our rapacious hands.

Despite the ongoing chatter, I realised my companion had not fully explained the reason for Trapaud's lie about her status. Encouraged by the easy back and forth we had so quickly established, I pushed a little more. 'So, you are *not* a Malay princess?'

She shrugged and smiled in a way that I would always find alluring. 'Francis likes to call me that,' she said with mock shyness. I took this to mean it was the kind of affectionate nickname men often gave their loved ones, similar to how my father used to call Mother 'angel face,' and I would occasionally whisper 'poppet' to Laura.

Martinha explained that it was an old-fashioned Malay courtesy to refer to someone like her, the child of one of the Sultan's entourage, as a princess, but that did not mean she was a blood relative or even Jiwa's daughter as had often been misconstrued. It simply meant that she was considered a lady of the court.

'That is not what Elisha Trapaud stated with certainty in his book,' I replied, my aggravation of that work palpable.

Martinha gazed over my head towards the veranda. She spoke so softly that it was almost as if she was speaking to herself. 'I find the motivations of some men unfathomable, James. But perhaps we all have a willingness to believe what we desire to be true for reasons that often remain secret to ourselves. A form of blindness, do you not think?'

I nodded, then muttered, 'And some men willingly misrepresent a situation because it suits their nefarious purposes.'

But why should Martinha be blamed for the deceptions that one of her husband's officers had perpetrated to give more piquancy to his book? It was not her fault if Light considered it advantageous to allow this exaggeration about his wife's status to stand—in the same way that he had not corrected Miss Davis and Mrs Beal, who had referred to him all evening as *Governor* Light.

Breaking into these thoughts, Martinha said, 'Francis is quite the practical joker, although some of his jests might be interpreted badly.'

'How so?' I asked.

She tittered charmingly behind her fan and looked over to the door as if expecting her husband to arrive back at any moment. 'Some years ago, the Reverend John Gottfried Haensel from the Church of the United Brethren visited my husband. I was staying with my sister at the time so never got to meet him, thank goodness. As you may know, Francis declared early on in the name of his government that he would protect the rights of Penang's inhabitants to practice any religion that remains consistent with the general good and peace of all. So, it is not as if my husband is intolerant of other faiths.'

She picked up one of the larger shells and began manipulating it between her fingers. 'This man, Haensel, was an almighty bigot and a bore; at least that is what I was told. To Francis, I am never sure which is worse. It appears he wanted to visit us again, but James Scott managed to intercept him, instructed by my husband to tell the Reverend that Captain Light had gone to Bengal and had lost his wife some years earlier, so he should not make the trouble.'

The two of us stared at each other for a moment, my eyes as round as saucers. Then we burst out laughing at that outrageous lie. I was filled with such desire to remain in the company of this lady—beyond the reason I had originally devised, to ingratiate myself further with the Light family—that I now would have forgiven either of them any deceit.

'No more games,' announced Martinha, at the end of my fifth loss. She began to gather up the shells into the silk bag with a flirtatious, 'I won.'

You certainly have, I thought to myself, since she had triumphed in more than just this game. I had surrendered myself completely to this masterful strategist who had helped me forget the mayhem that raged in George Town.

Pressing her advantage, Martinha said, 'Francis is a good man, James, and he has become very fond of you.'

'He has?' I blurted out.

'Of course, why would you doubt it? He has told me many times how much he appreciates your hard work and diligence; he would be lost without you. Please continue to help and support my husband. Do you promise?'

I almost wept, whether from gratitude, or joy, or just drunken exhaustion as the hour was now very late. 'I promise,' I pledged. 'But I fear there may soon be trouble concerning the Sultan of Queda. You probably know how envious he is that regional ships are now visiting Penang to trade, rather than his own ports. I worry that he may soon wish to reclaim this island.'

Martinha's face clouded over. 'My husband has realised a vision for Penang, with untold benefits for everyone who settles or trades here. By making this a free port and offering land to those who will clear and cultivate it, he provides people the freedom to determine their own futures, away from the jealous gaze and grasping hands of their former chiefs.' She lifted one of the larger shells and holding it between her fingers, deliberately snapped it in two. 'If Francis must break a few rules and ruffle the feathers of certain people for the good of the majority, so be it.'

I nodded, recalling the quote Light had shared with me from Machiavelli: 'For although the act condemns the doer, the end may justify him'.

Martinha gathered up the rest of the shells, placed them and the congkak board to one side, and said, 'Barely more than fifty people lived on this island before Francis claimed it, even though Penang had been well-populated at one time. Thousands were massacred here by an earlier sultan who wanted to end the piratical attacks on ships headed to and from Queda, even though that was the people's only means of subsistence because of their raja's demands for higher taxes and tolls.

'If you had been here in the early days you would have seen Penang for what it was: nothing but jungle, home to a few terrified families eking out their existence from fishing. Why then, when Francis has been the only one responsible for Penang's rising success, does the sultan think he has any right to it? Before we came, this island was of no value to Abdullah. It is pure greed and jealousy that impassions him now when he sees what this island could have become had he my husband's acumen.'

My envy of Captain Light constricted my throat and heart like bindweed. Oh, to have such a fiercely supportive, gracious, and intelligent wife. Now, at least, I had found someone apart from Pieter from whom I might learn facts that Light seemed determined to hold back.

'You have been refreshingly open and honest with me. As a newcomer to this island, I very much appreciate that,' I said.

'Never forget, James: Friends always tell friends the truth.'

My heart sang at the mention of the word 'friends'. From then on, I deceived myself, I would offer her the same truthfulness back.

'We would be more comfortable on chairs,' Martinha said, after a brief companionable silence.

I struggled to get up from the floor requiring Martinha's hand to do so, the two of us giggling like small children at my clumsiness. 'Where is your daughter?' I asked when back on my feet.

'Sarah is with my sister in Queda. Young people always find the allure of court more attractive than a place like Penang. But she will learn. Please, James, take that seat.'

I waited until she settled had herself into a chair, then sank gratefully into the one closest to her, worried that if I became too comfortable I would fall asleep.

'Do you have a sweetheart at home in England?' my companion asked.

For some reason, different from my reticence with Mrs Beal, I did not wish to speak of Laura. But before I had the chance to decide how to answer, we heard the sound of boots on the steps. Without conscious thought, I lifted my chair and positioned it further away from Martinha's.

The man who now stood before us was barely recognisable, his hands and clothing as blackened as a chimneysweep's, his thinning hair matted around a face that looked as if it had been too long in the noonday sun. Martinha rushed away, saying that she would bring water for drinking and washing.

I asked Light to share his news. The fire, he said, had started in Malabar Street, home to the Chulias. Too rapid to admit any remedy, the only thing he and his men could do was to prevent it spreading to the Chinese houses, and they would have failed at that had the wind not been in their favour, carrying the flames away from the town towards the water.

He explained that fifty-six houses had been burned and all of them had belonged to Indians. The Chinese living nearby had carried all their effects into their back yards, barred their doors, and armed themselves, while quietly resigning their properties to chance. No one had died, as far as he was aware, but many families would have to be kept in confinement until they recovered from their burns and breathing difficulties. As he sank into the chair Martinha had just vacated, Light said he estimated the financial loss to be around fifteen thousand Spanish Dollars.

'A dreadful accident,' I said.

Light looked across the room as if seeing me for the first time. 'This was no accident. No candle or lamp was in the house where it started. Someone on this island is deliberately trying to destroy us from within.' The captain continued to speak, more to himself it seemed than to me, as he rambled on about the men still searching for missing property. He would catch a few hours' sleep and then go back on the streets to help restore order and calm, for many scoundrels were using this as an excuse to riot or sail away with plunder.

I tried my best to concentrate on his words but was caught up in the human failing from which all but the extremely pious suffer, worried more about what Light had meant with his final words after dinner about wanting to speak with me. But just then, Martinha came back into the room with a bowl of water, a drinking cup, and wet rags with which she began to dab at her husband's burned face.

'I should go,' I mumbled, strangely affected by the small intimacies going on between them. Light and Martinha looked up at me in obvious alarm.

'I fear rioting will go on throughout the night and early morning, it is not safe for you to walk all the way to Malay Town,' said Light, who looked at Martinha. She nodded, handed him the cloths, laid down the bowl of water and dutifully left. 'You can have a makeshift bed here for the night. We need to speak at some point, in any case.'

'We do?' I said nervously. 'About what?'

Light shook his head and combed his fingers through his sooty hair. 'Not now. I must rest briefly then leave. In the morning. We'll meet again after dawn.'

Perhaps I had overtired myself or was too aroused by my earlier conversation with Martinha, but I swear I barely slept a wink, convinced that Light would lambast me at the very least for making public that he was illegitimate. I only hoped Martinha would appease him in some way, then groaned in envy at that thought.

Chapter 15

Spark of Purpose

I had not meant to eavesdrop.

Light and Martinha had been conversing for some time just a few feet away from where I pretended to be asleep, separated by panelling so full of gaps that had I wished to, I could have spied on them as well. Their words dipped and soared like a discordant musical score and held me fascinated by their exchange as I lay on the cot that a dark-skinned slave named I Boon had set up for me the night before.

The gist of Light's opening salvo to his wife was that Penang had become unsafe for his family, and Martinha needed to reconsider taking the children to live elsewhere. It was clear from their back and forth that this was a discussion that had happened many times. The captain's main argument, I gleaned, centred on his desire not to be worried about Martinha and the children when he had so many other things on his plate.

What alerted me to pay even more attention to their conversation was the mention of Pieter.

'You should not have to look very far to see who is behind all this mayhem on the island,' Martinha said. 'That awful Dutchman.'

'Reinaert?' replied Light, sounding sceptical. 'On the contrary, he has proven to be most helpful. Jim thinks—'

'Jim? Oh, for goodness sakes, Francis. He's a fine young man but so naïve. We should not be relying too much on *Jim's* assessment of anyone.'

My face reddened as if she had just slapped me across the face.

Light said something back to her I did not catch to which Martinha replied, 'Have it your own way, but don't say I did not warn you about him.'

Whether that was about Pieter or me, I could not discern.

Again, their conversation became muted until Martinha declared loudly, 'I will not leave Penang.'

'Whyever not?'

'Tell me—where do you suggest I go, Francis? Junk Ceylon, perhaps? Have you forgotten what happened in '78 when the Siamese ordered the massacre of Christians, which that capricious race could choose to do again? Or has it slipped your mind why we had to flee to Queda with Sarah back then?'

I heard what sounded like a deep intake of breath as if Light was preparing to speak, when Martinha continued, 'Or perhaps we should go back to Alor Setar where you tell me Sultan Abdullah is resentful towards you, my husband? Do you think I would be any safer there? Well, do you?'

I could only assume Light made some request for her to calm down as I heard only indistinct muttering for several minutes afterwards.

Then Martinha's voiced raised again. 'And no, don't think of suggesting I take the children to India where we know no one. I will not go there.' After a brief period of what seemed like silence she added, 'I have drifted from place to place like a rudderless ship for too long, Francis. This is my home now, my children's home. Where you stay, we stay. A family.'

'Don't forget, Martinha, we agreed this will not be William's home forever.'

I heard what sounded like a muffled cry and a subdued, 'Yes,' followed by, 'But he needs preparation, Francis. You cannot expect to uproot the boy and replant him in that foreign country, even one familiar to you. How will he fare so many thousands of miles away from us?'

'I told you, he will be well looked after. My good friend George Doughty and his wife Anne will see to that. And by that time, I may have amassed a sufficient sum to buy Golsberry Farm, close enough to Theberton Hall so I can reunite with William later on.'

I could not help but notice Light's choice of 'I,' not 'we,' and lifted my hand to my mouth as if I could have stuffed back the words that had come from him, that I was sure had wounded his wife as much as they had offended me. Clearly, any future plans to return to England did not appear to include her.

'But why upset yourself about an event still several years away?' said Light.

'And in the meantime?' Martinha countered. 'I have tried to engage European tutors as you suggested. Some come one day then fail to turn up the next; many have proven unsuitable to the task; others William says he dislikes. As you have pointed out yourself—'

'I know,' interjected Light, 'William is a mild-mannered boy and easily persuaded but has a certain obstinacy in him that does not willingly bend to harsh control.' The captain spoke in a manner that suggested he was proud of these characteristics in his son.

'None of these men had the slightest notion how to nurture William's curiosity and passion for learning new things,' Martinha continued. 'He's like the nutmeg you have been unable to cultivate successfully here, needing exactly the right conditions to thrive. How can I help prepare him when I have never seen England?'

Then the two of them lowered their voices such that I almost settled back into a dreamless haze when I heard my name mentioned.

'Where is that darned assistant of mine? Not awake yet? Jim needs to learn to hold his liquor better.'

Martinha's voice rose a notch as if scolding a wayward child. 'Francis! Remember what we talked about?'

'Then tell I Boon to wake him up. I need to speak to him before I leave.'

'I'm here,' I said, standing just inside their room, some feet away from where Light and Martinha sat adjacent to each other, feeling dizzy from having sprung from my cot so quickly to dress.

'Good morning James,' said Martinha with another of her inscrutable raised eyebrows. She gave her husband a strange look before exiting the room with, 'I'll leave you men to it.' Only later did I come to understand that she intended for Light to have words with me, just not the admonishment that I expected.

'Sit down, Jim,' said Light over the top of my apology. I claimed Martinha's vacant chair as he said, 'Forgive my outburst just now. You did a valuable service looking after Martinha and my son last evening, a sojourn she tells me was most relaxing under the circumstances. I am grateful to you for that.'

Then Light stood up abruptly and, turning his back to me, began to pace around the room. He coughed as if clearing his throat of some impediment. 'I have wanted to say for some time,' he began, then coughed again, 'not only how much I have appreciated your hard work and diligence these past few months—' Another cough. 'But that I have become rather fond of you. Martinha—or, rather, both of us— yes, both of us want you to think of yourself as part of our family. As a young man, your life in Penang should not be consumed only with work.' He turned to face me and asked, 'Are you happy here?'

'Thank you, sir, I am,' I dissembled. *Well, I will be when Pieter returns, and if I had not read Trapaud's book, and if your wife could be a daily joy in my life so I could prove to her I am not so naïve*, I wanted to say, but kept such thoughts to myself.

'Good. That's good. Yes, that is what I have tried to ensure. Scotty told me you would be easy enough to please. I think then that I have succeeded despite what others might think.'

Our joint embarrassment and the awkward silence that followed threatened to submerge us just as Martinha re-entered the room with William. With great relief I blurted out, 'Hello again, young man,' to which the boy beamed and ran over to me and held out his hand. I spontaneously crouched down so that our eyes were level. 'What, no pastry this time?' I joked as I shook William's outstretched hand. The lad laughed, and the tension in the room eased.

'It's my birthday on Monday,' William announced to great amusement from his parents.

'Really?' I said. 'In three days, eh?'

'Yes. But we won't be doing anything special. There's nothing fun to do here,' said the boy so forlornly it almost broke my heart.

'Did you know,' I began, in an attempt to hide my distress, 'that the ancient Greeks first began the ritual of birthday cakes with candles in honour of the goddess Artemis. And the Germans have a name for such an event: Kinderfest.'

'I would like a cake with candles,' declared William, looking sideways at his mother.

Martinha might consider me a poor judge of character but this was my chance to improve her assessment of my own. 'I hear Mrs Gray is quite the baker and perhaps can help make a tasty honey cake if we ask her nicely and she has the ingredients,' I said. 'And I'm sure I can find suitable candles in the Chinese quarter; I would like to help make your birthday a special one this year.' Avoiding his parents' gaze in case my suggestion would be rejected, I asked, 'How old will you be on Monday, William?'

'Five,' said the boy, which caused an explosion of retorts from his parents.

I sprung up at the surprise.

'You are *not* five years old this year, my son,' laughed Light, but did not seek to correct with his actual age. 'Do not tell fibs, William, or there will be no cake and candles for you.'

'Yes, Papa,' said the boy, in a tone that suggested he was clearly aware he would get his wish regardless of how many fibs he told.

'William is tall for his age and quite precocious,' said Martinha hurriedly, gesturing for the boy to come to her, which he ignored as he was by now holding my hand.

'Advanced,' said Light, as if believing I either did not know the meaning of the word his wife had used or wished to show a preference for his own. 'Take the day off on Monday, Jim. You and William have fun together; I'm sure you can discover something that isn't *too dreary* to do on the island.' At this, Light made a grab for William and began to tickle and tussle with him for several minutes. When he righted the boy back on his feet Light said, 'That's decided then. Come to the fort as soon as you've freshened up, Jim, for we have much work to do today to itemise the devastation from the fire. And I will expect you in tomorrow. But Sunday is your day off, which is most deserved. Then on Monday, it can be just the two of you.' And with that, Light tousled his son's hair, pecked his wife on the cheek, and left the house.

I had always liked the symmetry of a square. Light, Martinha, William and I were to be a family. That, sadly, excluded Pieter who, nevertheless, needed to be included because—as I soon discovered—he knew all the best adventures to be had in Penang.

Chapter 16

Dark Discovery

George Town, Sunday 26 April.

The amiable Mrs Gray had, as expected, leapt at the chance to bake William a birthday cake and I had just secured a number of small candles from an enterprising Chinaman. With my chest newly arrived from Calcutta, I decided to gift Light's son my copy of Daniel Defoe's *Robinson Crusoe*. I knew the boy could already read, but I looked forward to reciting it to him, as it had long been one of my favourite tales, and I hoped it would be so for William.

Walking along Market Street, I planned to buy some fruit before deciding what to do with myself this fine day. There was still no sign of Pieter but, given my elevated spirits, I had every expectation that he would reappear soon.

Eyes downcast to ensure I did not twist my ankle in a rut or trip over an oversized stone, I looked up when I heard a group of native sepoys laughing raucously on the opposite side of the road. I watched with disgust as this uniformed rabble ripped open the mangoes that moments before had been scattered on the ground and now sucked hungrily at their flesh. I called out, 'Hey! What is going on over there?' and would have left it at that but caught sight of Awang lying behind the upturned cart, the lad who had helped me after my skin had been bitten by the local blood-sucking gnats. He looked dazed and appeared to have a minor head wound that had bled on to his clothes. Why were these military men ignoring him? Naively, it never occurred to me they might be responsible for his plight.

None of these recruits was like the tall, high-caste Hindustanis whose ancestors had been pressed into the Honourable Company's service a century earlier. The regular pay, benefits after death, and guaranteed employment for their sons and other male relatives had purchased these Indians' loyalty at a cost considerably cheaper than shipping in hundreds of our own soldiers from England. The EIC had since used them to supplement our low military numbers in Bombay, Calcutta, and Madras, with no shortage of willing recruits.

This group hailed from the south of India and held to none of the taboos that prevented their northern counterparts from undertaking sea journeys. Light had complained, when writing his initial report to newly installed Governor-General Cornwallis, of being lumbered with one hundred 'ignorant and unworthy marines', undisciplined men 'who made frequent complaints of the hardships they suffer in being obliged to work'. Men who nevertheless opened a bazaar within days of their arrival in Penang, a much less laborious way of making money. Whether these were the same fellows or not, this smaller contingent appeared no less out of control. Why were they here and not attending the fort, given the danger of attacks by the Queda sultan's forces, a European enemy, or Bugis and Lanoon pirates?

Agitated by their lack of duty, I called out a second time. The insolent bunch quietened and gazed at me as if I were some kind of interesting insect. One of them tipped his head in my direction and said something in an Indian language I did not understand, then they all burst out laughing and carried on as before. I looked around at the nearby Malay hawkers and their customers. Most had stopped their buying and selling and averted their gaze, others had scurried away.

I strode closer, infuriated that these supposed guardians of law and order were not only blatantly ignoring the needs of this wounded young man but appeared to be helping themselves to the produce that had fallen from his upturned cart. One of them deliberately crushed the heel of his boot into a dozen or so eggs that had landed, happily unbroken—at least until now—atop a pile of fruit.

'Stop that!' I called out and strode towards them. 'Stop that at once.'

'Stop *what*?'

I looked up and, despite hearing the disdain in his voice, sighed in relief as Captain Robert Hamilton appeared, adjusting his breeches. While the officer had been relieving himself around the corner, it seemed, his men had taken the opportunity to act in this disgraceful way. I smiled at Hamilton in gratitude for his welcome authority. But my consolation was short-lived as moments later I watched an elderly native scamper past us like an abused slave. The day was dry and the heat already searing, but the man was soaked from head to feet, and the acrid smell coming off him was so overpowering that I turned my head in disgust. I knew this man had always been clean in his habits on those occasions when I had placed a coin into his palm in gratitude for his masterful playing of the *seruling* and exchanged pleasantries with him in Malay. These natives took greater pains with their personal hygiene than did most of my countrymen; at least *they* washed daily, especially before eating and praying.

A fresh thought assailed me, causing my eyes to widen in horror and my knees almost to buckle. 'Sir! Did you just—?'

I did not have time to search my befuddled brain for the right words before Hamilton replied with a grin, 'What? Piss on that worthless pond scum? Guilty as charged.' His sepoys laughed even louder and continued with their plunder.

Before I knew what was happening, Hamilton had me by the throat and hauled me off down the same side alley in which he had deliberately urinated on a harmless old man.

'Take your hands off me, sir,' I said, with false bravado.

Hamilton drew his contorted face closer, his foul breath almost causing my stomach to heave, although my throat was too tight with fear to have released its contents. 'Or what? You'll tittle-tattle to your good friend, *Mister* Light? Yet where will *he* be one black evening when you accidentally fall, dash your head upon the rocks and end up in the sea, only to be washed up blue and bloated weeks later, if at all?'

I had no doubt Hamilton would carry out such a threat if I blabbed about his conduct to Light. Gossip gleaned from the Chinese had it that once, while Captain Glass was sick and Hamilton had temporarily become commander of the garrison, he had pressed to have a Chinaman's wife severely punished without trial for some minor civil infraction. Light had refused to sanction this, of course, and happily, John Glass soon recovered and took back control. But if Hamilton would happily whip a woman still nursing her baby and out of his jurisdiction, he would no doubt enjoy doing worse to me. As it was, his knuckles pressed so hard against my windpipe I feared I would soon pass out from lack of air.

'I don't like you, *Master* Lloyd; nor did I from the moment we first met,' Hamilton whispered in my ear as he released his grasp and I sank into myself, having worried that I would piss my pants if he did not let go of me soon. 'But forgive my earlier outburst as I should really not like anything *bad* to happen to you while in Penang.' And with that he made a mocking gesture of straightening my clothing.

I had two choices: squirm like a coward or be found dead in a ditch. I kept my mouth shut as I rubbed my throat, breathing deeply through my nose in order to calm myself. Hamilton poked my chest hard with a long, well-manicured finger. 'A quick word of advice, Jim lad. Keep your nose out of my bloody business and *never* address my men again, do you understand?' At no immediate response from me he screamed, spittle flying into my eyes, '*Do you understand?*'

'Yes,' I mumbled.

'Yes what?'

As loathe as I was to give him any satisfaction and berating myself for never having kept up the boxing lessons my uncle had urged me to take when I was younger, I answered, 'Yes, Captain Hamilton.' He continued to stare with intense hatred and so I added, 'Sir.'

With a supercilious smirk that made me wish I could have knocked his teeth through to the back of his head, he pushed my shoulder sending me crashing against the wall, then turned on his well-polished heels and left.

It took me several minutes after Hamilton had gone to compose myself. When I managed to stumble back around the corner, I saw that a few of the locals who had witnessed this disgraceful show were attending to Awang. Others picked through the remains of his produce trying to find anything that had not been eaten or deliberately smashed. These were returned to his now righted handcart.

I knelt beside the young man, whom I guessed was perhaps fourteen or fifteen years old. I took the dampened cloth that one of the nearby women held out and began to dab at the blood on his face. He had a gash on his forehead that was already closing up, a swollen lip, and would likely sport a black eye for a week. 'You'll live,' I said in Malay and attempted a smile, although I was not entirely settled myself. 'Can you stand up?'

He nodded and I helped him to his feet, hoping that none of his bones was broken.

Holding on to his cart as Awang continued rubbing his head, I said, 'Let's get you home.'

Awang said he was fine and that he would return to the kampong alone as he did not wish to cause me further trouble.

'No,' I said firmly, 'I insist on taking you back to your family.' I could not repair Awang's hurt and shame, but I could at least show him some kindness to make up for the outrageous treatment he had received at the hands of those ruffians. Men in uniform who were not only dishonourable, but also led by a potentially dangerous East India Company officer whose dislike, if not hatred, of me was obvious.

Chapter 17

Murky Tales

On the walk home, I learned that Awang's father was the headman of Malay Town, whom the son wanted me to meet. 'How should I address your father?' I asked, aware that there were any number of honorifics I might use.

'My father is known here as Nakhoda Kechil,' answered Awang. 'But his name is Ismail.'

'*Nakhoda* meaning a ship's master or captain?' I asked, to which Awang nodded.

'My father was also once a trader and helped to develop Batu Uban in the south where locals and foreigners brought goods. My uncle, Nakhoda Intan, who has already left this world, was a religious teacher at the mosque there. But to answer your question, the correct way to address my father is Tuan Nakhoda Ismail.'

Once we reached the kampong I waited outside their rumah until the completion of the early afternoon prayer time known as *Dhuhr*. As they folded their prayer mats, I heard Awang inform his father what had taken place earlier. This was not the first time such sanctioned theft and destruction had occurred and both Malays seemed resigned to it happening again.

Once seated on the floor of their home, shoeless as was the custom, I apologised profusely as if personally responsible for Awang's misfortune. His father smiled and waved a dismissive hand, but I could see the barely constrained anger in his eyes. At a loss to know what else to say, I implored him to take his grievance directly to Captain Light, ashamed that I could not for fear of aggravating Hamilton again.

'Why would the superintendent believe me when his officer will say my son brought damaged produce to market and now seeks payment we do not deserve?'

I replied that I still thought they should not let this matter rest, for others if not for themselves. Tuan Ismail merely shrugged and looked over at his son in silent communication. I was about to protest further when we were interrupted by the arrival of a woman, whom I assumed was Awang's mother, who began applying ointment to the young man's wounds.

'My son tells me you like to write stories,' said the father.

I must have mentioned my interest in chronicling when Awang had first tended to the insect bites on my hands. 'Yes, Tuan Ismail,' I replied.

'Would you like me to tell you something about our lives?' Although couched as a question, from his tone the headman left me in no doubt that this offer was not to be dismissed.

'Certainly,' I answered. 'I would be delighted.' At Tuan Ismail's earlier invitation, I had gladly removed my jacket and now sat in shirt sleeves and breeches that stuck to my skin in the heat, awaiting the commencement of his tale.

His family, the nakhoda told me, had lived in the hinterland of Penang for decades, his ancestors—simple fishermen—having escaped there to free themselves from the feudal system to which they had earlier been yoked. His great-grandfather had been one of the few to escape the wrath of an earlier Queda sultan who had sent an army to the island in an attempt to clear it of pirates. Father and son laughed when I interjected that my countrymen castigated others as 'pirates' while anointing their own citizens, who undertook the same unprovoked raids on sea-faring vessels, as 'privateers'.

Awang's father had been one of fifty-eight Malays collecting the tree resin they call *dammar* near to the place that the British contingent had landed, he told me. After asking for and receiving Light's assurance of protection against the sultan they had offered their services to help cut back the jungle, which at the time almost reached the water's edge.

'Captain Light rejected my father's offer and we watched, trying to hide our smiles, as his men repeatedly broke their weak European tools on the slow-growing ironwoods,' added Awang.

'Also known as the penaga tree, I believe,' I said, then shared the same story I had mentioned to Pieter. 'I understand Captain Light became so frustrated by the lack of progress he rather cleverly thought to load a cannon with silver dollars and fired it into the forest so his men would have reason to work harder.'

Awang's father ambiguously said, 'I did not hear it.' That convinced me further of what Pieter had implied: the event had never happened except in Light's imagination to make himself look—what? Commanding? Ingenious? Despite his power and position, what a strangely insecure man my employer seemed to be.

I barely had time to think further on this when Tuan Ismail added, 'But Captain Light paid us one silver doubloon for every one hundred nibong palms we cut and took to his camp, as the penaga tree proved impossible to fell in large quantities and he seemed very eager to build his stockade.'

'You must have been happy to see the British arrive, hoping that it would help improve your life considerably,' I said, lulled by a sense of friendship. I noticed Awang shift on his haunches at my comment.

The older man's face changed to one as hard and unyielding as the ironwood tree and I immediately regretted voicing it. After all, his son had just lost the produce he had spent all morning collecting and taking to market not because of some accident, such as one of the wheels of his handcart becoming buckled by a pothole or large stone, but because an officer of the East India Company had deliberately encouraged his sepoys to overturn it so they might feast on its contents without paying for what they would claim, if confronted, were damaged goods.

Keen for my earlier contention to be true, I blurted out everything Light had told me about the corruption connected to the Sultan of Queda's court. I wanted to make the point that the Malays harboured evil men, too, we were not alone in that. Surely, I went on to argue, things were better under British rule than they had been before? I spoke too fast and talked too much. With an embarrassed jolt, I realised I must sound like a boastful, naïve fool.

Awang's mother had earlier left us but I was grateful that she now re-appeared. She laid down a large, rubbery banana leaf in front of each of us on which she spooned a mound of steaming coconut-infused rice, followed by several small fried fish, half a boiled egg and a spoonful of sambal. A boy a little older than William—I guessed the younger son—helped her with small bowls of water in which we washed our hands. He stuck his tongue out to his brother before running back outside. Seeing me eye the fiery red sambal, Tuan Ismail smiled and said, 'You may want to taste a little of that first, before you decide to mix it into your meal.'

I nodded, dipped my forefinger into the sauce and gingerly tasted it. '*Sedap*,' I said. Delicious. I had learned to enjoy spicy food in India and, grateful for this temporary escape from further conversation, we ate the meal in silence.

After every morsel had been scooped into my mouth, I thought it best to leave with some dignity still intact, after thanking the family for their hospitality. But then the wife, who had cleared away the remnants of our meal, re-emerged with three tin mugs filled with cooling water in which floated pieces of cut *limau kasturi*, a small green citrus fruit with orange flesh and many tiny pips. Before I had a chance to make my excuses, the headman spoke again. 'I am surely wrong in your case but it has been my experience—' he paused, studying me carefully before concluding, '—that we are thought of as less by European men.'

That I could not deny. Indeed, it was no secret on the island that Captain Light much preferred the Chinese to the Malays. He considered them Penang's most valuable acquisitions since they possessed any number of useful trades including carpentry, masonry, and different kinds of smithing that helped the new settlement to thrive. In one letter, Light had even communicated to Lord Cornwallis that the Chinese were, in his opinion, the only people of the East from whom revenue could be raised without requiring expense and extraordinary efforts of government.

I blushed as I realised that the village headman must be aware of the slights Light had perpetuated about his people and determined to stop trying to excuse the disgraceful attitude of my countrymen. I had come here to learn more about Malay life and religion and trusted that if I sat quietly, I would hear more. I did not have to wait long.

'Our way of life may seem strange to Captain Light and maybe to you because we are less interested than the Chinese in working all day and night to amass gold, silver, and property. But is it not important to live a life that most satisfies us?'

I told the nakhoda I agreed with him; some of us did not want the same things out of life as others.

'Then you may be wondering why we are seen by the Europeans here as layabouts and criminals.' The older man gestured to his wife who immediately refilled our mugs with more flavoured water.

While he took a long, slow draught, I used the opportunity to share a theory I had mentioned on an earlier occasion to Pieter, who had agreed with me. 'I believe something similar happened to my own people after the Enclosure Acts,' I began. 'I remember my grandfather telling me that making land private which had once been open to all Englishmen for centuries—to graze their sheep and cattle, to catch rabbits and other game—was a scandalous act of government that deprived common folk of their traditional ways of making a living, even to eat.'

'And what do people do when they are forced to give up essentials like food and honest livelihood, Tuan Jim?'

'They do whatever they must. Even acts deemed criminal by some.'

The older man looked across at his son as if wishing to instruct him in a lesson. 'We are *orang laut*. If we must pay taxes and dues on what we catch and cultivate so that it is impossible to feed our families, some *will* turn to piracy. Although, as you said, one man's pirate is another man's privateer.'

I nodded enthusiastically, grateful that we had found common ground.

'Our sultans have long experienced internal problems, which they try to overcome according to our ways. *Tetapi kemudian datang Belanda.*'

But then came…

'*Belanda?*' I said, not fully understanding the older man's meaning. I knew this only as the word for the red-haired, long-nosed monkeys common to the island of Borneo.

Tuan Ismail's face clouded over like the sky before the monsoon rains. 'Let me explain our relationship with the Netherlanders this way—'

So belanda was the word the Malays associated with the race they hated most of all, the Dutch; they likened them to long-nosed proboscis monkeys.

But I had no time to dwell on this as the headman continued. 'Malays, as you know, trade in elephants. To train the calf we tie it up so that it can move only a short way before being pulled back by the leg chain. Eventually the calf learns what it can and cannot do, according to its master's wishes.'

The image of Pieter as a proboscis monkey vanished from my mind, replaced by that of this cruelly restrained creature.

'When an elephant is old enough to work on the farm or carry weapons and men during war it never runs away. Why?'

I saw Awang open his mouth to speak but his father held up his hand and looked directly at me.

'Because it has learned that its movements are restricted. The creature continues to believe that, even though it is now free, there is only so far it can go before it will be pulled back,' I said.

'*Betul!*' said the village headman. 'And that is what Dutch tyranny has done to our people, after their strength and ingenuity reduced us for the purposes of their monopoly. Those who will not give in know their lives will be reduced if they are not feared. Our ancestors told stories about what had happened to the Bandanese people at the hands of the Dutch. And so, many fled to the sea to become pirates.

'A desperate man is a terrifying enemy. We have gained this reputation but not always from free choice.'

For a while the three of us sat in awkward silence. Wishing to assure Awang and his father that it was better to live under the British flag's protection than be ground under the heels of the Dutch, the French, or even his own king, I said, 'Captain Light may not always use honourable means to achieve his goals but I believe he is a decent man at heart.' I purposefully ignored Light's betrayal of the Malay sultan in service of what I hoped would be a reassuring point to my new acquaintances.

'I will wait before deciding,' said the headman. 'Only when tragedy befalls this island will we know if our new king puts the needs of others ahead of his own commercial interests.'

Tuan Ismail's royal reference to Light brought to mind a verse I had heard sung in the kampong but dismissed as the Malays' lack of appreciation that a prosperous Penang would benefit everyone: '*Pulau Pinang has a new town and Captain Light is its King; Do not recall the days that are gone, or you will bow down your head, and the tears will gush forth!*'

Before I could respond further, the older man rose up from the floor complaining to his wife that she should not have let him sit in one position for so long as his muscles ached terribly. Then he looked at me and said, 'However high the egret soars, in the end he descends to his perch on the buffalo's back.' At my puzzled expression he explained, 'No matter how great a man may become in life, in the end we all return to dust.'

He said I should visit any time, as we were already neighbours.

'My father can tell you more stories about our people,' said Awang.

'But do not feel you must listen,' added the older man with a shrug.

***

As I lay on my cot that evening reading the notes I had just made, recalling my conversation with Awang's father, an apparition projected itself on to my mind: The framed sketch I had looked at in Government House the night of the fire, drawn by Captain Elisha Trapaud to commemorate Francis Light's colonisation of Penang. I reviewed the illustration again through the imagined gaze of the kampong's headman.

There was Light, standing under the makeshift flagstaff, proclamation in hand, flanked by the captains of the *Valentine* and the *Vansittart,* those two company ships drawn faint on the horizon. A few other anonymous Englishmen traveling to Canton on those vessels were situated nearby. On the esplanade, the troops stood under arms with six cannons ready to fire the salute. Two turbaned youths sat under a tree, close to a Bengal marine holding a musket. The only other figure—the only one who might be considered Malay—was a woman with a water pot on her head. All others, including Tuan Nakhoda Ismail's family who had lived here for centuries and the Sultan of Queda's emissaries who had come to see what was being done in his name did not feature; they had been ignored. Indeed, the sultan had never even been mentioned in Light's proclamation.

I sat up so fast I felt dizzy as I teetered over to the table where I kept Trapaud's book. Within moments I found what I was looking for: His reference to the Act of Possession that Light had read aloud that day:

'*These are to certify that agreeable to my orders and instructions from the Honourable Governor-General and Council of Bengal, I have this day taken possession of this island, called Poolo Penang, now named Prince of Wales Island, and hoisted the British Colours, in the name of His Majesty George the Third, and for the use of the Honourable British East India Company—the eleventh day of August, one thousand seven hundred and eighty-six, being the eve of the Prince of Wales' birthday*'.[2]

With no mention of Sultan Abdullah, it sounded as if Light had chanced upon an uninhabited island and 'taken possession' without the need to consider anyone else at all.

Might a thoroughly exasperated sultan, losing hope over the military protection he had insisted upon, soon decide to claw back what was rightfully his?

Chapter 18

Pretence

My first six months in Penang had not been as fully satisfying as I had expected. The second six, with the addition of new and rekindled friendships, passed with an ease that I only appreciated when it wore off.

The sultan continued his near-daily correspondences which ran the gamut from the petty to the minor to the more serious. All were matters that Sultan Abdullah expected Light to deal with: the repair of a damaged watch; the provision of merchandise and ships that would help 'a group of poor pilgrims make their way for haj in the Land of the Arabs'; an order for fifty sets of small cannons; an immediate demand for warships to arrest the officers of a French ship that had docked at Kuala Muda claiming to have run out of food and water. Then there were the frequent and varied reasons why *koyans* of rice could not be sent: The sultan was facing financial difficulties as no ships were coming from India to buy elephants; there were less trading ships arriving at Queda's ports overall. Our administrative affairs with the owner of Penang continued very much in that vein.

Other than his frequent references to the demands being made upon Queda by Siam for rice, men, canoes, bullets, and opium, the sultan's fears about his kingdom coming under attack from its northern adversary seemed to have abated. Light helped calm those waters by writing to remind the sultan of the advantages of maintaining his relationship with the Governor-General in India: Sultan Abdullah could expect to see his own businesses profit, including selling rice at the price he set rather than imposed by the East India Company; he would receive taxes from John Company's profits in Penang; and Queda should have no fear of sea attacks since it was protected by the Company. All of it dissembling on Light's part. I was not aware that the EIC had sanctioned Queda to set its own price for rice; there were no profits to be had from this fledgling settlement, one of the reasons for Lord Cornwallis' wish to abolish it; and what good would a lone *jaga-jaga* or lookout boat be against Bugis and Lanoon pirates or a Siamese fleet?

I had become well used to Light's exaggerations and outright lies but passed them off as successful tactics. The superintendent had managed to hold everything together thus far, and I had convinced myself that he could keep Sultan Abdullah appeased a while longer.

One of several bright spots in my week were the dinners I had with Martinha, usually with her husband absent as he frequently claimed overwork. The others, of course, were my adventures with William and Pieter, as well as my burgeoning closeness to the nakhoda's family.

Pieter had returned to George Town not long after my run-in with Hamilton and way-laid me one day in July as I sauntered along Beach Street to return to the Malay kampong. He flung a hefty silk purse at me, which I delightedly caught in one hand, telling me this was my profit from the trade he had mentioned at our first meeting.

'Where have you been? I was concerned that you had left Penang and did not intend to return,' I said, trying to sweeten my bitter-sounding words with a broader-than-usual smile.

'Count it,' answered Pieter, falling into step alongside me.

I opened the silk bag and gasped. 'How did you—' I began, but Pieter interrupted, saying I was never to ask him specifics of his trades as going into such details bored him. Why worry where the money came from, as long as it continued to grow?

'Another opportunity is bound to come up again soon. Are you interested?'

'Certainly,' I said. 'What is my stake?' I held the money bag out to him, but Pieter waved it away, and this time I did not argue; I trusted him to deal with me fairly.

As we ambled along, I told him about my friendship with Martinha and regular outings with William.

'That must be boring, stuck with a child of his age,' scoffed Pieter.

'Not at all. I've always wanted a younger brother and the lad is very inquisitive. We've had a few adventures so far, but I worry about running out of ideas since it would not be wise for us to venture too far from George Town until William is older.'

Upon hearing this, Pieter offered to show us new places to visit, introducing some of Penang's inhabitants whose artisanship or activities he thought would interest us both. This included Nachiappan the Chettiar, who had recently journeyed from his home village, Kandanur, south of Madras in Tamil Nadu, across the waters to Ceylon, and from there overland through Burma, Siam, and Queda. He loaned money at a fraction of a per cent compared to the thirty per cent or more charged by European usurers on the island including, unsurprisingly, James Scott.

William had great fun that day, as I did in observing him. From this one visit, he learned how a moneylender keeps his accounts, and why in the month of Chithirai the Chettiars stamp their new account books three, five, or seven times per page with turmeric paste to invoke God's blessing. Sitting on the man's *mengkuang* mat enjoying tea and biscuits and with as full a rendering of the charitable and other activities of the Chettiars as I would ever need to know, I watched in amusement as William's fingers turned as yellow as a tobacco chewer's teeth as he used turmeric sticks to stamp the corners of each page of Nachiappan's account books in readiness for the next fiscal year.

I also came to appreciate not just Pieter's inventiveness but his generosity over these many months. Whenever he came back from a trip, he invariably brought back a toy that delighted young William while instructing me to tell his mother that *I* had purchased it at the harbour from some visiting traders. Pieter told me how Holland had once been the pre-eminent centre of European publishing, with every sizeable town or city boasting at least one bookshop and printing press. Then he handed me a rather fine first edition of Dr Johnson's that he had purchased while in Batavia, along with a copy of *Robinson Crusoe* to replace the one I had given to William for his birthday.

Beyond that, my Dutch friend proved to be a fountain of knowledge. While not admitting how or from whom he had heard this intelligence, Pieter informed me in late September that Charles Cornwallis had recently written to his younger brother, Commodore William Cornwallis, Commander-in-Chief of His Majesty's East Indian fleet. In that letter, the older Cornwallis admitted that he was looking for any reason to remove the establishment from Prince of Wales Island but, until he was successful in that regard, the brothers should keep this matter between themselves.

Perhaps hoping to catch the captain ill-prepared, the Governor-General summoned Light to Calcutta to address his concerns the following month. I had already informed Light of Cornwallis' duplicity, claiming I had discovered this news through secret sources to underscore my value to him. Light told me he knew as much already. Then, as was his habit, he dictated one of his exhaustive, point-by-point letters. Only with great forbearance did I prevent my eyebrows shooting up when Light intoned that Penang was capable of sustaining fifty thousand people and abounded in all the necessary materials for their service and security. How was this possible when the current one thousand inhabitants relied almost wholly on rice from Queda and were in constant fear of yet another embargo of goods by its mercurial sultan?

In November, after the monsoon storms abated, Light set sail for Calcutta on the snow *Indus* to directly address Lord Cornwallis' mounting concerns about the company's financial outlay. He left the island in the capable hands of Captain Glass, who turned out to be a much less demanding taskmaster. This gave me more time to myself and I daily imagined where we might venture next if Light were to lose Penang. After all, were we not family now?

I had amassed a reasonable amount of silver, thanks to Pieter's trading acumen, although not enough to earn me independence yet. As my treasure mounted, I asked Awang to show me hiding places near the kampong where I could secrete my stash. We used scraps of coloured cloth to indicate these burial places so I might find them again easily, and I gave the boy a small fee to be their guard. As we hid these bags of silver in the jungle, I thought of one day writing a story about a young lad—Awang's age or slightly younger—who finds himself shipwrecked on an island that shelters a gang of cutthroat pirates and whose only hope of returning home involves finding and stealing the pirates' treasure buried in the jungle. When I considered that the hero of my tale needed someone older to assist him in his quest, a character akin to Pieter came to mind.

Meanwhile, life seemed replete with options. I could always remain with the Lights, should we be forced to leave this island, but there was an additional allure to sail away with Pieter and have adventures on the high seas: he would trade and make money and I would write stories about our exciting lives. But I would not abandon William, at least not yet.

Then, as if in the blink of an eye, Christmas arrived. With the superintendent still away in Calcutta fighting for the survival of Penang, I sat at the head of Light's table gazing across at Martinha, William, and the recently arrived Sarah, and allowed my imagination full rein.

I had such high hopes for New Year 1790.

Chapter 19

Dark Secrets

Bukit Bendera. Tuesday, 16 February 1790.

'I…cannot do this. I must…go back.' Bent over, hand on one knee, I reached out with my other arm to grasp a nearby branch. Pieter, standing behind me, grabbed my wrist. Startled, I looked up and saw that my hand had been poised mere inches from where a regiment of ants, some as long as my pinkie finger, armoured in black and red, marched along the mottled wood. Inhaling deeply, I thanked my Dutch friend. How ill-suited I was to this kind of exercise after so many years stuck behind a desk, despite the long walks I made to and from Fort Cornwallis and the Malay kampong each day. At least they were on a flat surface.

I forced myself erect and Pieter's hands grasped my shoulders in support.

'Where's that young pupil of yours?' he said, his whisper blown warm against my ear.

I jolted to attention. I could not imagine what Light would do if I reported that his adored son had been gored by a wild boar, poisoned by a snake, or stung by ants while in my charge.

'William,' I yelled with the little energy I could muster but heard no response other than the incessant rattle of insects high above us and the chatter of hidden monkeys. As the boy had grown in confidence, he had become much harder to control. I began to appreciate the trials of parenthood and what my own mother and father must have had to contend with when I was young.

What I saw ahead filled me with dismay. I had to force myself to scale a slope that rose at the kind of angle that had already punished my body and spirit almost beyond endurance. I mustered my fear of losing William into a greater determination to round yet another bend and another after that.

'*Your* idea,' Pieter said, seeming to choke back amusement as I struggled up the arm's-width pathway that intrepid locals and sepoys had carved out of the verdant chaos of nature, in readiness for one day erecting a flagstaff and lookout on this hill with which to detect ships that sailed towards us from the south and west.

Annoyance surged within me like bile. Yes, an outing in nature *had* been my idea now that William was older, but I had not anticipated this assault on Penang's Great Hill. That suggestion had come from Pieter who told me he was looking to find some peace from the raucous Chinese New Year celebrations now underway. He had suggested this calmer, cooler diversion to great enthusiasm from William. I had merely gone along with the idea not realising how ill-suited my body was for ascending pathways that seemed as relentless as a life sentence. How I longed for the gentle meandering of Richmond Hill.

'That waterfall I described earlier lies not too far ahead,' said Pieter, interrupting my thoughts. 'I'll go on and forestall William. Once we reach there, we're almost halfway to the top.'

I groaned inwardly at the thought of covering the same distance or more with an even steeper incline. As Pieter edged past me and disappeared, I determined to trudge on. I had nowhere to sit and nothing I dare touch. While I had come to appreciate more of Penang's beauty, I never ignored its dangers—both natural and man-made. At least the air up here felt cooler than in town. Pieter, for all the exertion required to scale this hill, never took off his black overcoat, while I had reduced myself to shirt sleeves and the loose, cotton trousers Awang's mother had made me.

At a fork up ahead, I saw Pieter but still no William, unsure if the whooshing sound I heard heralded water from the promised waterfall or was merely blood rushing to my head. I needed a drink of water desperately. Pieter gestured me to follow him along a narrow clearing to the right, beyond which William sat, legs dangling over the edge of a huge granite boulder, with a sheet of paper unfurled on his lap and a plumbago pencil in his hand.

'The lad has a talent for drawing' said Pieter who, tugging at my sodden shirtsleeve, directed me to sit next to him, some distance from the engrossed boy. 'His pictures are very life-like for such a young age.'

I nodded before making my way towards the gentle torrent of the stream. Using my palms, I drank my fill and splashed the frigid water over my hair and face to cool off. I re-joined Pieter and wriggled my body into the most comfortable position I could against a large rock and said, 'The boy loves to draw mementoes of our days together but has also taken an interest in music. Now he is a little older, I have arranged for him to take lessons in the *kompang* from one of the Malays.'

'The hand drums they play at Malay weddings? His parents are going to love that!'

Pieter and I laughed like mischievous schoolboys.

'Do you know what William said to me the other day?'

'What?'

'I asked him what he wanted to be when he was grown up and he said—' I turned to Pieter with the same serious expression the boy had used with me. 'A naval man like Lieutenant Gray; a soldier fighting the French—at this, Pieter, I think he deliberately avoided mention of the Dutch because of our friendship—; an artist; the founder of a new settlement like his father; an explorer; *and* a man of leisure.'

'What did you tell him?'

'I said he can indeed become all of these things although perhaps not at the same time.'

Pieter nodded and said, 'I hope the boy doesn't lose that sense of possibility when he reaches England.'

William appeared engaged in his drawing and I wallowed in the chance to rest. I closed my eyes and listened to the restorative sound of the water rushing from some unseen height into the pool not far from our feet. From there I imagined it travelling down to where Light had dug two wells: one for the George Town community where I had first sat with Pieter, the other for his sole, personal use.

After some silence, I longed to hear Pieter talk. I found his slight Dutch lisp endearing and had noted over our months together that his tone was somewhat different with me—softer somehow, more gentle— compared to the gravelly way with which he conducted business with others. 'What have you learned that has delighted you most on your travels?' I asked.

Pieter did not answer immediately. With his upper lashes nestling on his cheek, I thought for a moment he had fallen asleep. Then he said, 'The natural resistance of chaos against man's order and the unwillingness of life to hold to only one truth.'

He opened his eyes and gestured around us. 'We accept as natural the many shades of green we see here and the variety of woods we put to different uses. But in men we desire uniformity. What I've learned from observing life in the East is how much Europeans do not respect let alone take advantage of our remarkable differences.'

I could not help but think again of my friend's deformity, although I barely noticed it now. The superstition about the 'Devil's bite' had set him apart and would always isolate him from much of accepted society. My hand twitched but I stopped myself from reaching out to cover his with mine.

Then Pieter said, 'I remember reading something Alexander Hamilton wrote in *The Federalist*. To the effect that there was sufficient diversity in the genius, habits, and manners of people that such dissimilarities should help oppose any single point of view or way of being. At least, he hoped that would be the case in his new country.'

I nodded in agreement, trusting that in liberated America a greater appreciation for differences might be more the case than could be found in England.

'Did you know that the Bugis of South Sulawesi and their neighbours the Torajan don't limit people to only two genders but believe there are as many as five? They freely engage in whatever associations they feel inclined. It is only Western bigotry and unfounded fears that severely punishes sodomy—'

I looked over in alarm at William, relieved to see the boy still engrossed in his work.

'—and it disgusts me the way pious men condemn diverse acts,' continued Pieter. 'These people they unfairly call *savages,* while they happily torture and kill those who flout their religious laws. Good Calvinists like my father believe his God saves sinners but refuses to assume such good intentions himself. He abandoned his own child yet is considered the very best of Christians,' he said, with such venom that I worried he might crush the rock he now held in his hand.

I had become used to these brief outbursts from Pieter which, the more I got to know him, evinced great compassion in me. Had he not been unfairly tainted by the Devil's bite? A man might be a bully or a gambler or even a murderous beast and escape social censure because such traits did not show up on his face. But Pieter, my thoughtful, generous, loyal friend carried this unfair stigma under his nose and would for the rest of his life.

'I was telling you about my adventures in the Dutch East Indies,' he continued. 'The practices my father and his kind abhor are common in the region of South Sulawesi. And while I can see from your expression the idea is abhorrent to you, I would ask: who are we to judge others' rituals, or even carnal desires?'

Pieter turned to me, his eyes no further than a hand's touch. I imagined I saw in them an expression of defiance, as if he challenged me to think badly of him for voicing such views. He had done this many times during our year-long friendship which always puzzled me. Mistaking my expression his face fell in disappointment as he called out, 'Gather up your things, William. Come, I'll race you to the top of the hill.'

As the boy waved to indicate he had heard him but remained intent on finishing his drawing, Pieter said to me, 'It is interesting, is it not, how disgusted men are about some deeds over others.

Do you ever think how often acts of cruelty by men upon women are not condemned with the same intensity as fond acts of men upon men?'

I shrugged my shoulders, having never thought of that before.

'When men in London, Paris or elsewhere don a dress and paint their faces for the stage why is that acceptable when presented as art yet prosecuted as an everyday inclination? I have no time for society's laws or any religious dogma that restrains who we truly are. Do you?'

Pieter did not wait for my response. 'Look around you at this chaos, Jim. I believe that is the true urge of life, not the order men try to impose upon it. But perhaps I am merely predisposed to seek it out. After all, the greater the chaos the more opportunities there are for people like me. The ones served badly by *normal* society. You surely cannot blame us for wanting to tip the scales in our favour when men's laws unfairly obstruct our success.'

Pieter's views seemed no different to that of Machiavelli's or Light's in determining that doing wrong is acceptable—even if those actions are contradictory to society's laws—as long as one's self deems them justified. Yet, having read *The Prince* many times I was reminded of the Florentine's warning that, 'A people who can do whatever it wants is unwise, but a prince who can do whatever he wants is crazy.'

I followed Pieter's lead and stood up. My troubled friend looked over at William as he gripped my shoulder tighter than before. 'Your young student looks ready for the last leg. We'll leave you to reach the summit at your own pace, Jim. There's only one pathway up so you won't get lost. I'll make sure William never leaves my sight.'

Without waiting for my agreement, the two of them set off at a pace I knew I could not match. I followed as fast as I could, hindered by dark thoughts. Was Pieter intent on pushing me away as these occasional attempts to shock me seemed to suggest? Or had he made an indirect admission of *his* 'natural inclinations.' Not just towards sowing havoc but the fluidity of his relationships, perhaps with other men. Was he testing me to see whether or not, twelve months into our intimacy, I was of the same mind?

Chapter 20

A Dawning

Finally reaching the top of the hill, I joined Pieter and William who sat on the ground in a clearing. From this vantage point we could see most of the island to the south, the straits that separated us from the land of Queda on the other side of the water, as well as smaller, verdant islands in between. My young charge was listening to Pieter compare the Dutch stronghold, Batavia, with our 'sorry specimen' of Fort Cornwallis, 'a fraction of Kasteel Batavia's size and strength.' As Pieter referenced the Vereeidge Oost-Indische Companie, or VOC, Holland's equivalent of the English East India Company, I remembered the epithet our officials in Bengal had used to describe our enemies and competitors: The Violent Opium Company.

The name of their stronghold in the Dutch East Indies, Pieter explained to William, was in honour of the Germanic Batavi tribe that had occupied a series of islands in the Dutch Rhine delta which the conquering Romans had called Batavia. The VOC's founding governor, whose name I did not catch, had wanted to give the settlement the name Nieuw-Hoorn in celebration of his birthplace—Pieter's also, I noted—but had been overruled on this matter by the VOC Board.

The streets of Batavia were similarly laid out as George Town's in a grid pattern, Pieter continued, with the high walls surrounding the city

securing it from enemy attacks. Kasteel Batavia, the fort from which
the VOC Governor-General ruled, had been thoughtfully planned
and laid out to the north of the city it protected, Pieter opined, 'not
rashly positioned, as with George Town, on a sand bank that becomes
submerged by twelve inches of water during the spring tides.'

I could understand my Dutch friend's pride in his countrymen's
achievements but became uncomfortable at his constant sideswiping
of Light in front of his son. From the moment he had landed Captain
Light had been afraid of attacks, writing to the Fort William Council
mere months after his possession to report how a Siamese general was
in the process of destroying a nearby state. All men, children, and
old women were to be tied to the ground and trampled to death by
elephants. Light had expressed his belief that if similarly threatened
Sultan Abdullah would have no qualms about sacrificing his new
settlement to the avarice of the King of Siam. He had also been
concerned about pirates jealously eyeing us to see what they might
raid and had informed Lord Cornwallis that the two thousand Spanish
Dollars the fort, its storehouses, and barracks would cost to construct
was a much-needed outlay.

I had barely time to draw breath in order to interject when William
said, 'Where would you have situated the town instead, Uncle Pieter?'

My Dutch friend gazed over at me, smiled or smirked—I could
never tell the difference with him—then looked back at the boy. He
appeared to love it when William called him Uncle Pieter. 'There's a
healthier place some three miles south-east as the crow flies, called Battu
Lanchon, where there is an elevated dry plain large enough for a fort
and a city. That would have been a better location for both mercantile
and marine uses since all ships sailing up the channel would be obliged
to steer directly towards it. It could be defended by crossfire from
batteries positioned on Pulo Jerajah near where I oftentimes anchor my
ship.' Pieter turned the boy so he could look across the water to where
that uninhabited island lay between Penang and the mainland. 'Jerajah
could provide a defence of docks, stores, and ships to some three or
four leagues. How far in miles is that, William?'

'One nautical league is about three miles, Uncle Pieter.'

Pieter patted the boy on the back. 'Well done. Almost three and a half miles to be accurate. Whereas George Town's positioning only offers a defensive range of one or two miles.'

'You have a camp on that other island?' asked William excitedly.

'Not on Pulo Jerajah but at Battu Lanchon. A *secret* camp,' replied Pieter, then lowered his voice to a whisper so I could not hear what he said next.

I moved closer to my loquacious Dutch friend and nudged his arm to convey that he should change the subject. I had noticed William's wriggling as if desiring to be freed from further lectures. As I moved closer, the boy got up and whispered to me that he needed to relieve himself. I told him to go squat behind one of the nearby bushes, but only after he was certain nothing lay in the undergrowth that might bite his bare backside. With a merry laugh, the boy ran off.

I said, 'You are very knowledgeable about Batavia.'

'Of course,' Pieter replied. 'Its first governor, Jan Pieterszoon Coen, is an ancestor of mine.'

Governor Coen, Pieter continued, had ruled Batavia from 1619 to 1623, and again from 1627 until his death in 1629; the only man in VOC history to have done so twice. These were the company's 'glory days,' in my Dutch friend's estimation.

As William bounded back, I asked if he would be interested in a more personal Dutch history lesson from Uncle Pieter and so the three of us huddled together on the ground to be regaled by the story of 'King Coen'. With no particular love or admiration for Holland, England's long-time enemy, except of course for my fondness for one of its countrymen, I nevertheless thrilled to hear how King Coen—a term Pieter used a lot—had overseen a vast commercial enterprise that managed shipments from places like the islands of Banda to Europe, via Batavia. Pepper from Banten had been traded for textiles from the Coromandel coast; silver from Japan exchanged for Chinese goods; each compensating the other without the need to drain the Netherlands' home treasury. Providing Hollanders with goods at low prices that nevertheless earned huge profits for the VOC and its shareholders.

'The Company established a complete monopoly in the Malay Archipelago until the recent emergence of the English,' Pieter concluded.

I rested a hand on my friend's arm as if to remind him of my heritage and that while William had been born in Queda his education in England would undoubtedly ensure he would be thought of as an Englishman, too, in time.

'How did the VOC manage that?' I asked, hoping the answer might divert my friend from making any more contentious utterances about my countrymen.

'The local chieftains will promise any amount of goods in exchange for protection against their enemies. That's how we enforced our monopolies. We would offer to support rival princes in exchange for exclusive concessions. Although if any of them took liberties by going behind the VOC's back and selling to competitors the company would not hesitate to give them a taste of our military superiority to bring them back in line.'

I wondered if Pieter knew about the governmental constraints that Light had duplicitously ignored in order to make Sultan Abdullah believe he could expect similar offensive military support from John Company.

'Holland had the entire Malay Archipelago sewn up, from Riau to Tanjung Pinang and Malacca. Until, of course, your father, William, managed to establish this settlement—' Pieter slapped a hand on the ground beneath us, 'and showed himself to be such a clever man!'

As if signalling that we should bring our conversation to a close, William's stomach rumbled, and I realised how hungry I was myself. After our exertions I looked forward to Awang's mother's cooking, then an early night. My only concern at that moment was how my limbs would feel in the morning.

'Let's head back,' I said, winking at William who sidled over to show me the drawings he had made earlier. They truly were impressive, particularly one of an inquisitive looking black and white-faced monkey with her young clutching her chest. I gave the boy a hug, aware of Pieter watching us.

The Dutchman got up and strode off in the same direction as William had earlier, I assumed for the same reason. He stood, his back towards us and I mused once again why he never seemed to take off his great black coat. When Pieter returned, he stopped alongside William, jingled his pocket and withdrew a silver coin which he handed over saying, 'Don't mention anything to your mother about me joining you today. Good boy!'

I opened my mouth to protest, disapproving of Pieter bribing William in order to stay quiet, since we both knew Martinha loathed the Dutchman for reasons I had never prised out of her. Whenever Pieter's name came up in conversation, she would only say that while there was nothing she could do about whomever I chose to consort with, she did not want him anywhere near her son. But before I could chastise him, Pieter extracted a rather fine brass spy glass from his coat pocket, which he handed to me, and pointed in the direction of Fort Cornwallis.

Through the lens I could better see George Town, the Indian sector now thankfully recovered from the fire of ten months earlier. That vista appeared to illustrate Pieter's earlier point about order and chaos, with the town sandwiched between the narrow strait that separated this island from the mainland of Queda and a jungle as vigilant and dangerous as a tiger waiting for its chance to raid a village. From this vantage point our feeble attempts to restrain nature seemed very vulnerable indeed.

I extended my gaze to the opposite coastline, where three vessels flew the horizontal red, white, and blue stripes of the VOC flag at the mouth of the Prai river. 'Why are they here?' I asked Pieter as William joined us, all thoughts of the earlier bribe displaced. Had war broken out again between our two countries?

'It appears Superintendent Light has conjured up fresh trouble for himself,' said Pieter.

Light had been back in Penang less than a week after three months in Calcutta where he had successfully eased Lord Cornwallis' concerns about the company's financial investment, at least for the time being. Now three Dutch warships had arrived.

At my look of concern Pieter said, 'You are surely aware that Sultan Abdullah earlier implored the French at Pondicherry to help him with the military assistance your employer seems incapable of providing. The French turned him down but the sultan seems to have had better luck with my countrymen,' said Pieter, with as calm an air as if he had been reporting a fine day.

'What do you mean?'

'Exactly that,' shrugged Pieter, retrieving his spy glass and handing it to an eager William with instructions to be very careful with it. 'Sultan Abdullah has offered Penang to the Dutch in exchange for ousting the English from his island. You can hardly blame him given the way the Malay raja has been deceived by Light.'

I pulled Pieter away so William could not hear us. Trying to suppress my alarm I whispered, 'How do you know all this?'

My friend smiled and said, 'Knowledge is power, Jim, and war means money. A wise trader stays ahead of potentially disruptive events.'

'My God, what are we going to do if the Dutch attack?' With this new risk of war literally on the horizon, my disdain for Light's actions—ones I had kept in check first because of ambition, later because of my affection for his family—overwhelmed me. It was one thing to be concerned about a *potential* Malay attack, quite another to see Dutch warships on the horizon.

Pieter and I would have continued but William bounded up to join us and inquired what we were whispering about. Despite his young age, the boy was intensely observant and intelligent.

'We'll speak more later,' Pieter told me. 'Come with me, young man,' he said to Light's son, pulling him away.

I watched the two of them begin their descent, Pieter playing chase with William who pretended not to want to give him back his spy glass. Presumably emboldened by their burgeoning friendship, the boy asked what had happened to Pieter's face.

'One day, although not for the first time, my ship was attacked by pirates,' answered Pieter, drawing William towards him. I hurried close behind. 'Their leader was the most fierce, ugly monster I have ever seen. He said I was so pretty I looked like a girl and that he would take great pleasure in cutting my face to make me more of a man. We fought long and hard and at one point he got so close that he did indeed cut my upper lip, just so, with his keris. I told him I would proudly declare it my battle scar, just before I bit off his ear.'

'What happened then?' asked William in wonder.

'I stabbed the pirate in the guts, cut his throat, and threw his body in the drink to rest in Davy Jones's locker,' said Pieter, mimicking each action. I heard William howl with laughter, but lost sight of them both temporarily as they scampered around a bend.

'That's enough of that,' I called out, aware that I sounded like a chastising mother. I intended to ask Pieter not to deceive the boy about his disfigurement, although I could understand his reasons; who would wish to get into a discussion with a child about the Devil's bite? But what concerned me most as I scampered after them was that if it came to a fight with the Hollanders, in which direction would my Dutch friend's allegiance lie?

At the base of the hill, before we parted, Pieter drew me to one side out of William's earshot. 'Of course, if my countrymen retake Penang on behalf of the sultan, you should know that we are kinder to our prisoners than the Siamese or Malays.' He then pulled out a keris from inside his coat and made as if about to cut his own throat.

My thoughts turned immediately to William. Surely Europeans would not torture and kill young children with the same lack of concern as the Siamese, whom I knew had no qualms about trampling women and babies to death under the feet of their elephants, along with their menfolk. But then I remembered the horrors James Scott had described, that went on in Batavia's prison: decapitation, scourging, and branding among them.

At the expression on my face, Pieter began to laugh. 'Oh, forgive me,' he chortled and punched me on the shoulder as he returned his keris to its hiding place. 'I find it amusing to see you squirm. Trust me, those Dutch warships won't anchor in Queda much longer than a few days, a week at most, so you need not wet your breeches. And surely you know that should the need arise, I will protect you.'

Without a farewell to either William or myself, and with no backward glance, Pieter strode off. As I watched him fade into the distance, I felt William's fingers encircle my hand. I wondered if the boy was hurt that our mutual friend had not formally said goodbye, but he uttered simply, 'This is for you,' and handed me the drawing of the monkey and her baby I had earlier admired. As I gazed at it again, my breath caught in my throat. Near the bottom of the sheet the boy had written, 'I love you, Uncle Jim. From William'.

I drew the boy closer, my eyes misting up. 'Thank you, William. I love you too—' I almost added 'son' but caught myself in time and merely said, 'young man'.

***

Pieter was wrong. The Dutch warships anchored at the mouth of the Prai river refused entry or exit to any ships doing trade between Queda and Penang for much longer than a week. We were embargoed again. The consequences of Light's lies and dissembling were no longer speculative. The notion that something *could* happen not an abstract thought now that danger was physically present in the form of three Dutch warships.

The next few weeks were hellish, with reality setting in just how dependent on Queda we were for our sustenance. I no longer had faith that by sheer power of will or kharisma or whatever he thought would deny the truth of our situation, Light could hold on to Penang.

Soon after, the settlement began to collapse from the inside out. First came the complaints, not just made directly to Light and me but followed up with letters to Bengal. As superintendent, they claimed, Light was abusing his position by securing monopolies that made it impossible for others to compete. Gentlemen who had planned to trade here had written to Lord Cornwallis to say it was fruitless for them to attempt breaking into the superintendent's privileges.

As tensions heightened at the prospect of being attacked by a combined Dutch and Malay force—one far greater than the four hundred men Light had at his disposal—the effect on us all became more dire. Landowners saw no point in trying to grow much-needed crops like rice and pepper if their investments were soon to be trampled under the feet of marauding mercenaries. Without cultivation, we would be even more dependent on Queda. Without trade, as merchant captains became fearful of being caught in the middle of a skirmish if not all-out war, Penang's financial fortunes would sink.

As much as my employer needed the support I had promised Martinha I would give him, I could barely look the man in the eye, infuriated by his intransigence. I had originally been concerned with buttressing my professional reputation and value in the eyes of my father and Light, but I never expected my life would be at risk as a result; that I might *die* here because of one man's belief that he always knew what was right. What was it Dr Roxburgh had once accused me of: *Often mistaken, never in doubt?*

Francis Light had imperilled this community with his exaggeration and dissembling. Perhaps doing so fitted his Machiavellian self-justification but a thousand innocents now faced the consequences, including Martinha and William, including me. As easy as it would have been to jump on the first ship back to India, despite the dire consequences of having no prospects and insufficient money when I reached there, I would not abandon the boy.

I had backed the wrong horse and was now foolishly associated with Captain Light. But what could I do about that now? And would I live long enough for my reputation even to be a future consideration?

Chapter 21

Enlightened

The mood between Light and myself could best be described as tepid during the time those Dutch warships remained anchored two miles off our shores. I answered my employer as was sufficient and inquired of Martinha whether her husband would be joining us for dinner before accepting her invitations; I did not wish to see him any more than was required.

One morning in late February, almost two weeks after our trip to the summit of Bukit Bendera, I had been frostier with him than usual. As I pored over papers recently arrived from Calcutta, I pointedly avoided looking at the man seated not two feet away from me. Then, forgetting myself, I responded with a sharp, 'What?' when my employer spoke my name, presumably prior to asking me a question or giving me an instruction. This caused Light, hands on his desk and leaning back in his chair to bark, 'Okay, Jim, enough of this! Out with it.'

'What?' I repeated in a less agitated tone as if, as my mother would have put it, butter wouldn't melt in my mouth.

'You know very well *what*. Spit it out, man, for God's sake.'

I wished to avoid a full-blown argument and merely said that I had been wracking my brains trying to come up with a solution to our problems concerning Sultan Abdullah's embargo.

'Hah!' scoffed Light, 'You think *you* can avert this likely war?'

'Just as well as you it seems,' I answered. Up to now Light had put forward no plans, other than the usual offer of opium and silver, which even Captain Glass said the sultan was likely to send back if the Dutch did not purloin it. 'Why can't you admit you were wrong and tell the sultan that military protection will not be forthcoming? You know the raja still expects good news from London but is frustrated by the delay. Why else would he have risked defying the king of Siam's brother when he marched on Queda to collect the triennial *bunga mas?*'

Tuan Ismail had earlier explained to me that Siam considered its southern neighbour a suzerain and demanded tribute in the form of a gold and silver tree every three years, known as bunga mas. 'Thinking we would support him, Sultan Abdullah refused to offer tribute and it was only the Siamese surprise at being faced with ten thousand Malays ready to repel them that caused Prince Jorasi to back away. That would have been the ideal time for you to come clean but, no, you continue to evade the sultan's questions and give yet more excuses for the delay in receiving a ratified treaty. So why are we shocked when, after being forced to bow down to a superior Siamese force later and pay tribute because they saw through his ruse, Sultan Abdullah wants to reclaim Penang for our not acting in good faith?'

'Don't be naïve, Jim,' Light said. 'Telling Abdullah the truth would cause him to attack us for sure. I still have hopes that London will come back with the right answer.'

I sank in my chair, unable to grasp why Light could not see what was as plain as the nose on his face. 'But what if London says no, as Cornwallis has already told you?'

I was familiar with the letter the Governor-General had written to Light in January 1788—more than two years ago—that stated quite clearly, '…*with respect to protecting the King of Queda against the Siamese, the Governor-General in Council has already decided against any measures that may involve the company in military operations against any of the Eastern princes. It follows therefore that any acts or promises which may be construed into an obligation to defend the King of Queda are to be avoided.*'[3]

Yet Light had never conveyed that decision to the sultan but maintained his subterfuge. Did Cornwallis even know that Light had not only failed to avoid an obligation to defend Sultan Abdullah but led the raja to believe military support was all but certain?

'What do you intend to do about the people who have put their trust and hopes in you?' I railed. 'They are not goods you might risk on a perilous sea voyage; they are people dammit!' I had not meant to raise my voice but could not quell my frustration.

Light seemed to collapse into himself. He spent so much time these days running his fingers through his thinning hair it was a miracle he still had any on his head. Then he chuckled but not, I thought, in a humorous way. 'You are spending too much time with Martinha; you sound just like her. She is forever accusing me of looking at everything as a transaction.'

'She is right,' I murmured. 'You do.'

Then something I never expected happened.

'I received a letter recently from my brother, James, telling me that our mother, Mary Light, is ailing and will likely not last out the year,' murmured Light.

'I'm sorry to hear that.'

He shrugged, eyes gazing within his memories. 'Don't be. I haven't seen the woman in over thirty years and we parted on less than happy terms.'

Not wishing to tackle that directly I said, 'I did not know you had a brother.'

'Two brothers. Peter died in infancy the year before I was born. I was amazed to hear there was still life in the old dog when my friend George Doughty informed me about James' birth. William Negus must have been fifty-seven and had been married to Margaret Nadauld for over twenty years by the time Mary bore him a third son. James would be around your age by now, twenty, maybe twenty-one.'

'I'm sure there were reasons why your natural father did not give you his name,' I broached. I tried to make a joke of it, saying, 'Perhaps the local vicar put in his pennyworth. One should never underestimate the callousness of Christian clergy, after all.'

Light did not respond as he continued to reminisce. 'I blamed her for everything. She defended herself by saying that she loved my father which was why she was willing to bear him the sons he craved, even knowing we would be bastards. They gave no thought to that when they engaged in their affair. As far as I see it, they both struck a transactional bargain and as much as Martinha likes to claim otherwise I doubt love had much to do with it.'

'Why would you think your mother did not love William Negus?'

Light scoffed. 'Think about it. Mary Light was a servant girl who took up with the master of the house. It was the only way she could better her lot. I was their transaction: she got more money in her pocket and he got to boast having sons his wife was unable to bear.'

'You don't think your parents stayed together all those years out of true love?' I ventured. 'A love forbidden because they came from different strata of society and could not marry? Imagine how your mother must have had to endure the opprobrium of her class, who are more vicious in my view than any landed gentry in perpetuating the lie that some humans are inferior to others. If it had been a mere transaction, either could have got their needs met elsewhere.'

Light did not bend to my suggestion. 'You are inexperienced in these matters, Jim, being a young man with no wife. But bear this in mind for the future: When a woman says she loves you, it's to entice you to provide her with a home and protection and to sire her children. Indeed, if you scratch the surface of any so-called love relationship you'll find a transaction lurking; that is just how life is and has always been.'

I wondered if that was the case with Martinha. Remembering what James Scott had told me about how she and Light had met I now regarded their union in a different light. But I merely said, 'We must agree to disagree,' to which Light laughed and looked me squarely in the eyes.

'So, what else is on your mind, my young assistant?'

With all the drama that had gone on this past year, including the three months Light had been away in Calcutta, the notion of my being his chronicler had obviously been swept from his mind.

'Nothing more.'

'Friends again?' said Light.

We were never, nor could we ever be, friends.

'Yes, of course,' I replied.

Chapter 22

Exposure

One day in mid-March, having apparently come to the conclusion that Sultan Abdullah's demands were too costly and his needs too prolonged to remain, the Dutch sailed off. Most inhabitants in Penang breathed a sigh of relief while the pragmatic among us waited for the next stage of the Malay king's frustration. Like the aristocrats we had heard were being executed in France during their Revolution, all we could do was wait our turn for the guillotine blade to drop.

As if to celebrate this lull in our ongoing drama, one Sunday in April, Pieter took me to his hideout at Battu Lanchon. We left Malay Town just after sunrise and traveled on a bullock cart handled by an elderly Malay with a face like a gnarled tree trunk, who took us as far south as the rutted tracks allowed. After that, we traipsed for miles through dense jungle, with me ever vigilant for what could sting, bite, or kill me. Just as I began to think my aching legs could take me no further, Pieter parted another doorway of thick, rubbery leaves and there it stood, cleverly concealed. A rudimentary yet solid wooden hut perched within trees some six or seven feet above the ground. I could not imagine how Pieter remembered where this place was or that anyone would ever find his hideout—although I had taken pains to ensure I could do so again, even if Pieter were not around.

Using a ladder hidden in the nearby bushes, we climbed up to the narrow platform. I followed my friend into the darkened room then shrieked in alarm as something jumped out of the gloom, close to my head. Pieter laughed as a tiny, ochre-haired monkey with a face like a wizened old man and bat-like ears landed on his shoulder like Blackbeard's parrot. Pieter introduced the creature as Raksasa Kechil, which, despite a deformed paw, began grooming Pieter's hair as it chattered in high-pitched squeals.

'Raksasa is inquiring why I have allowed an interloper into our home,' my friend said as the two of them embraced like long-lost lovers. Pieter had named his pet Little Monster, a maimed macaque he told me had been abandoned by its mother, and he had nursed back to health. As small and misshapen as this one was, I had a fear of monkeys—as Pieter knew very well—and determined to stay as far away from its bared fangs as the cramped space allowed.

Once my eyes were fully adjusted to the dimness, I could see the place was furnished with a hammock, a chest that appeared to do double-duty as a small table, two wooden boxes big enough to be used as seats, a second sea-chest, a large jug inside a bowl, and assorted tin receptacles for eating and drinking. I detected a number of confusing odours: rusty nails; dried fish; something as sickly sweet as an Arab's pomade; along with the faint putrefaction common to the jungle. Pieter kicked away a roll of narrow, undyed cloth that had partly unravelled and invited me to sit down on one of the boxes. The place reminded me that I had longed for a treehouse as a child, although there had been no sturdy oaks left in the part of Mayfair in which we lived and, even if there had been, no one was willing to build such a hideaway for me. For Pieter, skilled enough to live off the land and unconcerned about the dangers pervading the jungle, this place could have kept him safely secreted for many months, perhaps even years, with no one knowing his whereabouts.

The tiffins we had carried from George Town were soon emptied of the congealed rice, cold fried fish, and soupy vegetables on which we feasted, with Pieter alternately fingering food into his own mouth and the monkey's. Parched from the salty fish, I asked Pieter for water.

Settling the monkey on the hammock, he jumped up, took the empty jug and within moments had returned with fresh water that he said came from a rain barrel at the back of his hut. He ladled the welcome liquid into my cup.

'How are you and Light getting along?'

'Better,' I offered. 'In many ways, I feel sorry for him.'

'Why?'

I recounted the conversation I had had with Light, in which he revealed his antipathy towards his mother and how that had coloured the way he saw the world in transactional terms. 'I have been thinking a lot lately,' I went on, 'about the wounds that most often occur in childhood and grow out of all proportion. Such as the constant belittling of my efforts that caused my obsession with proving myself worthy in my father's eyes. Although that seems less important now.'

Pieter nodded. I needed to feel closer to him. 'From what you told me during our hill walk, it seems you had issues with your father.'

'No,' said Pieter, stroking the chin of his monkey, having moved back to the hammock where he sat with his legs over the edge. 'It is my *moeder* I hate the most.' The way he uttered the Dutch word for 'mother' sounded almost like murder. 'You expect a woman to show greater love towards her children. Yet she abandoned me easily and is the most evil in my eyes.'

Neither of us said anything for a while, and I basked in this new intimacy, the strange joy of sharing one's deepest thoughts and concerns with a friend.

Then I said, 'What am I to do, Pieter? Nothing here has turned out as expected. Light appears to have given up all thoughts of engaging me as his chronicler, and I would need to write the same propaganda as Elisha Trapaud to present him in any kind of positive way, which I am not prepared to do.' I related the contents of the letter Light had received over two years ago from Lord Cornwallis, telling him that no English military support should be given in the sultan's ongoing feuds with the Siamese.

'That's because Cornwallis sees the bigger picture,' said Pieter. 'He wants the company's commitments limited to Penang to avoid straining relations with the Dutch and the Siamese. The Governor-General is hoping to establish a trading alliance with the King of Siam or at least negotiate more concessions for English traders, which they have never been as willing to do as the Malays. Cornwallis is not going to antagonise the Siamese by having your company involve itself in Sultan Abdullah's ruinous political affairs.'

'Then Light has backed himself into a corner from which I fear there is no way out other than aggression.'

'Perhaps, perhaps not. I suggest we continue sharing intelligence. Keep me apprised of Light's plans, and I'll see what I can find out from other sources as to the sultan's future intentions.'

Pieter's monkey—which up to this point seemed to have fallen asleep in his arms like a baby—suddenly roused itself and, seeing me so close to its master, bared its tiny fangs. Amused at my fearful reaction, Pieter said, 'Raksasa is jealous of you, Jim,' and laughed. 'Silly monkey!' he chastised his tiny pet. The renewed attention seemed to calm my would-be attacker.

'Keep your ear to the ground in the kampong. I know you have become friendly with the headman and his family, but ask yourself: If required to choose between their ruler who would have the bigger fighting force, and Light, who will the Malays on this island support?'

'I don't believe Tuan Ismail would betray us,' I said.

'Don't be so sure,' said Pieter. 'People are fickle. They look to see which side will win before joining it. Surely being around Light has taught you that?'

'The Malay headman has suggested there is a European traitor in our midst, working secretly against Light,' I confided.

'Has he? Who?'

'He doesn't know but says that he will share that intelligence with me when he finds out. I believe it's that blackguard Hamilton; he would like nothing better than to see Light fail and to precipitate a fight with the sultan. The man is a devil.'

'Another problem for Light.'

'That is why I cannot help but feel sorry for him: A traitor in his own ranks; Cornwallis won't support his endeavours; the traders complain about his monopolies; Sultan Abdullah won't parlay with him. If the natives on this island turn against Light, he will be fighting on two fronts with a mere four hundred men and will lose Penang for sure.'

I recalled something my grandfather had once shared with me. A line from Milton's *Paradise Lost*, part of a conversation between Satan and Beëlzebub, which I recited to Pieter:

> **Here we may reign secure, and in my choyce**
> **To reign is worth ambition though in Hell:**
> **Better to reign in Hell, then serve in Heav'n.**

'Grandfather said this was perhaps the greatest challenge we humans face: To choose whether to serve in heaven or reign in hell. I clearly remember how he had intoned, 'But first, my dear young Jim, you will need to learn which place is which'. I fear Captain Light has never made that distinction.'

'Or perhaps he has. For some, like Satan, reigning in hell is their preference,' replied Pieter. He turned his gaze to the sea chest lying at the edge of the room and added, 'Of course, you may not choose to pity the man if you knew certain things about him.'

'What things?' I said.

'That he is not honourable when it comes to his wife, whom you adore so much. Of which I have proof.'

I thought seeing such proof would settle my mind once and for all about Francis Light, so I urged Pieter to show me. Not only did it fail to help matters, but one day that decision would make matters much, much worse.

Chapter 23

Disheartened

Pieter manouevred himself out of the hammock. Lifting the lid of the sea-chest, he scrambled among waves of papers before extracting several hand-written sheets which he held aloft. 'Love letters,' he announced. 'From several of Light's women in Junk Ceylon. Including—'

'Oh, I don't think I want to see them,' I resisted, turning my head away as if by doing so those letters would magically disappear. Negative evidence concerning Light was one thing, but I did not wish to learn anything that might make it hard for me to face Martinha or cause me to have to lie to her any more than I already did.

Pieter shrugged his shoulders and looked as if he were about to return the papers to the chest. 'Several are from his other wife.'

Stunned, my exclamation of 'What?' caused Pieter's pet monkey to shake its furry head and place its undamaged paw over one ear.

So Light was not only a liar and a cheat in business but a philanderer in his private life. With a great sigh as if he were forcing me to read them, I snatched the letters out of Pieter's hand, noticing that each one had been written in the same careful script:

From Bun Kaeo, 2 November 1786[4]

'These days I remember with gratitude what you did for me once upon a time. I shall never forget it. But it is my sad fate not to be connected with you any more. It is not like when we used to gather flowers together. I am short of money these days and feel I should put myself under your protection. I have no clothes to wear, nor rice to eat. Please look after me and do not let me die.'

From Chao Ratt, 20 April 1787[5]

'This is to let you know that during your long absence I have been in great distress and I cannot find any happiness. I have been trying to make a living, remaining faithful to you, and I raise my hands to you in salutation every morning and every night when I lie down to sleep. Now I am like a nestling or a tiny fawn bereft of its mother. I have to hide myself away, faithfully waiting for you. I sent a letter by Captain Scott and another one by Ma Lim but I have had no news of you. There is a crisis at Thalang at present and we are very short of food. I have had to use the articles you gave me to buy food at a high price. I had nothing left except my clothes and a robber stole all those.'

From Mae Prang, 4 January 1788[6]

'I think unceasingly of you. I was going to send you some things but the Westerner was in a great hurry and I could not get them ready in time. I have only got ten melons for you. At present I am in great distress and I think of you night and day…'

I handed the letters back to Pieter with a scoff. Women might write anything, but it did not mean their love was reciprocated. I knew only too well, having never worn a uniform myself, how women in Europe and here in the East were drawn like moths to a flame when they came upon men wearing the attire of a naval or military officer. Just because such letters were written to Light did not mean those feelings were returned.

'This all looks rather one-sided to me,' I said. 'And where is the proof of another wife?'

Pieter sorted through more papers until he found a document that he held up. 'This is a note written by James Scott in which he refers to the payment of money for a transaction involving Chao Ratt. Notice the date: August 1785, some thirteen years *after* Light married Martinha Rozells. Yet in Scott's very hand it says the payment was ordered by Captain Light, *Chao Ratt's present husband.* Go on, read it.'

I shook my head and told him there was no need; I had heard enough. Why would Pieter lie? The specificity of what he had just shared made clear to me that this was the unfortunate truth. I turned my head towards the makeshift door with a sudden desire to leave. The room was too small, the atmosphere oppressive. I did not like being in such close proximity to the macaque. While adoring of Pieter, the monkey continually bared its fangs at me.

Pieter interrupted my indecision. 'Luckily for Light, Chao Ratt is no longer around. She died some years ago.'

With a jolt, I remembered the story Martinha had recounted during our first night together, the night of the fire. How her husband had told Scott to inform the bigoted German pastor that he could not meet him because Captain Light was in Bengal, his wife dead. Martinha had laughed, assuming this to be one of Light's practical jokes. Now I knew it was not; he had not been referring to her at all but to this other woman, Chao Ratt.

Pieter shrugged at my silence and began to return the letters and other documents to the chest.

'How— Why do you have these letters in your possession?' I challenged.

'Simple,' he answered as he reached further into the wooden crate and pulled out a wooden pipe with a small metal bowl at the end, together with a container filled with small balls of opium. 'Smoke?'

'No, thank you,' I mumbled.

'You look upset, Jim. Don't tell me you're that naïve. Men cheat on women all the time. Why would Light be any different? And don't look at me like that. It would take a lot more tears of the poppy than this to kill you. Indeed, a puff or two might help ease your obvious distress.' Raksasa squealed and jumped on to the hammock as Pieter began to create a spark using two pieces of flint, to light his pipe.

'I very much doubt that, and I just said no.'

'Okay, don't bite my head off. You'll excuse me if I do.'

'I think I should go now, to reach Malay Town before it gets dark,' I said, as the hut began to fill with the heady vapours from Pieter's pipe.

Inspired by the signs Awang and I had made so I could find my hidden silver in the jungle near the kampong, I had begun our journey with a pocketful of thin strips of coloured cloth with which to mark the way from where we left the bullock cart to this secret place. My Dutch friend, bounding ahead, had seemed unconcerned by my dilly-dallying. I had had an inexplicable desire to find my way home without needing to be dependent on him.

'I thought you might stay the night—' Pieter began.

My eyes drifted to the single hammock that the monkey had just vacated, and my heart raced, remembering the confession Pieter appeared to have made on Bukit Bendera.

'Perhaps then you will see certain things differently.' He could have been talking about the business between Light and the sultan, or Light and his lovers, but I heard another suggestion in his voice.

'I just remembered that I'm due back at Martinha's for an early dinner. But there is no need for you to return with me,' I said hastily, suddenly desperate to leave this place where I felt intensely vulnerable.

'Keen to leave me then,' Pieter said, with one of his ambiguous smiles.

'No, just to ensure no one worries when I don't arrive at Martinha's on time.' I swear that monkey smirked at me as I began to gather up my belongings. 'But you never answered me as to why you have these letters since they were clearly meant for Captain Light.'

'No need to accuse me of underhandedness,' said Pieter behind a screen of wispy smoke. 'I've long delivered letters to and from the women Light keeps on hand at Junk Ceylon. At least he did until settling here in Penang. That's why I imagine his half-caste wife detests me; she must have discovered my role in his deceit.'

'Don't call her a half-caste,' I snapped. 'And that still doesn't explain why *you* have these letters.'

Pieter sighed and stroked his monkey under its chin, the creature's eyes now as dull as an opium den dweller's. 'They're copies. And not just love letters. They're also records of promises made and financial transactions for which Light has, in the past, borrowed a great deal of money from me. Some of it still to be repaid.'

He took another puff of his pipe, inhaled the smoke, and blew it out gently. I knew it was time to go but curiosity impelled me to stay.

'Do you not see a certain pattern among the few letters you read?' He began to mimic a high-pitched woman's voice: 'Please provide fifty muskets, cloth, sandalwood oil, and rose-water'; 'I am in such a poverty-stricken state I ask for your sympathetic assistance'; 'I am a woman and there is no-one else to turn to'; 'I am so poor, I cannot repay you'; and so on. They're clever these ladies of Thalang, having gained a reputation for being very beautiful, very alluring, and as cunning as hell.'

Light believed that there were no love relationships, only transactions. Perhaps these letters had convinced him of that since they were filled with so many demands for commodities.

Whether or not I was being seduced by the effects of the opium I wanted to reach out and touch Pieter, thinking his scornful tone meant that he had been hurt by a deceitful paramour in the past. But I dared not in case he misread my fraternal intentions.

'Light's women have expensive tastes and he has a tendency to say yes when he should tell them no; he thinks with his cock like all men,' scoffed Pieter. 'My Siamese being poor I gave my translator these letters so he could make copies in English before I handed over the originals. That way I could keep track of the goods I had loaned to Light and the money I advanced him.'

Then Pieter cocked his head to one side and stroked his deformed monkey. 'You do know by now how to tell when Light is lying?'

I shook my head.

'He repeats himself, often in the same moment.'

I thought back to how Light had originally told me about shooting silver into the jungle to encourage his lazy sepoys to work harder, a story that both Pieter and Tuan Ismail could not verify. It seemed to me now as if he had been trying to persuade himself that it was true.

'Once you know, you'll see how often he does it. He can't help himself; the man is predisposed to lie. Save your pity for those who truly deserve it.'

The pungent smell of opium, sickly sweet and rather fishy at the same time, began to dull my senses. 'I have to go. But there is no need for you to come along; I can find my way back to George Town.'

'Yes, it was clever of you to mark the trees as you did.'

I startled.

Pieter continued, 'Oh, come now—haven't you already realised I have eyes in the back of my head?' He laughed. 'We'll leave those coloured strips there for now, in case you need to find your way here without me; no one else will know what they mean. Are you sure you will not stay the night?'

'I'm sure,' I said. 'I don't like being around monkeys. Your pet obviously does not like me and is likely to attack me in my sleep.'

As if to confirm such intentions, the macaque made a move as if it were about to jump on me, and I shooed it away.

'Have it your own way.'

And that was how we left it, with me trudging through the jungle following ribbons of red and orange until I reached the rutted tracks that led to Malay Town. I could still hear Pieter's scathing laughter and the chattering agreement of his deformed monkey long after the hideout was out of earshot. I had been stupid to antagonise him and would later apologise for my hasty retreat. For without his friendship, one that a boy the age of William or a woman with such a strong allegiance to my errant employer could not replace, I believed life in Penang would be very desolate indeed.

Or so I thought.

Chapter 24

Harrowing Tales

The letters I dreaded arrived, one in late June, the other in early July. The first, from my father, berated me as was only to be expected for what he considered an ill-thought-out decision to relinquish my position with the Honourable Company. In hindsight, I knew he was right. But, my father continued, if Captain Light's possession of Penang was as successful as I had painted it, he trusted I would soon return to Calcutta of even greater value to the EIC and thus our ambitions would be accelerated rather than delayed. Father looked forward to an update on my achievements on the island. I thanked the Lord that letters took a year or more to travel back and forth between our two countries.

Laura's letter was no less painful to read, despite its more earnest support. She had no doubts that I had made a wise decision to place my destiny in the hands of the accomplished Captain Light, although her parents did not see this matter in quite the same way. Laura looked forward to my glorious return to England as a wealthy, independent man with my future as a biographer and journalist assured.

Unable to answer either letter in the way their writers expected, I tried to put them out of my mind; I would no longer lie. As summer beckoned, this became easier, not least when the Light family left. In August, the captain succumbed once more to the fever that had bedevilled him since first arriving here, and he went to his Suffolk estate south of George Town to recuperate. Martinha and William joined him after discovering the boy had chicken pox.

Left to handle all the work-related matters, I began to see what I had been blind to earlier—because of Light's hubris. Fort Cornwallis needed some serious reconstruction, although nothing could be done about its location. Its limited size could not be expanded because all the surrounding land had been taken up by speculators; expecting its value would rise as the settlement grew, they would not sell.

There was no regular procedure for the granting of land or titles. Those who claimed free land were certainly willing to clear it, as was their obligation for receiving it in the first place. But few had bothered to cultivate the ground, especially since we lived in constant fear of a Malay invasion.

There were no government funds for loans or purchases, which is how usurers such as James Scott were able to make a killing. When men found themselves unable to repay their debts, they invariably lost their properties and Scott soon became the biggest landowner on the island, caring little for the misery his extortionate interest rates caused. Whenever I had the opportunity, I spread word about Nachiappan the Chettiar and suggested—particularly to the Chinese, whom I found to be notorious gamblers—that they borrow sums of money from him to cover their debts instead.

I had seen Pieter once, briefly at the end of June, during which I set things right between us. Since then, no one seemed to know where the *Fame* had sailed or when she would return.

I missed William.

My one solace was Tuan Nakhoda Ismail's family. I took every opportunity I could to question the Malay headman. On one occasion, I asked him why he had sat down to his evening meal at the time he usually laid out his prayer mat. He responded in his usual common-sense manner that it was better to think about praying while eating than to go through the motions and attempt to pray while distracted by a growling stomach.

I revelled in the man's stories, eager to learn more about the Siamese and why the Sultan of Queda was so afraid of them. The tale

Tuan Ismail told next occurred after we had eaten; I'm not sure I could have consumed anything had it been beforehand.

'Let me tell you about the nature of the Siamese,' began the nakhoda. 'How the usurper king, Phetracha, freed himself of the previous heirs and supporters of King Narai.'

Awang, Othman, and I ventured closer to their father, whose voice lowered as if he was about to tell a ghost story.

'After claiming the throne, Phetracha seizes forty-eight royal members of the Siamese court loyal to King Narai and orders his men to cut small pieces from their bodies every day for twelve days, although not enough to kill them. This meat is sent to the kitchen, where it is cooked in a variety of spicy sauces. Phetracha forces the prisoners to eat their own human flesh before impaling and disemboweling each one of them in front of their families.

'The tyrant then gives their land to his followers, and the dead men's relatives become slaves. All of this happened more than a hundred years ago, but similar atrocities occur today. The Burman is no better.'

Awang and Othman pulled faces of disgust. I could hear a faint ringing in my ears. I reached for more water and drank as if my life depended on it.

The headman had not finished.

'Phetracha was known as the Elephant Prince because of his ingenuity with killing his enemies that way. Execution by elephant does not always end quickly. I have seen a man tied to an elephant's leg and dragged along the ground until one by one his bones tear from their sockets and he suffers the greatest agony. People to be punished are tied to poles and elephants brought to look at them.'

Othman shuddered next to me. I drew him closer and put my arm around his shoulder, holding him tight.

His father continued, 'On command, the creature pulls the pole from the ground into the air with the prisoner unable to escape. Sometimes a man lands and is stamped upon. Other times, the suffering lingers as the elephant forces him on to its ivory, then soars him into the air repeatedly until the guard directs it to squeeze the man's body to death.'

All I could hear, beyond that distant ringing in my ears, were Othman's deep breaths.

'Malays are fierce warriors, but we do not torture women and children. We also believe in giving a man a clean and quick death while the Siamese enjoy torturing him for as long as possible,' continued the headman.

As if sensing we had all had enough of torture and death, the nakhoda said, 'But I will not talk any more about these matters. I think you now understand why Sultan Abdullah does not wish to offend the King of Siam without the guarantee of help from your King George. Everyone is afraid of an invasion by the Siamese. Protection by the British is important to Queda.'

Wishing to keep the conversation going but eager to lighten the mood, I pointed out that Captain Light had once been on friendly terms with the Siamese governor of Junk Ceylon, before being driven off that island. 'When the governor died, I understand Light stayed in touch with his widow, Lady Chan.'

'Ah, now there is a story you must hear,' exclaimed the headman. 'Of Lady Chan and her younger sister, Lady Mook.'

I released my grip on Othman, but the boy continued to sidle close to me.

'How do you know this story, *ayah*?' said Awang.

'Because the mother of Lady Chan is Malay, as is her first husband Nahum, a distant relative of my friend who lives in Kuala Muda,' his father replied.

'A story from the past?' Othman asked.

'No. Four or five years ago. The Burmans invaded the island of Ulang Salang just before Captain Light came to Penang. Like Sultan Abdullah, Lady Chan asked the East India Company to help defend her people, but they did not. The Siamese under her care fought the colonizers but were cut down in large numbers.'

Tuan Ismail paused to look at his eldest son and me. 'Now think, Jim and Awang: you are a helpless woman about to be ruled by a devilish enemy with only a few old men and many women and children to protect. How do you avoid a slaughter?'

Awang spoke first. 'Negotiate a ceasefire, ayah?'

His father shook his head.

'Perhaps through subterfuge or diversion?' I offered. I was thinking of a victory General George Washington had achieved near Boston during the American Revolutionary War. He had positioned a few cannons at Cambridge and began firing them to keep the British occupied while he secretly hauled the rest of his munitions up to Dorchester Heights. That gave him a much better vantage point to attack his enemy even with fewer, less experienced men. 'Could the Lady have used some kind of ruse against the Burmans?'

'*Benar tu*, Jim. Cunning offers the only advantage when attacked by a stronger force.' He took a long drink of coconut water and continued. 'Lady Chan told her people to hold spines of coconut fronds on their shoulders as if they were muskets and carry them in and out of the fort by night until the Burmans believed they were well protected. The colonizers left soon after, and King Rama gave a title of honour to Lady Chan and her sister Lady Mook in recognition of their success.'

Othman squealed with delight, obviously relieved by a happier ending than being trampled to death by elephants.

'But that, I think, is enough storytelling; it is almost time for our final prayers of the day,' said the father.

'Before I leave, Tuan Ismail, I have one request. Your sons have expressed an interest in learning English, and I would like to teach them if you would agree.' I had not realised how much I missed my informal tutoring of William while the boy convalesced.

With the headman's agreement, so began some of the happiest days of my life. The next morning, I found Awang and Othman hard at work under their father's watchful gaze. Othman was busy whittling hollow reeds known as *resam* into pens. Tuan Ismail held up a writing board and explained how he and Awang had spent the previous evening cutting large squares of a fine-grained, cork-like wood called *pulay*. They were about to complete the task by whitening the board's surface with pipe clay. I marvelled at the nearby receptacles that appeared to contain black ink and was told that the boys' mother had burned rice until it resembled charcoal which she then soaked in water and strained.

Tuan Ismail wanted his sons to take their education seriously, which was why he insisted they prepare their own instruments of learning. He told me I would, from then on, be known as 'Munshi James', teacher of languages.

We did not spend all our time on English words and grammar, however. As with William, I wanted the boys' learning to be fun and easily retained, to have informative adventures rather than squat in front of their writing boards. I had hated my schooling and was determined these boys should not similarly suffer.

Othman turned out to be like a hive of bees continually flitting from one blossoming interest to another. Small and wiry, he smiled constantly, revealing an endearing gap between his two front teeth. Like William, he showed his tactile nature by constantly nestling close to me but was otherwise the joker of the kampong, carrying out japes and telling funny stories, the meaning of which I did not always understand which amused him even more.

The younger son was also intrepid and had a particular fascination for jungle creatures, fearless despite my warnings of their poisonous bites and stings. Othman squealed with delight as I allowed him to drop his collection of live centipedes, spiders, and even small snakes into jars of arrack, a trick I had learned from a Chinaman. Two days later, having drowned, they were such perfectly preserved specimens they looked as if they were still alive. Othman made a pretty penny selling these mementoes to sailors who stopped in Penang and wished to amaze their friends at home with exotic creatures. My heart swelled with love for this little boy such that the loss of William's company became easier. A loss that was only temporary, or so I believed.

Awang, albeit much older, taller, and more muscular than his sibling, mirrored William's artistic side. Quiet and shy, he revealed an equally skilled ability to draw life-like pictures of the fruits and flowers that grew abundantly in the jungle. I taught him about angles as we crafted frames for each of his masterpieces, which he also sold to foreigners coming to the port. Thanks to Nachiappan the Chettiar's instruction, each boy now kept a notebook with a running tally of his earnings. They learned how to set prices, write descriptions of their wares, and negotiate as ably as any Arab merchant. Tuan Ismail appeared delighted with their progress, which in turn boosted my desire to please.

Such teaching was not all one-sided, however. I discovered the immense knowledge of the Mussulmen regarding astronomy and certain forms of mathematics that helped them determine the direction of Makkah. From observing the appearance of the first pale light on the eastern horizon, through the rise and fall of the sun until it sank below the western horizon, each devotee also knew the correct time to pray.

Now intimate with the family I became aware of small changes, joking with Awang about the downy black wisps that had sprung up on his upper lip and chin, while rubbing my own smooth face ruefully. That was one of the things Pieter and I joked about, our seeming inability to sprout facial hair. Pieter had explained that this lack of hirsuteness was common in his family. His ancestor, Jan Pieterszoon Coen, had apparently once been insulted by a prominent East India Company captain for having no beard at the age of twenty-six. The point being made was that Coen had neither the right nor the wisdom to challenge the older Englishman.

Even if not physical, a more profound change came over me. I experienced a previously unknown sense of purpose and joy from these simple interactions with Tuan Nakhoda's family. With a sudden bolt of insight, I realised that I had been asking myself the wrong question all along. I was now Munshi James, a respected and able teacher and had never felt happier. I needed to concentrate less on how to make others proud of me and more on what I needed to do to be proud of myself.

When Captain Light returned from his convalescence, I had to extricate myself from this duplicitous adventurer. Even if that meant facing the consequences my father would undoubtedly mete out, and trusting that Laura would go against her parents and elope with me.

Chapter 25

Re-kindled

George Town. Friday, 10 September 1790.

'Uncle Jim!'

As I ambled towards the fort, my spirits sank with the dread of revealing to Light my intention to leave Penang. At his cry, I looked up and saw William galloping out of the guardhouse and down the glacis that ran around the perimeter of Fort Cornwallis. I was so thrilled to see the boy that I temporarily forgot my resolve. The excited lad almost knocked me over. I tousled his black, curly hair as his arms curled around my waist and said, 'I'm glad to see you have recovered from the chickenpox, William, and that it hasn't robbed you of your energy.'

'I missed you, Uncle Jim. We must never be apart for so long again. Promise that we won't!'

I laughed at the serious demeanour of this precocious child. 'I promise,' I assured him. It had been a month since I had last seen him, and that length of time to a small boy must have seemed like an eternity; at his age, it had certainly felt so to me. Then I remembered what I intended to do as I continued towards the fort and wished I had not made such an impetuous promise.

William's chatter interrupted my thoughts. 'Why is it called chickenpox, Uncle Jim, when Mama says my illness did not come from chickens?'

I released his arms from my waist and placed one hand on his shoulder. 'Ah, now that's an interesting story, William,' I replied. 'But it will have to wait for another time; your father is expecting me.'

'Papa is with some angry men and everyone is shouting. He told me to tell you to take the day off because you've been working so hard in his absence.'

I had no doubt what the shouting was about, given the range of matters that had unsettled everyone again. Rumours continued to spread that Lord Cornwallis was about to withdraw all financial and military support from Penang because of his preference for the Andamans. There had been rumblings that the Sultan of Queda was very agitated, tired of waiting for ratification of the treaty Light had promised would be approved by London. The raja was now parlaying with other Malay states to support him by amassing a sizeable armada to retake his island. And Lanoon pirates had been spotted at Pulau Kra, eight miles south of us, although no one was sure of their intentions.

At my lack of a reaction to this free day, William continued, 'Mama needs extra time to rest, with the baby growing inside her, and Papa says it's not good for me to only be around women and slaves.'

So, the rumours I had heard about Martinha's pregnancy were true. A confirmation that lifted my spirits concerning her relationship with Light. He already had his heir. Surely this addition to their family showed that they loved one another, even if their union had seemingly begun as a transaction.

At my further hesitation the boy said, 'Do you not want to have adventures with me any more, Uncle Jim?'

'Of course, just not—' The innocent, pleading face that looked up at me shattered my resolve. I glanced over at the guardroom and shook my head. It would be a relief not to be in the midst of all that handwringing and blaming. I would speak with Light as intended another day. 'Then if your father says so, let's begin. There is someone in the Malay kampong I would like you to meet. A boy close to your own age named Othman. He needs to practice his English and can show you his skill with the kompang.'

'I'm going to have a little brother,' William said as if he had not heard me. He had placed his hand in mine as we began walking down Beach Street in the direction of Malay Town.

'Are you quite sure of that?' I said.

'Papa says so; he's even chosen a name,' replied William, as if that were the end of the matter.

'Then I'm happy for you,' I said. 'Brothers are much better than silly sisters.' We laughed in unison at our shared belief.

'Can I have a piggyback?'

'Alright. Just don't choke me like you did last time by holding my neck so tightly.' I knelt down so the boy could climb on to my back.

'You said you would tell me why it is called chickenpox.'

This was one of those pieces of information that had come to me quite by chance. I explained to William that my Uncle George had been friendly with William Heberden, a fellow physician, whose patient had been none other than the famous Dr Samuel Johnson. Heberden had discovered that this common childhood ailment was quite different from the deadly smallpox so Dr Johnson decided to name it 'chickenpox' to indicate that it was a more cowardly, harmless disease.

'Of no great threat to anyone other than pregnant women and the elderly who might already be weak,' I said, adding quickly, 'I trust your illness did not affect your mother or father.' The boy replied that he had stayed out of their way most of the time, being looked after by the family slave, I Boon, and his wife. Which, William told me with dramatic effect, had been *very, very boring*.

We chattered non-stop during our journey. I was tempted to tell William that I had visited Pieter's hideout at Battu Lanchon and to describe the Dutchman's strange pet but decided against it in case the boy hankered to go there. It would only be under the direst of circumstances that I would visit that place again.

When we arrived at the kampong neither Othman nor Awang were to be seen. I thought they had perhaps gone fishing with their father, although this was late for their return. 'Another time,' I told William, who seemed less disappointed than I was. 'Come see where I am living. We can take some refreshments then walk back to George Town. There is something amusing I want to show you.'

After a brief visit to my lodgings, William and I trundled back the way we came. It was childish of me, I knew, but I thought it would amuse my young charge to see the antics of a relative newcomer, an Arab, to the Penang population. I also wanted to use the opportunity to educate William on the meaning of the Arab's name. 'Tunku Sayyid Hussain is a pepper trader, said to be related to the Sultan of Acheen,' I told William as we walked along. 'Sayyid—or Syed as some spellings would have it—means that this follower of Islam is descended from the Prophet Muhammad through the lineage of Husayn, the Prophet's grandson.'

William's silence told me he was not much interested in this new knowledge but I was proud of my increased understanding of Islam, as relayed to me by Tuan Nakhoda Ismail.

'Look over there,' I nudged William as we sauntered close to the Arab's George Town residence. 'Why do you think the richest man on this island lays out his gold and silver like that?' We both stared at the outrageous display of wealth being aired on mats outside the pepper trader's home.

'Why does he wash his money?' asked William.

'Perhaps he is afraid of touching anything that has been soiled by plebeian hands,' I laughed.

'Or he needs to give his bloated entourage something to do all day,' a familiar voice behind us said.

I had not seen or heard from Pieter for some time and was delighted he was back in Penang. Standing alongside my Dutch friend and William, I felt as if life had returned to some semblance of balance. To see Martinha later would surely make the day complete.

'I'm glad I met you. Here.' Pieter thrust a bag of money into my hands. 'Good trading, although nothing as grand a sum as that Arab prince makes in a day.'

'Are you in Penang for some time?' I asked, trying to keep the note of hope out of my voice.

Pieter shrugged his shoulders under that great black coat of his. 'Perhaps. But I cannot linger. I have some business to attend to. I will seek you out another time when you are on your own and we can talk.' He looked over at my young companion. 'Hello, William.'

'Hello,' the boy said in return, the reticence in his voice sounding rather odd.

Pieter pulled me away from the boy and whispered in my ear. 'Have you heard any more from your Malay friend Ismail about the identity of the traitor in our midst?'

I shook my head. 'Not yet. But I'm sure it will be soon.'

With a slap on my shoulder, the Dutchman strode off without another word.

Now considerably richer, William and I went in search of the Chinaman who sold kuih, and we partook of several of the sticky rice cakes, some of them coloured blue from pea flowers and sweetened with *gula Melaka.* My young charge was particularly taken with the *kuih talam,* a layered confection with the green part flavoured with juice from *pandan* leaves and the white layer made from coconut milk. While seated on the ground, enjoying our sweet feast, I asked the Chinaman to package some kuih in banana leaf so William could take the treats back to his mother. As we gorged ourselves, I realised with a jolt that my earlier determination to release myself from Light's employ would not be as easy as I had thought now that his son had re-appeared.

'Time to go home,' I told William once the last piece of kuih had been consumed, feeling guilty at potentially having spoiled the boy's appetite for dinner. I wanted to return to the Malay kampong to find Tuan Ismail before dark to see what intelligence he might have for me that I could share with Pieter.

After two long walks and a belly full of sweetened sticky rice, Light's son was quiet as we trundled to his mother's house. At the steps of her bungalow, I paused and asked William what to do, since I did not want to disturb his mother if she was resting.

'Mama told me to tell you she wants to see you,' he said, almost dragging me up the steps in a renewed bout of enthusiasm.

I entered Martinha's rumah, but soon wished that I had not.

Chapter 26

Torched

Something had changed in her.

After greeting his mother with a kiss, Martinha told William to find Esan, her personal slave, who would take the boy to Mrs Gray's house where they would treat him to High Tea. After William ran off, Martinha pointed to the chair opposite and ordered me to sit, using a tone more fitting to commanding a dog. Alongside her on the sofa lay several large sheets of paper, faint signs of colour seeping through from the other side. I noticed that she looked fuller in the face and thought being with child suited her very well.

I was about to say so when Martinha spoke. 'I have never known anyone to understand my son the way you do,' she began, with no smile in her eyes or on her lips. 'His interests and range of knowledge are much broader now, and William takes pleasure in so many things, full of excitement after what you call your 'outings'.'

'I am glad,' I replied, hoping I had misread her demeanour and that Martinha was merely tired. Women in her condition, I had heard, were often erratic in their behaviour. She did not seem at all like my old friend but, then, I had never been around her when she was with child.

'That is why I am especially sad today,' she said, turning over the sheets of paper that lay next to her so I could see the pictures on the other side. Martinha tapped an index finger on a painting that depicted a short man in a long, black overcoat. 'Uncle Pieter, William calls him,' she said, so quietly a chill coursed through my veins.

'I can explain—' I began, but her raised hand stopped me, as did her expression.

Martinha lifted a second painting depicting an unnaturally large figure I did not recognise, with a crown on his head. The title of the drawing, in William's handwriting, was 'King Coen'.

'My son was quite taken with the tale your Dutch friend told him some months ago. But allow me to relate the true story of his *glorious* ancestor,' she spat. She paused, then continued. 'The Dutch were always greedy and wanted to monopolise the spice trade, given how Europeans had been duped into believing that nutmeg in particular is a cure-all for everything from the common cold to the bubonic plague. The best, some would say the only source of nutmeg at that time, came from the island of Banda. You know the place to which I refer?'

I nodded, aware that she was referring to a tiny speck in the ocean that lay between the bigger land masses of the Dutch East Indies and Papua New Guinea and was barely discernible on any map.

'You might think, as many Europeans do, that the Bandanese were merely ignorant fishermen. But they were expert traders and navigators who managed a successful entrepôt to which the Chinese, Malays, Arabs, and others sailed, not just to buy nutmeg but to trade in other goods. They had no wish to fall under the subjugation of a European power, forced to accept useless items in exchange for their crops, so they resisted all Dutch negotiation attempts. But Coen had other ideas. In 1621 he led an expedition of thirteen Dutch warships, over sixteen hundred Batavian soldiers, and eighty Japanese mercenaries to Banda, where they proceeded to round up the villagers—men, women and children—many of whom chose to escape being butchered or enforced into slavery by throwing themselves off the cliffs into the sea.'

I listened in wretched silence as Martinha related the horrors attributed to Jan Pieterszoon Coen. It was only when I felt a stab of pain in my right hand that I realised I had been pinching the skin with my fingers and my nails had dug so hard I had drawn blood.

'By the time the Dutch were done with their slaughter the population of Banda had been reduced to barely a thousand people. Scores of island elders who had come to Coen to surrender were beheaded and quartered by his mercenaries.'

'Martinha,' I pleaded. 'Please stop. You will distress yourself.' I saw no obvious sign of that, however. What I really meant was that she was distressing me.

'I know I should not be uttering such stories in my condition, but this is one I heard from my father in childhood and you need to hear it now,' she replied.

I lowered my eyes. Martinha continued and I forced myself to listen as she described how the Dutch had kept a certain number of natives on Banda rather than ship them all to Batavia as slaves because the Hollanders were not as skilled in nutmeg cultivation and required their expertise. But conditions under the Dutch had been so bad that within sixty years the native Bandanese population had been decimated to just one hundred survivors. This required the *perkeniers* to import slaves from other parts of Java, as well as India and China, to maintain a population sufficient to plant, nurture, and harvest the crops. 'All they ever cared about,' Martinha said.

My eyes pleaded with her to end this horrific tale, but she continued on. 'The Dutch were so intent on monopolising the nutmeg trade they wanted to control the Bandanese island of Run, which the British maintained. The Dutch and English East India companies had, by this time, come to an agreement not to poach each other's trade but that was not enough for Coen. He waited until the British left Run undefended then invaded that island and chopped down and burned down every nutmeg tree so none was left standing. Legend has it you could smell the aroma of nutmeg across the ocean for months afterwards.'

'But why?' I gasped.

'So that would be the end of British designs on the spice trade which Coen was fanatical about controlling entirely,' Martinha answered. 'As well as to demonstrate what others could expect should they choose to defy the Dutch. That was the nature of the man your friend Pieter Reinaert admires so much.'

We sat quietly for a moment as the horror of what she had told me sank in. I did not doubt she spoke the truth, remembering Pieter's comment that day on the hill about the way the Dutch effected their treaties with local sultans: '*If any of them took liberties … we would give them a taste of that military superiority to bring them back in line.*'

'That cruel oppressor would never be called King Coen in this region, except by Pieter Reinaert and his disgusting ilk,' Martinha said, at length. 'Ask anyone who has heard of Jan Pieterszoon Coen, who never received any rebuke from the Dutch for his atrocities and is still thought by them as a 'statesman', and they will utter his true title: 'The Butcher of Banda'.

I would have closed my eyes to block out her stony stare but knew that if I did all I would see would be scores of Bandanese lying on blood-soaked beaches and bloated bodies washing up on their shores.

'Please, Martinha, forgive me. I promise it won't happen again.'

'In that you are correct,' she said. 'My son will doubtless achieve much in life for which we will always be grateful to you for igniting his passion for learning. But your association with this part of our family ends today. You will not see William any more, James; I can no longer trust you with my son.'

Her face told me that words, excuses, pleading, were useless. The boy adored me, as had been evidenced earlier when he had insisted I promise we would never be apart for so long again. Why would she be so cruel to William, knowing how close we had become these past eighteen months? I felt the same pain in my wrists as I had as a writer in Calcutta. I looked down at my hands and found them tightly balled into fists. I spread my fingers out to relieve the ache and placed my right hand on my knee to stop it from bouncing up and down as if it had a mind of its own.

'You have proven yourself to be a poor judge of character, James,' Martinha continued. 'And not an especially fine one yourself. For you not only encouraged my son to lie to me but allowed him to accept bribes from that man. How dare you!'

Anger, shame, fear, confusion mingled in a torrent of mental turmoil. Without thinking what I was saying—indeed, believing at first that I had not spoken these words out loud—I mumbled, 'Perhaps the same might be said of you, given that you have long lived with a man who has betrayed you.' I could not look her in the face but heard her sharp intake of breath from across the room.

'What did you say to me?'

I raised my hand and sucked the blood that trickled from it. Perhaps I had been misled by Pieter to think his ancestor was a hero. And, yes, I had defied her by allowing the Dutchman to join us on our adventures. But what harm had come to William as a consequence? Why was Martinha blowing everything out of proportion? Was she so perfect to never make a poor decision herself? I had meant to berate Pieter for giving William that money, but the arrival of the Dutch warships had distracted me.

I felt a desperate need not only to defend myself but to attack, as she had done unfairly to me. 'Aside from all the lies and deceit your husband has used to possess this island, did you know that he once had another wife? After he married you?' I said, immediately regretting my outburst.

Her response was not what I expected. After a moment's thought she said, 'Are you speaking of Chao Ratt?' At my shocked expression, Martinha threw her head back and laughed so raucously I worried for her health. 'It seems I must re-educate you once again, James. You *have* heard of debt slavery, I take it?'

I nodded.

'In this case, the injustice was all the more monstrous because the debt alleged against Chao Ratt's husband, a minor Siamese official, had been invented by a jealous Chinaman with imaginary scores to exact against the man. As disgraceful as the practice is, that lady was to be made a debt slave, likely forced to labour in the tin mines which the Chinaman owned. Francis, with my full knowledge and blessing, not only cleared the debt fully but took her as an unofficial wife to ensure there would be no further disputes.

'As you must be aware by now, James, men in this region keep several women. Sultan Abdullah has three wives and four favourite *gundeks* with which he has amassed more than a dozen children, I hear.'

James Scott, I knew, kept at least two women at his rumah in George Town, with goodness knows how many others throughout the region. Certainly, it was common enough practice, but—

Martinha looked away from me and sighed. 'The arrangement with Chao Ratt and her husband, the Khun Thalakang, benefited everyone: the Chinaman received money; the Khun was free of his debt, Chao Ratt was no longer at risk of demeaning servitude, while Francis increased his stature in the eyes of those who mattered by carrying out this good deed.

'You see, James, sometimes a story cannot be fully known merely on the face of it. It is wise not to judge an act until you know the full circumstances in which it occurred.'

'But there were others, and—' I began.

Only then did Martinha raise her voice to me, eyes blazing. 'Do not insert yourself between Francis and me, James, or you will be crushed.'

She closed her eyes, stroked her belly as if calming the child inside and said more quietly, 'Relationships are complicated, as one day you may discover for yourself. But, yes, if you are accusing me of being a poor judge of character then I admit my guilt because I never expected *you* to betray me, having always treated you not just as a friend but as family.'

I felt as if my bowels were about to give way but dare not move or say anything in case I provoked her further. This anger would surely pass, if only she would look at me and see how genuinely contrite I felt.

'As for my husband, I imagine you will betray him also. Perhaps even desert him in his time of greatest need.' She smiled with the coldness of a grey English dawn. 'Oh, don't look so surprised, James, Francis will not banish you for this. He finds you far too valuable, and that is his choice.'

'Why?' I said, aware of how petulant I sounded. 'He has James Scott to support him, he does not need me.'

Martinha tipped her head to one side. 'Did you know that Francis had a mind to buy Golsberry Farm near his good friend George Doughty's estate in Suffolk, England, having long become disillusioned with governing here? He planned to send Mr Doughty a further three thousand pounds to move forward with the purchase but discovered through his Calcutta agent that this could not be done. My husband's expenses have exceeded his pittance of a salary by a factor of two to one. It is only Scott's merchanting efforts that have kept this family afloat and is the reason why Francis cannot disband their business, although—as you well know—he is continually slandered by other traders for what they say is his unfair advantage.'

Martinha cast her eyes towards the shutters and sighed. 'But I can tell you that Francis *has* lived up to his promise to be a sleeping partner, it is James Scott's underhandedness that causes such discontent. I fear the Scotsman will remain loyal to Francis until my husband's dying breath but not a moment longer. He has already cast his covetous eyes on everything Francis might leave me, including our Suffolk estate.'

As I had many times before, I felt pity for Light so trapped by his ambitions. And for his wife, living with the consequences. 'Reigning in hell,' I murmured, to which Martinha snapped back, 'What does that mean?'

'It's a reference to Milton's *Paradise Lost*,' I replied, my bladder now fit to burst.

'Ah, *Paradise Lost!* That would seem an apt end to our conversation, James,' she said, standing up. I dared not touch her, that much was obvious from her glare as I moved forward to take her hand. 'It is indeed a pity you can no longer see the boy you claim to love. And I would be lying if I told you I will not miss you, too. But I am tired now, so please go. I believe there is a saying in your country, 'You've made your bed, now lie in it'. William will be distraught, but the young get over things much quicker than we do.' She flicked her hand in the direction of the doorway without looking at me. 'The pieces of silver with which your Dutch friend bribed my son to lie are on that table. Take them with you, then go.' I moved a step closer and took a deep breath before intending to beg her forgiveness once more. But she held up an arm as if trying to shield herself from an assailant and turned her head away. 'No! I don't want to hear another word from you or see your face again. You are dismissed.'

***

I stumbled down the wooden steps and squinted in the late afternoon sunlight, like a drunkard falling out of a back-alley alehouse after a night-long drinking spree. I struggled to make sense of what had just happened and what I might do next. As unintentional as it had been, I had betrayed Martinha by allowing her son to fraternise with Pieter. Among my many teachings, I had taught him to lie and take bribes. What had I been thinking?

I found a nearby bush and relieved myself. The stream of urine alleviated the tension in my body but did nothing to calm my tormented mind. I walked back to Malay Town as weighed down and wretched as any tin mining slave. To remain here in Penang, no longer allowed to see my dearest William and assist in his progress, would—I knew—be nothing short of reigning in hell for me. Yet what would Martinha think, how much further would I fall in her estimation, if I left Light in the lurch now? Only by staying here could I hope to put right my past wrongs and hope Martinha would forgive me once she had her baby.

But on Monday, I would have to face Francis Light.

Chapter 27

Dark Descent

Not finding the headman or either of his sons at the Malay kampong, I confined myself to my room, refusing the food makcik tried to coax me to eat. My shame soon shifted to fury; Martinha's reaction had not just been unreasonably harsh but spiteful. Caused by her condition, for sure, but unforgiveable just the same. She knew how much I loved William, above and beyond what teaching the boy had meant to me. Over the eighteen months we had shared adventures my passion for sharing knowledge with him had crept up on me like Christmas. It meant no longer waking up to just another humdrum day, but hours filled with newly discovered gifts; the nourishment of laughter; the intoxicating lightness of bonhomie. Nothing I had done for or with Francis Light had come close to that. I doubted that chronicling the man's life, as I had once believed I desired above all, could compete.

Frustrated, I silently railed against Pieter. I had never asked him to join us or turn the boy's head, spewing insolence about his father's failures, telling outrageous lies about his ancestor. King Coen, indeed! He was to blame, yet I was the one being punished. I stayed indoors and determined to cold-shoulder the world.

As one candle after another burned down to a stump, I took some solace in the belief that once Martinha had birthed her baby she would go back to being her kind, understanding self. Time, people said over and over, was a great healer. I just needed to wait things out. But that meant until next March at the earliest—six months away. What would I do with myself in the meantime? What if she remained moody and weepy after the birth, as I had heard some women were? The list of whats and what ifs seemed interminably long as I racked my brains to find a way out of my dilemma. Although I was not someone who gave much credence to praying, I hoped for some miraculous change to occur. When it did, it plunged me even further into hell.

***

There are more ways to kill a dog than hanging, as the old proverb says. I had to force myself to forget about William until Martinha came to her senses. In the meantime, I would continue tutoring Awang and Othman. I was 'Munshi James'. The title fortified me. By Sunday morning I decided to wash and dress myself then venture out to find my Malay friends, when knuckles rapped on my door. I opened it, fully expecting to lambast Pieter.

'William! What are you doing here? Did your mother send you?'

I looked over his shoulder and could see from the expression clouding I Boon's face, as the slave shifted from one foot to another among the hens, cocks, and dogs of the kampong, that she had not. William told me with an air of pride that this visit had been his idea.

'So where is your mother?' I asked.

'At home. Growing fat and ill-tempered,' said the boy, pushing his way into my room.

With some amusement I said, 'Do come in.' Then, remembering the slave said, 'What about I Boon?'

'Oh, he has some chores to carry out in George Town. I told him to come back for me later.'

I waved to the slave as if I had a white flag in my hand and tried to look sympathetic to his plight, then closed the door so I no longer needed to feel guilty about William's ruse.

The boy began to bounce on my bed and looking imploringly at me with those large, brown eyes asked, 'Why did you not come for me yesterday or this morning, Uncle Jim?'

I could feel the tell-tale signs prick my eyes and, turning away, I swiped a palm across my upper face. 'What did your mother tell you?' I croaked, sounding more like a boy in puberty than a man.

'Just that you're very busy. But that's not what Papa said because these are days you are not expected to work. Did I do something wrong, Uncle Jim? Don't you like me any more?'

I wanted to scoop him up and hug him. 'Far from it, William. The fault is mine.' I wondered if I dare tell him the truth when his mother appeared to have chosen not to. Or should I go ahead and compound her white lie? 'It's a grown-up thing, William,' I offered. 'Complicated. But nothing at all to do with you. It's not your fault, I promise.'

I somehow found myself sitting next to the boy on the bed. With heart-breaking innocence, he leaned into me and before I knew it my arm was around him and I kissed the top of his head. 'You need to wash your stinky hair, young man,' I said, in the hope of lightening the moment. He punched me playfully in the stomach and replied, 'Make me!' We began to tussle, like siblings.

Moments later, I jumped up in alarm. What was I doing? His mother would be furious if she knew he were here. 'William, you shouldn't have come. You mother will be angry if she finds out.'

'Oh, who cares? She doesn't need to know,' he said, now lying on my bed with his hands behind his head, looking like the king of the castle. 'The slaves do whatever I tell them to.'

I grimaced. 'We've talked about this before, William, remember? It's one thing to give a slave an instruction, quite another to involve them in lies, especially when—in this case—it means deceiving your mother. Think what it's like for poor I Boon caught between you, young master, and her. That's not really fair to him, is it?'

William seemed to consider this for a moment, then sat up. He always appeared older and wiser than his years. 'When I'm a man, everyone will do what *I* say on this island,' he responded defiantly.

Amused, I said, 'Oh, really, how so?'

'Because princes must be obeyed,' the boy continued, in a tone that alarmed me.

'And what has being a prince got to do with you?' I asked, already fearing the answer.

'Because that is what I am, a prince of the East. My mother is a princess of Queda and so that makes me a prince, doesn't it?'

His question put me in a quandary. I responded with one of my own. 'What makes you think your mother is a princess, William?'

'Everyone says so,' he replied, somewhat petulantly, as if he were surprised that I was questioning him. 'She was the daughter of old Sultan Jiwa and one of his lesser wives.'

I opened my mouth to correct him but thought better of it. I needed to listen further to hear exactly what the boy thought he knew.

William began to bounce up and down on my bed again, obviously excited. 'That is how Papa came to own Penang; it was part of my mother's dowry. That's a gift, isn't it, Uncle Jim?

'A dowry is a settlement made by the bride's family to her husband upon their marriage, yes, William. But can you stop doing that; you'll damage my bed.'

The boy obeyed and sitting still said, 'Well then, Papa was promised this island by Sultan Jiwa, but then the bad men at the East India Company—the *Dis*Honourable Company my father calls it—made him give it up. Seeding it to them. Does that mean like crops?'

'Ceded,' I corrected. 'C-E-D-E-D. It comes from the French word 'to yield'. It's when one party gives up or transfers the rights of property to another. But—'

'Papa was fooled into ceding Penang to Bengal for money, but then they have been defrauding him ever since.'

It was obvious that William was spouting words he had heard somewhere but did not fully understand. 'Do you know what 'defrauding' means, William?'

The boy looked at me blankly. Then, because of how I had taught him, he grasped at a likely definition. 'Trickery, isn't it, Uncle Jim?'

'Something like that,' I said. 'Again, we can go back to the French: *defrauder* means to cheat, a form of deception.' Oh, how much of that there was in Penang.

'Well, when I'm growed up—'

'Grown up,' I said.

'Grown up, then,' the boy shouted back, rolling his eyes at me. 'When I'm a man like you and Papa, I will take my case to the King of England. And if he doesn't give me back my island, I will fight his army for it—and win.'

His face was so contorted with impassioned pique that it took all my self-control not to laugh, although I found none of this amusing in the least. What had Light been telling the boy about his dubious inheritance? Had William heard snippets of gossip and conversations and created his own version of the lie that Penang was part of Martinha's dowry? Should I leave the boy his dreams of future glory or tell him as kindly as possible that his father did not own this island and never had? That his mother was no princess, except in her husband's eyes.

As if a hand had forced its way down my throat and was now squeezing my heart, I gasped, trying to control an array of disturbed feelings: concern mixed with anger tinged with dismay. William's next comment did not help.

'I want us to go on an outing today, Uncle Jim,' he implored. 'Please hurry up and get ready. Mama thinks I am helping I Boon with his chores and won't look for me because she is always sleeping because of the baby.' He looked at me expectantly with no idea why I could not go along with his plan. Looking at his innocent face, my already bruised heart shattered into pieces, forcing me into a decision of even greater import than telling him he was mistaken about his parents' status.

I closed my eyes and took a deep breath. I had never known such pain in my chest. 'I cannot do that, William—not today or in the foreseeable future. I'm sorry but I have fallen out of your mother's favour for not telling her the truth. You must go home now and not come here again until she says you can.'

'But—'

'I said no, William. I'm sorry.'

'Why not?' he challenged.

'Because—' I stopped, then smiled at him, but he only scowled back. What excuses could I proffer, and would they ever be enough? William, I knew from experience, was an obstinate boy. The retort used so often by my elders, 'Because I said so', had never worked with me and it would not with him. William would not let this go until he had beaten me down, and I had succumbed to his wishes, defying his mother and lying to her again. What lesson would that teach him? I would not have William become a bully like Hamilton.

I thought back to similar instances in my childhood when I had wanted my mother or favourite uncle to agree to something that they, but not I, knew was wrong. How I had harangued them, not letting my arguments rest. At least, not until—

Now I understood with a strange, fearsome clarity why at times adults appeared to be so unkind to children; reason and loving words do not often win the day with intransigent young boys.

'I want us to go on an adventure today. You promised!' William actually stomped his foot and glowered at me.

'That's enough!' I responded roughly, although the pain of doing so could not have been more intense had I been disembowelled on the spot. 'You will leave right now and catch up to I Boon. You need to learn to listen to grown-ups and do as you're told, William. We won't be going on our outings, and I can't teach you any more, at least not until your mother agrees to it, so don't come here again.'

William shot off the bed and stood with simmering defiance in front of me. It took all my powers not to scoop him up in my arms and tell him I was sorry for shouting.

'You are a horrible person and I hate you!' he screamed, before opening the door and slamming it behind him.

I dropped down on my bed like the victim of a firing squad and wept with what felt like infinite grief.

Chapter 28

Overcast

I burrowed under the covers of my bed, fully clothed. When Monday morning came, I did not bother to get up. To hell with Light and Penang. The sound of the monsoon rains reflected my mood. Like the grey clouds that had undoubtedly blanketed the island I remained shrouded in desolate gloom. I had no desire to eat, just sleep my life away; what purpose did it have?

On the occasions when I awoke, lips stuck together, throat parched, I leaned over to the jug that contained days-old water and made do with sips. I did not even want to expend the energy to piss. Sweating in the fetid, humid air of that room, I must have reeked like a galley slave but did not care.

I thought of my life in Calcutta and what I had given up for *this*. That had been a boring humdrum life, certainly, but one that was relatively safe. One that pleased my family, Laura's family. One I now sorely missed.

I lay naked in the oppressive humidity of that room for one day, two days, perhaps three days, I could not have said. Then, like the occasional ray of sunshine or glimmer of hope that streams through shutters after the rains, a stray thought grasped at my earlier idea. I might no longer have access to William, and that was indeed a great loss, but I would not allow Martinha's spiteful decision to deprive me of my new-found passion for teaching. I had to find Awang and Othman, whom I had not seen for days. After rising, washing, and dressing I became aware of my growling stomach. I could not to wait for the Malays to conclude their mid-day prayer time called Dhuhr and so decided to venture first to George Town, to a place where the locals liked to eat fire-roasted chickens.

Upon reaching where Chulia Street joined Beach Street, just beyond the outer reaches of Malay Town, the raucous chatter of European sea-faring men stopped me in my wake. My first thought settled on Hamilton and his sepoys, whom I certainly had no wish to meet. But as my feet continued moving, urged on by my hungry belly, I saw—surrounded by a small group of unsavoury-looking characters, scarred and tattooed—a familiar face.

He caught sight of me just as I was inclined to step back around the corner. Too late, his familiar gruff, Dutch-accented voice rang out. 'Jim! Come, join us.'

I was still angry at Pieter, believing him at least partly responsible for my predicament. He had after all been the one bribing William. not me. Yet I felt I had little choice, now he had seen me, but to accept his invitation. Besides, I was starved from not having eaten for so many days.

I ventured over as Pieter elbowed the ribs of the blond dishevelled looking man sitting next to him and said, 'Move over, you piece of Danish scum. Make room for my English friend, James Lloyd, Esquire.'

I dutifully sat down to the left of Pieter and heard names being uttered as introductions, to which I nodded in half-hearted response. The proprietor came over and before I could say a word, Pieter took charge and ordered our meals. Almost immediately, many spit-roasted kampong chickens, much smaller but more delicious than anything I had ever tasted in England or India, were placed on the table before us. One of the men reached across, but Pieter—quick as a whip— slapped his hand away. 'Leave it, you ignorant pig. Where are your manners? Guests are served first. Jim—please, help yourself before this motley crew makes off with the lot.'

Pieter appeared different in front of these men. The thought crossed my mind as to how well I really knew him.

The other sailors laughed and poked fun at their companion, who had reddened at Pieter's rebuke. 'Well, get on with it, lad,' the man muttered in the manner of a dog that had been kicked and was now keen to bite the weakest creature it could find. I did as I was told and broke off a piece of steaming crispy breast then blew on my fingers to cool them.

I remained quiet, having nothing to say to Pieter while we remained in this company, yet struggling to think how I might broach my aggrieved feelings after these lively men left. Judging by the amount of food and drink that had been brought to our table, I knew this would be many hours yet. I determined to eat quickly, make my excuses and leave. I wanted to see Tuan Ismail before it was too late to call on his family. My ire concerning King Coen would have to wait another time.

One of the men seated opposite, his mouth dripping with chicken grease, piped up, 'Finish your story, Reinaert.' Then, looking directly at me said, 'Your ugly friend was about to tell us how he got that misshapen mouth of his,' in a manner that made perfectly clear—as would anyone with sight—that Pieter was anything but ugly despite his deformity. Indeed, I had always thought his constant sneer lent him a sensual, almost seductive air.

Pieter leaned back, away from the man, and studied his face as if conflicted about whether to continue his earlier tale. Then he spoke. 'As I was saying I had, or so my mother told me much later, been far too cosy in her womb.'

'Aye, who doesn't love being inside a woman?' said a man with teeth so blackened it almost looked as if he had none in his mouth. As he began thrusting his hips in a suggestive manner, I could feel my face reddening. Pieter grabbed my shoulder in what I thought was his attempt to prevent me from bolting. He leaned closer, conspiratorially, and in a stage whisper said, 'Ignore this lewd rabble.' Then, louder, he retorted to the man, 'Do you want to hear my answer or not?'

'Go on,' the seafarer said, sending a spray of chewed chicken across the table. My stomach lurched. What disgusting individuals these men were. I could not understand why Pieter would admit their company.

'So, there I am, all cosy in the womb, not much interested in being born,' continued Pieter.

'I know how that feels,' added a weasel-faced man with rheumy eyes.

'They called the doctor when it appeared my mother's life, if not my own, was in danger. He declared mine would not be a natural birth.'

'An' there's been nothing natural about you ever since,' declared Black Teeth, which seemed to delight his cronies.

Pieter shot him a look that immediately quieted the grimy sailor, who cast his eyes down and began to pick at his chicken which he mixed into a plateful of rice and vegetables. The Dutchman picked up two tin forks and waved them in front of the man's face. 'According to the doctor, I needed to be pulled out headfirst with pincers.'

As he crossed the forks in the manner of makeshift scissors I offered, 'In the medical profession they are called forceps.'

'Forceps, then. Thank you, Jim,' said Pieter, squeezing then releasing my shoulder. 'All seemed to be going well until my mother, eager to see what she was about to birth, grabbed the doctor's arm just as my head was popping out, causing his hand holding the forceps to slip. The contraption tore at my mouth and this lip has been my battle scar ever since. But, then, isn't all birth and the life that comes after it a battle? It's just that I have a reminder of that daily on my face.'

The men seemed to sober up at that and nodded sagely. I turned to look at Pieter, brow furrowed, at the same moment he turned to look at me. Our eyes met, and I caught something in them that I thought I understood but was just another example of my interpreting what I already had half a mind to believe: why Pieter had uttered that propaganda about his ancestor, Jan Pieterszoon Coen.

When reality is too unpalatable—whether admitting to one's natural deformity, or the atrocities perpetrated by a notorious ancestor—are we not inclined to make up stories that better suit our needs? Had I not seen this happen many times, including in my own family, when rakes and gamblers and ne'er do wells of all stripes were spoken of with fondness, if not delight? One might wish to keep the activities of a law-breaking father or a drunken grandfather quiet but was there not a perverse pride in having an infamous ancestor when so many of us are denied even memorable ones? Wasn't Pieter's selective recounting of King Coen's actions understandable? Poor Pieter suffered daily from that reminder of life's inhumanity marked upon his face. As his friend, did he not deserve my compassion rather than my indifference? I reached over and squeezed his arm in a gesture of support, feeling a sudden surge of what I chose to think at the time was brotherly love. His glorious eyes—more indigo than azure in this light—seemed to dance in amusement. He really was the most inscrutable of men.

The conversation turned to the rumblings coming from Queda and of Sultan Abdullah. Black Teeth reported that the Malay ruler had been amassing a large number of armed prahus, by allying with the sultanates of Trengganu, Johore, Indragiri, Siak, Sulu, Kota Karang, and Siantar. They were undoubtedly getting ready to attack Penang.

'I hear there's been an infestation of Lanoons at Pulau Kra, too,' said Rheumy Eyes, repeating intelligence that Light and I already knew.

The men began discussing among themselves what they thought this pirate activity meant, weeks prior to *musim perompak*: the robbery season between November and April when anyone sailing close to the coast with valuable goods risked their lives.

Pieter leaned across to me and whispered, 'Sounds like it might be a good idea to get away from here for a while. I'm headed to the Dutch East Indies in the morning. Why don't you come too? I can show you Batavia. I think, compared to this place, you will be impressed. Come see how the Dutch do things.' His eyes smiled in a most disarming way.

I opened my mouth to speak just as I felt his hand rest upon my upper thigh, placed higher than it should. I held his gaze a fraction too long. His eyes were so beautiful, so deep and I needed that connection with someone I cared about. But then came the stirring. Nothing like that jolt when Pieter and I had shaken hands at the harbour on the first day we had met; this sensation was far more unsettling. I shifted in my seat, discomfited by the unexpected bulge in my breeches. My face reddened, my mind swirled with impossible explanations. I should not have felt this for another man.

Trying to control my rising panic, I wiped my grease-smeared mouth with the back of my sleeve and jumped up. 'I must go! I need to reach the Malay headman's rumah before it is too late. Something important. To discuss with him.' My earlier hunger had left me. Indeed, I felt quite sick.

'What say you to my proposal?' asked Pieter, staring up at me.

'What proposal?' I said, startled.

'About coming to Batavia with me, fool. What did you think I meant?'

I *had* to leave.

'Yes, yes, of course,' I gabbled, almost falling over the stool in order to break free. 'What time and where?'

'Join me on board the *Fame* any time after ten. I expect we will weigh anchor by eleven. No need to bring much with you, you can buy whatever you need there. I'll look after you for the rest.'

'Thank you,' I answered, more stiffly than I had intended. With a cursory nod to Pieter's companions, I bolted. Not to Tuan Ismail's, for I could not face anyone in my current state, but back to my lodgings to ponder what that unexpected sensation in my groin had meant. I knew of men in India and at sea who engaged in such practices and appeared to enjoy them. From the descriptions I doubted very much that I would. I had allowed Pieter to corrupt me in many ways, not least lying to Martinha and making a deceiver out of William, but I would not allow him to corrupt me towards *that*.

***

At eight o'clock the following morning I set out for Bukit Bendera. By eleven I reached the summit where I stood, alone, and watched with mounting despair as Pieter's ship sailed towards the horizon, sensing that I had lost something ineffable.

My life was now untethered, all avenues of comfort—Martinha, William, and now Pieter—closed off to me. How could I remain friends with the Dutchman given my concern about the kind of relationship that might have taken place in the cramped quarters of his ship? What was wrong with me that I should have had such a reaction to his touch?

Chapter 29

Glaring Mistakes

Fort Cornwallis. 3 January 1791.

We all breathed a collective sigh of relief when the *Crown* anchored off the coast of Penang.

Back in October, Light—who had treated me as if nothing untoward had happened between Martinha and me, in the same way that I chose to suppress what had happened between me and Pieter—had dictated a letter to the Council at Fort William informing them of the Sultan of Queda's burgeoning armada. Four hundred prahus carrying eight thousand men with an artillery of six, nine, and twelve pounders in addition to blunderbusses, muskets, and swivel guns, lurked at the mouth of the Prai river less than two miles away. The land forces were estimated at twenty thousand men, although Light believed half that number to be nearer the truth. I did not know if his figure was more accurate or another example of his preference for fiction. Regardless, Sultan Abdullah appeared ready to retake Penang.

Light concluded his letter to Bengal with, '*I am very unwilling to solicit any reinforcement at this juncture but request if one of His Majesty's frigates can be spared she might come over here for a month by which time we shall be in a better state of defence and be able to judge the views of our neighbours.'* All we could do was hope that this request, unlike so many others, did not fall on deaf ears.

But Bengal did not just send one of His Majesty's frigates to aid us. None other than Lord Charles Cornwallis' younger brother, Commodore William Cornwallis, Commander-in-Chief of the East Indies Squadron, arrived with three companies of sepoys. Which proved at first to be more a curse than a blessing.

In the ten weeks or so between Light's letter and the *Crown's* arrival, the Lanoon pirates had been on the move, raiding villages in Perak. Captain Lorrain of the *Princess Augusta* was dispatched to send them packing. Although he and his company succeeded in forcing the Lanoons further up the Queda coast away from us, they appeared to have a different purpose than a raid in Penang. The sultan had once again prohibited provisions from reaching us, with such a strict watch kept on ships that not even the smallest article could be exported here. We were embargoed once again.

When Commodore Cornwallis' men disembarked, they were as sick and emaciated as any sailors I might have ever encountered. We did what we could to supply them with fresh provisions to restore their health but were aware that if the Sultan of Queda did not end his embargo soon these additional demands by the naval men would bring us to starvation even faster. Commodore Cornwallis assured us that the four thousand maunds of rice Light had requested from Calcutta would arrive soon. We trusted that since the Governor-General's brother was now with us this promise would be swiftly carried out. In the meantime, we had to make do with whatever our vessels could purchase and bring back from Malacca.

Light knew very well that we could not survive another extended embargo and would either have to re-negotiate terms with the sultan or comply with his requests. I realised my wish to visit the sultan's palace in Alor Setar when Light instructed me to join Commodore Cornwallis' delegation as his translator. We were to take the frigate to Queda to inform Sultan Abdullah that he must permit supplies to be brought here as usual or his refusal would be considered a declaration of war. Light hoped that receiving this message from such a luminary as the British Navy's regional Commander-in-Chief would have a salutary effect.

Although I was initially awed by the presence of Commodore Cornwallis, my host proved to be a very down-to-earth and affable gentleman. He certainly did not appear as portly or fiercely imposing as his older brother Charles did in the portraits I had seen of him hanging inside Fort William. That first evening on board the frigate, as we sat together in the captain's quarters ostensibly to discuss our strategy once we arrived at Alor Setar while partaking of the wines on offer, I took the opportunity to ask the commodore questions about his own life and career.

While only four years younger than Light and a fellow Suffolk man, 'Billy Blue', as he was affectionately known among the rank and file, benefited from one of those round, line-free faces that suggest a youthfulness belying his years. Having a full head of wavy, light brown hair helped. Cornwallis sported what my father had once referred to—when describing a business enemy—as a 'facial belly-button'. However, I preferred to think of his chin as having an extra dimple.

After several pleasurable hours listening to the commodore recount his adventures against the Frenchies during the American Revolutionary War, having begun his naval duty in North America at the age of eleven, I gently directed the conversation towards our purpose in Queda. We carried five thousand Spanish Dollars and several chests of opium, together with various other gifts that Light had given us, to smooth our path with the king. From Light's descriptions of previous meetings, I knew that the ceremonial gift-giving could last for quite some time and that men like the Laksamana and Bendahara also expected to profit from the loot. I wondered aloud whether the offer of silver and opium would be rejected out of hand as it had been many times before. William Cornwallis agreed that this was likely, given the sultan's current state of agitation.

'My orders are to negotiate a peaceful resolution as best I can,' he began. Sipping a glass of Madeira he paused and said, 'I hope to persuade the sultan to disband his armada and accept the current terms.'

'I know that the Governor-General informed Captain Light several years ago that he should avoid entering into any discussion that might lead the King of Queda to believe we would defend him militarily should the need arise,' I said tentatively.

'Although the cat is out of the bag in that regard,' Cornwallis said, making obvious by his vocal tone and facial expression that he knew of the foolish promises Light had made in order to secure his possession of Penang in 1786.

'Given the stakes for the settlement, might the Governor-General not be persuaded to provide at least some military support to the sultan? Indeed, is there any hope that word will come soon from London agreeing to the terms of the original treaty? Light's previous offerings have been rejected because what the sultan desires, above all, is confirmation that we would come to his aid if Siam or his southern enemies attack him. I do not believe this would tax our forces greatly.'

The commodore said nothing for a while, seeming to savour his Madeira as he gazed through the grimy leaded windows, out to sea. I feared I had overstepped my boundaries and silently berated myself for speaking so bluntly. Then he said, 'Are you familiar with Prime Minister Pitt's India Act of 1784, James?'

'Yes sir,' I said, hurriedly adding, 'Although not in any great detail.'

'Then perhaps you are unaware of a particular clause that makes Captain Light's position untenable when it comes to securing any kind of military support for his quondam friend.'

I waited with trepidation for William Cornwallis to say more.

'Following the East India Company's follies in North America, the Pitt Act prohibits them engaging in any—and I believe I am quoting the regulation directly here—'treaties, or alliances that might lead to war, measures repugnant to the wish, honour, and policy of the nation'.' He took in a deep breath and added, 'Yet here we are.'

'But acting Governor-General Macpherson—'

'—likely knew of the Act's provision,' interrupted Cornwallis, 'and elected to ignore it. As it seems did your employer, Captain Light.'

This went beyond Lord Cornwallis making his own decision about the matter. The Governor-General was forbidden by an Act of

Parliament from ratifying the sultan's terms as originally agreed to by Light. The very first article of which clearly stated that should he be attacked by an enemy, internal or external, the Honourable Company must come to the sultan's aide at its own expense. I wondered if Light and Macpherson, perhaps in collusion, had used as justification for ignoring the Pitt Act a particular letter. The one dated February 1786 from a Mr Prince to the Governor-General, that I had found among Light's papers. The Bengal Council had seemingly been concerned about the viability of Penang before fresh negotiations had gone too far and had sought third-party opinions. Mr Prince—I suspected a good friend of Light's or James Scott—had responded that he preferred Penang to the Negrais in Burma: '*As it is an island sufficiently detached from the continent to prevent surprise or even attack from the natives and being a free gift from the acknowledged and rightful owner, can never give cause for war.*' As Light knew well, at no time had Penang been a 'free gift' to him from either Sultan Jiwa or his son, yet he appeared never to have corrected that falsehood. The 'never give cause for war' was now likely to be proven illusory too.

Light, knowing all along that he was never going to gain agreement to that first article, had strung the sultan along through outright lying and indirect obfuscating for close to five years. His assumption that the sultan would accept the irregularly offered bribes of money and opium and forget about his most important demand had been proven wrong. His expectation that takers of land in Penang would not just clear that land but also cultivate it, was highly misplaced since we were still so dependent on Queda for essential provisions like rice. The 'man on the spot' had overstepped his mark once again.

'Then what are we doing here?' I asked Commodore Cornwallis after his second-in-command announced that we were about to drop anchor off the Queda coast.

The naval man shrugged on the blue and gold jacket that had hung over the back of his armchair and emptied his wine glass before striding towards the door that would take him up on deck. Before leaving, he turned to me and said, 'What we are doing is attempting to maintain your employer's illusion, James. Perhaps when Sultan Abdullah sees a frigate flying British colours on his horizon and is made aware of my position, both in terms of commanding His Majesty's Fleet in the region, and as the brother of India's Governor-General, he will believe that we will offer every support to Captain Light in defence of Penang. However, currently there is no confirmation of that from Bengal.'

Left alone in the captain's quarters, I helped myself to another glass of Madeira. Slumped back in my chair I tried to reason how I had come to be so taken in by Light. For it was not as if there had not been plenty of red flags during my first meeting with James Scott in that alehouse in Calcutta. One story in particular came to mind.

Light had been captaining one of the rice transporters sailing from Calcutta to Madras during the last Anglo-French war when the French fleet led by the infamous Admiral de Suffren captured him. The Frogs stole our rice and would have made off with our ships too, but the Admiral declared the seized vessels too slow and had them all burned. All except for Light's ship, the *Blake,* which was not only fast but well suited to navigating shallow, coastal waters.

I remembered how Scott had lowered his voice so as to increase the dramatic tension of his tale.

'A rumour went out one moonless night that the French and English fleets had come so close to one another off the coast of Cuddalore that one of our frigates had happily retaken the *Blake.* On being asked the position of his French captors who were dangerously close by, Light reported to the commander of the East India Station, Rear Admiral Sir Edward Hughes, that the Frogs were refitting in the harbour at Trincomalee, some two hundred and eighty nautical miles to the south.'

A flagrant lie, one that James Scott assured me Light had told in order to *save* Admiral Hughes from embarking on a naval battle during which the superior de Suffren would likely have destroyed even more of our English fleet. But that had not been Light's decision to make, despite his unwavering conviction that he always knew best. I could also see now that there was an alternative explanation for Light's actions: he wished to save his own skin by avoiding being in the middle of a fresh fight.

Unless William Cornwallis could overawe the King of Queda and persuade him to disband his armada, Light would set us all in the middle of a bloody battle this time for sure. In which case Captain Francis Light *would* get his deepest wish to be remembered—but for infamy, when the sultan attacked and massacred Penang's population of one thousand souls.

Chapter 30

Hard Truths

We were welcomed at Kuala Queda with such fanfare and enthusiasm that I felt sure we were destined for success. The Malays fired one cannon after another in honour of Commodore Cornwallis' visit, followed by the lengthy, obligatory gift giving. Only several hours later, after being fed and watered by our hosts, did we board the boat that took us by river to the sultan's capital, Alor Setar. The river ran along the rear of the royal palace, the *Istana Pelamin,* where we were met by the sultan's *Penghulu Bendahari*, the courtier in charge of royal functions, who guided us through the grounds of the palace complex.

The Queda palace looked little different, albeit bigger, than a traditional Malay house. I had expected the raja's residence to be set behind a great wall to protect the royal family from the rakyat. Instead, it sat in an open area where any person might walk. Indeed, the entire complex gave the impression of a village, of similar size to some near my father's estate in Buckinghamshire.

The istana was a two-storey building with a pitched roof, the entire thing constructed—as the sultan's functionary explained—from *cengal emas*, a golden-brown local wood. The ground floor—he informed us while sharing a brief history of the building, including attacks on it during Sultan Jiwa's time by the Siamese and the Bugis—was where rice and firewood were stored.

When we reached the front of the building, I could see that the istana had been designed in a sort of T-shape, with an open veranda at the front flanked by two sets of steep stairs on either side that lead up to the public space where we would have our audience with Sultan Abdullah. We removed our shoes and ascended behind the Penghulu: William Cornwallis, me, and the three naval officers who accompanied us.

At the top of the stairs we entered a wide, open hall. Inside, huddled in groups to the left and right, sat an assortment of chieftains, nobility, and *tunkus* or princes, those positioned closest to the sultan's raised dais having the highest status. We were invited to sit on a slightly elevated platform in the centre of the room. Low stools for seating had been provided for Commodore Cornwallis, the naval men, and me, as they had for the rest of the audience. I positioned myself just behind Cornwallis, so I could translate the sultan's words and whisper them in his ear.

'Where do the sultan and his family live?' I asked the Penghulu while we waited.

He gestured to a closed-off area behind the sultan's dais where, he said, passageways led to two separate but connected wings, one facing north, one facing south. One wing was the private quarters of the sultan and royal family, and the other housed his gundeks or the women of the royal harem.

As we had been warned to expect, we waited for some time for the sultan to appear. I tried to observe as much as I could in order to describe everything to young William when I saw him next. Also, to calm my nerves. I had lived in Penang for two years and felt reasonably fluent in Malay. As Light had once warned me, there was a difference between the language of the court and the language spoken by the local people in the streets. I did not want to let Commodore Cornwallis down or be the cause of some dreadful diplomatic incident because of my failure to translate their conversation accurately.

After what felt like an interminable amount of time, the sultan's entrance was announced by six fierce-looking chieftains holding long spears who positioned themselves in threes on either side of the raised canopied seating area. Then came the Laksamana, who had earlier made off with the proffered silver and opium and now took his seat to the left of the dais, and the Bendahara who had accepted our other gifts on behalf of the king and sat on the right.

When the sultan entered everyone stood up. He was dressed from head to toe in golden yellow to signify his royal status. His silk brocade tunic was set off with a gold chain around his neck and a heavily jewelled gold belt around his waist. Light told me that Abdullah had ascended the throne, after the passing of Sultan Jiwa in 1778, at the age of around 30 years. I estimated that he was a few years younger than William Cornwallis. Clean-shaven and with no distinguishing features, he nevertheless looked like a man with the weight of the world on his shoulders. Two downward folds ran from either side of his nose to his mouth like parentheses, dragging his face down into a solemn expression. Nevertheless, I was overawed by the ruler's presence. During one of our many conversations, Tuan Ismail had informed me that Sultan Abdullah, who was said to be a descendant of Merong Mahawangsa, was the most recent ruler of a single dynasty. The Merong had been shipwrecked off the coast—at that point called Langkasuka— during a voyage from Rome. This legendary figure had become the inhabitants' king and his progeny had ruled Queda ever since. This man who had been deceived by Francis Light was head of one of the oldest kingdoms in the entire region.

I had already noted all the different arrangements of traditional Malay headwear that the court officials and princes wore, squares of heavy brocaded cloth folded and styled in arrangements that denoted where they hailed from and their status. In keeping with the rest of his outfit, the sultan sported the *tengkolok diraja* instead of a crown. Its peak rose high to his right and in the middle, above a splendid sun-like crest, rose a fan of diamonds to represent paddy, since Queda was known as the rice bowl of the region.

I took a series of deep breaths and sat on my hands to stop them from shaking during the interminable rounds of salutations and pleasantries. Then Commodore Cornwallis was invited to speak. He explained to the sultan, through me, that the British government was prepared to pay him ten thousand Spanish dollars annually for the lease of Penang. Sultan Abdullah merely nodded but made no remark to that. He wanted to know if Commodore Cornwallis' presence meant that Queda was now to be given the military support he had originally been promised. I have never known an Englishman, no matter how high-born, to be as adept as William Cornwallis at skirting the issue without directly saying 'No'. There was no need for me to soften his language as I had thought I would need to, given that in this culture everyone exudes politeness even when issuing threats. The commodore raised the issue of the piratical force currently amassed at the Prai river. Would the sultan show his good intentions to the British government by disbanding them? Equally skilled in diplomacy, the Queda ruler implied in a roundabout way that he could make no such commitment at this time. After what seemed like an eternity of back and forth with nothing settled, the sultan rose and left the audience hall to converse, he said, with his advisers.

'I need a stiff drink after that,' Cornwallis whispered to me and left the hall with his officers. I knew he would find none unless he had brought such a flask with him. Before I could gather my things and follow them, the Penghulu hurried over and told me that refreshments would be served presently if I would like to call my master back. I merely smiled in acknowledgement. The act of translating while in such a terrified state had exhausted me and the idea of eating anything made my stomach heave. What I needed more than anything was fresh air and the chance to calm my nerves. I only hoped that this break signified the end of negotiations for today as it was now late afternoon when, I assumed, the sultan and his entourage had gone to pray.

I left the meeting hall and stood on the veranda, clutching the balustrade to steady my still-tremulous hands and watch the comings and goings of the brightly attired courtiers milling around in small groups. Standing under a nearby plum mango tree, among an assorted group of rough-looking men, I thought I recognised Tuan Ismail. After a few minutes, all but one man in that group was left, who remained deep in conversation with the Malay headman. Taking the opportunity to waylay a nearby youth, I asked if he knew the name of Tuan Nakhoda Ismail's companion.

'That is Syed Ali,' came the reply. 'The sea lord of Siak.'

This was the man whose Lanoon allies had been looting villages in Perak, the kingdom directly to the south. Recent intelligence had revealed that the sultan would pay Syed Ali twenty thousand Spanish Dollars if he and his allies joined the Malay armada against Light's meagre force in Penang.

I watched as Tuan Ismail and Syed Ali huddled together in what looked like an earnest discussion. Then the Siak sea lord patted his companion on the back and strode off. Confused, I raised my hand and waved to try and catch the village headman's attention. He looked up and saw me. I had been right; it was indeed my Malay friend whom I hoped might come over to say hello. Instead, he remained rooted to the spot, his expression one of nervousness—or was it fear? He looked as if I had caught him in an assignation that he had not wished me to see. After all, why was he speaking so intently to the pirates' leader? Eager to know the answers I began to walk down the steps. Tuan Ismail turned and hurried away; he obviously did not want me to confront him.

I barely had time to think what his reaction might mean when one of Cornwallis' officers called out from the bottom of the steps, 'We are preparing to leave. The commodore has been informed that the sultan is not happy with their conversation and sees no point in continuing. He has refused the money we brought but—'

'—will keep the opium,' I guessed as I walked towards the naval man.

'Right,' smiled the officer. 'Sultan Abdullah plans to send a letter to Captain Light in the next few days to let him know his intentions. The commodore wishes us to be on our way; he worries about outstaying our welcome here.'

I looked around at the fearsome-looking pirates and cut-throats who seemed to have suddenly populated the palace complex. I agreed we should not delay.

Our sail back to Penang was a dispiriting one. I respected Cornwallis' wish to be alone so he could catch up on outstanding correspondence. Feeling isolated and constrained I ventured on to the gun deck in order to think. I recalled what Pieter had said about the Malays on the island and where their loyalties might lie in the event of a war. I even began to doubt what Tuan Ismail had told me about a European traitor. Perhaps he had wished to distract me from his own treachery, and this false tale was a ruse to throw me off the scent. That seemed out of step with what I knew, or thought I knew, about the man. But how else was I to interpret the intense conversation he had been having with the Siak sea lord? What could they possibly have in common other than the demise of the British in Penang? I had been blind for so long about the true nature of Francis Light, why did I think the Malay headman had not deceived me also? Martinha had accused me of being a poor judge of character. It seemed she was right once again.

We arrived at Penang just as dawn broke, passing local fishermen heading out for their daily catch. I thought once more of the nakhoda. It was likely no longer safe for me to lodge in Malay Town if, as I now feared, he had sided with his king. *Kerajaan.* There was no government in Queda *but* the king. Loyalty to their raja was of paramount importance to the Malays. It had to be, given that the ruler controlled every aspect of their lives. Why would the Malay headman change his allegiance just because of a few pleasant dinner conversations with me and my tutoring of his sons?

After landing and being dismissed by Commodore Cornwallis so he might discuss matters later with Captain Light alone, I hurried off to Chinatown and knocked on the door of the kuih-seller whom I knew to be an early riser. I asked if he might know of a room I could rent straight away. The few belongings I had left in the Malay kampong I could easily replace.

As I settled into my new lodgings, exhausted and desiring to sleep for a week, I realised Cornwallis and I had accomplished nothing. The embargo would continue, for what did the sultan gain by ending it? Indeed, he could save himself the twenty thousand Spanish Dollars he had promised to pay his pirate allies if the entire population of Penang starved before they could invade and slit our throats.

Chapter 31

Glimmer of Understanding

It was Light, not the sultan, who escalated matters. The promised letter arrived from Queda telling him nothing more than Commodore Cornwallis had already shared. Sultan Abdullah was keeping his rivers shut to trade with Penang. Some thirty thousand Spanish Dollars' worth of merchandise that should have found its way for trade here was being held at the sultan's main port. The forces encamped at the mouth of the river Prai would remain until his demands were met. Our stores of rice and other provisions dwindled perilously. The Superintendent of Penang had to do something.

On 15th January, Light sent the cruiser back to Queda with a letter stressing once again that if Sultan Abdullah did not permit supplies to be brought here, this would be considered a declaration of war. What we received in return was a sort of ultimatum: Light must either adhere to the original demands of the agreement they had made concerning the ceding of Penang or evacuate the island immediately. But the sultan left the door open for further discussions, saying he had no wish to antagonise the English as he recognised us as his biggest potential ally against his many enemies. Commodore Cornwallis surmised that the Malay ruler would not take offensive action while he and his men remained in Penang but reminded

Light that he would soon be sailing back to the Andamans. We had expected the *Crown* to keep us safe for a month. Cornwallis and his men had now stayed for almost two.

Without a further role to play, William Cornwallis spent increasingly more time on his ship. I missed our discussions, having been enthralled during our encounters by his tales of adventures in the West Indies and his brief command of the royal yacht prior to joining his older brother in the East Indies. Light's company, on the other hand, I avoided as much as my work allowed. His unwillingness to accept the impending dire consequences of his duplicity was like impregnable armour and infuriated me. Light had not given up lying but believed he could continue to dupe Sultan Abdullah now that we all had full bellies again, the promised supplies of rice having arrived from Calcutta at the end of February. The pirates at Prai had been warring among themselves for weeks, so we heard from local fishermen, and were now preparing to sail north to pick a fight with their long-time enemies, the Siamese. When Light promised the Malay ruler that he would write again 'seriously' to Calcutta about their agreement, I could no longer stomach his deceit.

It was in this frame of mind that I found Pieter one late afternoon in early March sitting on the top step outside my lodgings in Chinatown. Had it not been for my simmering fury with Light and continued concerns about the intentions of Tuan Ismail, I might have asked him to leave. As it was I desperately wanted someone—anyone—to provide consolation and perhaps some advice.

With time, I had convinced myself that I had been emotionally drained and starving that evening I had last seen Pieter, deprivations associated with hallucinating. I wanted to believe that nothing had happened between us, at least not as disturbing as I had once believed. Like Light, by ignoring a reality I did not wish to face, I had learned to fool myself.

I was about to ask Pieter how he knew that I now lived in Chinatown but realised that was pointless; the man knew everything that went on in this town. As weary as I felt over Light's intransigence, there was a certain elation in seeing my Dutch friend again.

'Back from your travels, Pieter?' I said as I gestured for him to enter my cramped lodgings, then nodded in admiration at his top knot, a fashion reminiscent of two Japanese mercenaries I had spotted some days earlier in the harbour. Their appearance had prompted my interest in the Edo period shogunate and the way the samurai wore their hair as a mark of their status. 'You certainly look well rested and appear to have adopted a new look. Gone up in the world, have we?'

'I don't know about that,' answered Pieter. He sat down on the room's solitary chair while I hovered in the doorway. 'Martinha taken you back into the fold, has she?' he said.

So, he knew about that too. 'Not yet,' I said, then asked if he would like some tea.

Some minutes later, with two cups and a strong brew courtesy of my landlord's wife, we sat in uneasy silence.

'Where have you—?' I uttered at the exact moment Pieter said, 'You look troubled, Jim. Is there anything you wish to share?'

I shook my head, although I hoped Pieter would insist that something was the matter and force it out of me. Instead, he changed the subject. 'It looks like this business with the sultan will be resolved soon enough,' he said, blowing on his tea to cool it.

'You have heard something?' I said.

'The chiefs at Prai wrote a letter to the man whose name you English mangle as Datoo Pongawa Tilebone, a wakil of Sultan Abdullah's who lives here, which I managed to intercept before it was delivered.'

Ignoring Pieter's jibe, I set down my cup. 'What did the letter say?'

'You know their language: That the English agreed to many things not one of which they have performed and that many of the English do much evil to their king. More specifically it stated—and here I am quoting from the letter directly: 'We therefore make known to our Brother and all Muslamen that with our Brother they will separate from these English'.'

'Meaning what?'

'That Tilebone will pay or otherwise persuade your friend Ismail and the rest of the Malays living here to incite riots or directly attack the fort when the sultan invades. Certainly not to give you English any support.'

The light outside had dimmed, dusk shrouded Pieter and me in grey gloom. I rummaged around my scant belongings, unsuccessfully as it turned out, to see if I could find an unspent candle. While I did so I described how I had seen Tuan Nakhoda Ismail in earnest conversation with Syed Ali at Alor Setar. How he had looked at me with a strange expression on his face before striding off in the opposite direction in order to avoid me.

'Really?' said Pieter, his face now almost obscured.

'Yes. But I cannot believe Tuan Ismail is the traitor responsible for all the troubles that have beset this settlement since Light founded it: The murder of those two Siamese around the time I arrived, an increase in the number of suicides—which I believe were only made to look like that to foment distrust and unrest—and the fire started deliberately on Malabar Street last April,' I said. 'As well as all the rioting and other mayhem that has gone on for years. He had convinced me that the perpetrator was a European who has long spied for the sultan, passing intelligence back and forth to help undermine Light's success.'

Pieter cocked his head to one side and said, 'I agree. It does sound unlikely that your Malay friend could be responsible for such misdeeds. That would require a cunning I think he does not possess.'

My tea cooler now, I sat on the bed and absorbed the brew's subtle fragrance and taste. 'Who would, then? Hamilton? He's a nasty piece of work and has always disliked Light.'

In the fading light, I barely saw Pieter flick his fingers as if Hamilton was not even worth a swat of his hand. 'I assure you it is not him. That man may be a pompous ass, but he is without the wiliness to pull off such artful variations in these crimes. Murders of such different stripes, incitements to riot, arson? To show such ingenuity while leaving no clues and never getting caught takes a far keener mind than Hamilton's. As devilish as it sounds, it's hard not to admire such deviousness.'

'What I don't understand is why Tuan Ismail looked at me in that way, as if *afraid* of me. If he was not passing intelligence to the Siak sea lord, then—'

'Maybe the pirate leader was sharing something with him? Something he believed you are complicit in.'

'But what could that be?'

Pieter stood up, blocking what little light still shone through the shutters. I needed to remember to go out tomorrow to purchase a fresh supply of candles. 'I don't know. But you can be sure I will find out.'

'I think I should make a visit to Tuan Ismail and ask him directly. I don't believe he would be foolish enough to attack me with the commodore and his three companies of sepoys still here,' I said. 'I can use the excuse that I've come back to the kampong to collect my belongings. I always got on well with the old man and may be able to talk some sense into him if, indeed, he is intending to side with the sultan.'

'When will you go?'

'Right now,' I said, eager to unravel this mystery.

Pieter drained his cup and said, 'Not a good idea. I actually came to warn you to stay indoors this evening; villainy is likely in the streets tonight. I don't believe it has anything to do with what is going on with Pongawa and the Malays, but it would be best for you to remain here for now. Old man Ismail isn't going anywhere, at least not for the moment.'

'But should I not tell Light of my plans? To get his perspective?' As much as I detested the man, I could not shake off the hope that Martinha would learn that I was still on her husband's side and allow me to make amends.

'Much good it will do if someone attacks you on the way to Fort Cornwallis,' Pieter said. 'Don't risk it while it's dark. Tomorrow will suffice.'

'You think so?' I said.

'Yes. Leave it until first light to go and visit the Malay headman. Determine whether or not he is telling you the truth about his loyalties before you mention anything to Light.'

I stepped towards my friend and hesitated only briefly before clasping his hands in mine. No stirrings of an unnatural kind occurred, thank goodness, only gratitude for this chance to see and talk with him again. 'A good plan, Pieter. I need a full night's sleep, in any case, to clear my head.'

'Good. Stay safely inside 'til morning Jim, then go to the Malay kampong. We can rendezvous later in the day if you like.'

A new thought struck me and I hesitated to voice it, in case Pieter thought I was hinting for him to stay the night. But my friend's welfare concerned me. 'What about you, Pieter? Is it not dangerous to venture outside now that it is dark? You just said that there is mischief afoot in the streets.'

I heard Pieter laugh, his features swallowed up by the darkness. I could just about see his hand as it reached the top of his head to draw out what looked at first like a very long hat pin. His sun-bleached hair cascaded down beyond his shoulders as he held up a wavy metal blade that glinted in the scant moonlight shining through the shutters. The sort of ornamental keris I had seen Martinha hide in her hair for protection. 'I always have weapons at the ready,' he said as he opened the door. 'There is no need for you to worry about me.'

As I discovered soon enough, he spoke the truth. It was others I had come to love, along with myself, I should have been afraid for.

Chapter 32

Pitched

The next day, the Fates devoured my old life as a tiger might a child. I awoke with a sense that something monumental was about to happen and deluded myself that it would be all for the good.

I knew Tuan Nakhoda Ismail to be a decent, honourable man. The Malay headman had railed many times about how *adat,* the customs to which Malays adhered, had become whatever a powerful chieftain decided suited his own desires. Surely he would not side with the sultan against us? I recalled the conversation we had last October after his family returned from their extended trip to the mainland, and Tuan Ismail had appeared more pensive than usual. We had sat together on a fallen tree trunk, and I asked what troubled him.

He began strangely, saying that he was grateful to have neither wealth nor daughters, for those who did live in perpetual fear of loss. 'A man I knew well had a very beautiful daughter and was approached by a chief known for abusing his wives; he wanted to make her his fourth wife. My friend refused and was found murdered shortly after. The girl missing. No—taken against her will.'

The headman's grief had been palpable. 'Build a nice house and it will be claimed by a chief if he chooses it, without hope of return. Wear good clothes or shoes, and you may be penalised as these are meant only for royals. Ordinary people cannot lift themselves up or show originality in case they offend their rulers.'

Tuan Ismail had paused and stared into the fetid destruction of the jungle, wiping his fingers across glistening eyes. 'No one dares bring the chief who killed my old friend to justice. Avoid such villains, and you may live a long and peaceful life, unless your daughter becomes too pretty or your wealth is too obvious. Cross them and not only are you accused of treason, but your house is also destroyed and your wife, children, and all other relatives gone.' Then he had added, almost in a whisper, 'A man must be careful whom he displeases. Even those once considered allies or friends.'

I did not seize on that particular comment because I wanted to know why the Malays were so resistant to improving their circumstances.

'We have a saying: 'Some are like the frog beneath the coconut shell who thinks the shell is the sky',' answered Tuan Ismail.

'What does that mean?'

'That most men do not realise how ignorant they are. Despite being presented with new ideas, they are afraid to break free from the customs of their fathers. That is why gaining an education, such as you are providing for my children, is so important.'

Before trundling off he had shared another Malay saying: 'When the tiger is dead, his stripes remain; when the elephant is dead, his bones remain', to which he added, 'However, when a man is dead his reputation lingers on among later generations.'

Had he been thinking of his own reputation, or Sultan Abdullah's, or Light's? It never occurred to me that he might be talking about mine. But the time had come for a direct confrontation so the nakhoda might explain his behaviour at Alor Setar. Once I knew what he had discussed with the Siak sea lord, I would inform Light who, impressed by my initiative, would tell Martinha and that would surely lead to a reconciliation with her and William.

None of which happened.

In the space of a few hours, I found myself squatting alone in Pieter's dank hideout, grieving over four loved ones dead. Either my pursuers would find me and dispense justice, leaving my hidden body to rot somewhere, or I would be shipped to Bengal to face trial before being dropped from the gallows.

With sweat pouring, heart pounding, lungs aching, and legs straining I had hacked my way through the jungle, hunted like a wild boar. As the blood-congealed keris I held severed bracken and enormous leathery leaves as easily as it had earlier sliced through human flesh, the same relentless question rattled around in my head: *Dear God in Heaven, what have I done?*

Unseeing, I must have run around in circles for hours; where I was headed, I had no idea. This was an island, and I had no boat. Word would have reached everyone by now and they would be searching for me in all the usual spots. Then, like a beacon, I saw a scrap of scarlet ribbon and began to follow the barely discernible trail I had laid out for myself months earlier. Strips of fabric that were pointers but also resembled splashes of blood.

Scrambling over rotting tree stumps and through dense foliage was like running the gauntlet, a punishment I had witnessed on the ship delivering me to India from London a lifetime ago. When a crew member had been caught stealing an extra noggin of rum, his shipmates had lined up on both sides of the deck to whip him collectively as he passed by. As low branches tore into the skin on my shoulders and back that is how nature's indictment felt to me. I shrugged off the pain because I deserved it—and more.

Nearby, I heard the grunts of wild boars. Looking around in panic, the next moment I found myself face down in a bed of fetid soil and putrefied leaves, tripped up by a tangle of rope-like roots nearly invisible on the jungle floor. The keris that I had been holding, a tiny yet lethal murder weapon, catapulted into the teeming mass of life. Too afraid that I was about to be gored to pay attention to my skinned knees and grazed forehead and hoping to steer clear of leeches, I beat the ground desperately trying to recover the dagger so I could defend myself.

It *had* to be here somewhere. As, I knew, were snakes and gigantic poisonous centipedes and armies of copper-coloured fire ants whose bites would cause me to break out in pus-filled blisters and the life-threatening swelling of my tongue. Desperate to find the weapon,

I searched for several minutes. That keris was a vital piece of evidence as well as my only form of protection. I could carry on without it and leave myself vulnerable to what I believed lay ahead or risk becoming the victim of boars, insects, or vipers. I gave up, exhausted; the dagger, like me, was lost.

Eventually, I reached Pieter's hideout, which from the outside appeared as silent as the grave. I had no plan for what I would do if he were there. Or his darned monkey. I found the ladder hidden in undergrowth and ascended as quietly as I could. The space seemed more dark, dank, and confining than the infamous Black Hole of Calcutta.

I threw myself on the floor, startling a few cockroaches that scuttled away as I pounded my fists into the black, rotting planks. *Please God, let this just be a terrible dream.* But the ingrained russet stains beneath my fingernails and my clothing drenched in blood made clear that it was not.

In a daze, I ventured over to Pieter's sea chest. Beneath narrow rolls of light cloth and a strange, funnel-like apparatus, I found what I was looking for. Extracting the pipe, tin filled with opium, and flints to create a spark, I succumbed to the alluring desire to escape.

Becalmed by the tears of the poppy, a weakness to which I had once vowed never to succumb, four figures haunted the shadows. I squeezed my eyes shut but they remained. The same scene assailed me. A terrible, spectral play.

Chapter 33

Tragedy

The kampong is eerily quiet. The men out in their boats, the women at the market with their children, the elderly asleep, or so I think. The door to the Ismail family's rumah stands slightly ajar, a good sign. A dog, a scabby, half-starved creature, has its paws on the bottom step looking up. *Shoo, shoo.* The cur limps away.

With a deep breath, I break into a broad smile, kick off my shoes, mount the seven steps, and call out, '*Selamat pagi.*' I am confused why the door does not open easily as I struggle to step inside.

Legs lie at unnatural angles. Tuan Ismail, like a slain sentry, partly blocks the door. His hands a bloody mess, one eye gouged out. Mere feet from his father's resting place, Awang clutches a broom handle. A puny weapon insufficient to save the lad, lying with a grinning gash across his throat.

In the farthest corner. a small boy—*Othman*—curls like a foetus, his head haloed with black ooze. Time shifts. The child is alive; his spectral killer squats down, a palm pressed against the terrified child's mouth and murmurs, 'Don't worry, it won't hurt. It will all be over soon.' Then he draws his dagger swiftly from ear to tiny, shell-like ear, forcing the boy's head back to speed his release. The black-coated killer disappears like the illusion he always was. Othman is cold. *Mati.*

Turning away from that horror, I feel something soft beneath my feet. I am standing on the hand that reaches out towards her youngest son. *Dear God in heaven!* Fresh blood springs from her neck in slow spurts. She groans—the mother whose name, for shame, I never knew.

I kneel down and grasp her upper arms to pull her close. 'Who did this? Who did this to you?'

She exhales, '*Orang belanda.*' Then, '*Kawan awak, Tuan Jim.*' As the last syllable gurgles in her throat, I take off my jacket and fold it in almost religious reverence beneath the mother's head. I hold the hands that once cared for her sons, her husband, her neighbours, and for me, until they become like marble.

I fall back, one hand on my chest to stop it from exploding, the other slams the floor. Something sharp presses itself into my palm. An item concealed by her blood. I pick it up. Incontrovertible proof beyond dying words that I might have tried to reason away. The keris that Pieter had worn in his hair to hold it in a samurai bun.

A monsoon of tears mingles with blood as I rub my red-stained hands across my eyes in a futile attempt to clear them, face distorted like a gargoyle's. *So much blood. Dear God, so much blood.*

My empty stomach heaves, lungs crave fresh air. I stand up and somnambulate to the doorway. Like some rufescent monster emerging from the depths of hell, I emerge on to the top step, the still dripping keris loose in my palm. A piercing scream, accusing eyes, mouths distorted, movement towards me. An instant decision. I stagger down the wooden steps and flee into the jungle. My only thought: run, run.

Chapter 34

Clarity

Hunched in Pieter's hideout, the poppy's effects worn off, I yearned to bask longer in its dream-like embrace. I had always thought opium dulled the senses and perhaps it does, over time. But my thoughts had become sharpened. Another spectral scene emerged, one inspired by those two words: Kawan awak. *Your friend.* I now understood the reason for Tuan Ismail's fearful expression when he had seen me at Alor Setar.

The Siak sea lord must have revealed to him the name of the traitor working for Sultan Abdullah against Light. A man who was known by most on our island to be *my* friend: Pieter Reinaert. So many horrors had been perpetrated since my arrival, from the murder of the two Siamese traders to the fire started in Malabar Street. I was likely spotted running away in the opposite direction, guided by the Dutchman, on the morning that young Chinese woman had supposedly committed suicide.

When the Malay headman looked at me, he must have believed I was complicit, if not a willing accomplice, in Pieter's crimes. Failing to return to the kampong after our brief encounter likely confirmed my treachery in his eyes. Tuan Ismail had always intended to remain loyal to the British in Penang where he enjoyed greater freedom than under the rule of Sultan Abdullah. The nakhoda had been true to his word regarding rooting out whoever among us was putting the settlement at risk. Pieter—that very traitor—always so clear-minded and cunning, had deduced that he was about to be exposed and killed the Ismail family before his treachery could be revealed. Because I had found them so soon after he had slaughtered them, I would pay for his crimes, as Pieter had no doubt intended.

In my despair, I toyed with the idea of ending things right then and there. But all I could find were a tin fork, a bent spoon, and a rough-bristled hairbrush lying atop a fresh batch of Pieter's clothing. I laughed like a Bedlam inmate. No, I would have to see this through to whatever end I was fated to experience. For I knew one thing for certain: that I had to prove my innocence in the deaths of the nakhoda's family and bring Pieter Reinaert to justice. I would, one way or another, avenge my Malay friends.

What a naïve fool I had been. Four innocents—people I had admired and loved—had been slaughtered because I trusted a man who was not who he purported to be. Had not Pieter long hinted that he thrived on mayhem and chaos? Had not Martinha underscored that by exposing King Coen as the 'Butcher of Banda'? I had allowed Pieter's lies to blind me to the truth of who he really was. To what our faux friendship had always been: just another conduit of intelligence to enable his nefarious deeds. I was so obsessed with Light's deceit of Sultan Abdullah that I had not seen how Pieter had duped me.

Enraged, I tore off my blood-befouled clothing. I rushed outside naked like a crazed lunatic and found the barrel of rainwater at the back of Pieter's hut into which I stared at my distorted reflection. In that dark water I did not look like a man but a monster, one who had naively befriended a proud agent of chaos. I was no better than the fallen angel Beëlzebub blinded by Satan's lie that there is virtue in rejecting service in heaven in order to reign in hell.

Was I not the most hellish of creatures, face smeared with the blood of my friends? I plunged my head into the barrel but lacked the courage to drown myself. I climbed in nonetheless and sank down until my head became submerged as if taking part in a baptism. Lungs burning, I sprang up, slithered out of that watery womb and ascended the hut once again.

I could not die, at least not yet. Certainly not at the hands of weapon-wielding villagers or despicable men like Hamilton. I would not endow this White Man's Grave with my infamy. But there was something worse than being ended by a wavy-edged dagger or the rope: Living with soul-crushing guilt.

I smoked another pipe, then another, in an attempt to forget and to clarify what to do next.

Someone in the kampong must have seen Pieter. Perhaps that was why so many villagers had hidden away when I arrived; I must have just missed him. A black-coated, diminutive Dutchman visiting the friends of his friend. But even if I could convince one or more of the Malays to speak up in my defence, Hamilton and his corrupt cronies would not believe them; they never did.

I stared at my arms and legs and wondered where the fresh blood had come from. Was it even real or another hallucination? But the blood was mine, oozing from angry red streaks on my skin. I must have picked up the brush in my delirium to excoriate myself. Corporeal mortification, meagre penance for my sins of naivety and arrogant ambition. How I longed for the boredom of Calcutta. Had it really been all that bad? Was I not foolish to desire something more for my life than being an EIC lackey, since becoming John Company's Governor-General had been nothing but a fantasy of my father's? I could not stop thinking. Until I must have passed out once again.

When the blackness paled to grey and glimmers of golden daylight shone through the bamboo walls, when the lacerations from the relentless harsh brushing of my skin began to crust over and crack, and each nerve tingled with pain, I knew I was alive for a reason and that is how I must remain.

Days passed, but I had no desire to count how many. I ate nothing and could not bring myself to drink the water in which I had washed off their blood. I only smoked opium and relished its clarifying release.

Strange, disjointed recollections occupied my thoughts. I had read a book in Calcutta by Sir James Porter: *Observations on the Religion, Law,*

Government and Manners of the Turks, in which the author referred to a Turkish proverb claiming that 'a fish stinks first at the head.' I had once mentioned this to Tuan Ismail, who had told me this was inaccurate; to know if a fish is fresh, one should look at its belly because a fish first rots from the guts.

Guts. *Courage.* Yes, that is what I needed to garner now, regardless of consequences. Otherwise, I would be no better than Light.

Captain Francis Light. The man who had come to know me, over twenty-six months, as someone who was petulant and prone to idealistic outbursts. But also loyal and hard-working. He had heard me speak many times of my fondness for Tuan Nakhoda Ismail and his sons. He surely knew I was incapable of slaughtering that family for no reason. Besides, I needed to warn him about Pieter's treachery.

Rummaging in the chests, I found fresh clothing and a felt cocked hat. I might end up dead by morning but had found fresh purpose in the meantime. The opium had induced what I can only describe as a mystical experience. I now embraced a truth from which I determined never to waver: That from this moment on I would care less about when or how my life ends than how I feel about myself when it does.

Chapter 35

Leaden

The hours I spent skulking from Battu Lanchon to George Town gave me ample time to rehearse what I would say to gain entry to Fort Cornwallis. But as I followed the path across the esplanade to reach the guardhouse, my mind suddenly went blank. Staring at the palisade, I had a sudden urge to relieve myself. Would Light believe me as to why I had fled that room of bloodied bodies in Malay Town? With legs that began to buckle from fear, only the urgency to warn everyone about Pieter spurred me on. As I began to walk across the bridge built over the shallow, dry ditch that provided no real protection for the grandly named fort, I pulled the hat down over my eyebrows and kept my gaze low.

Deep in thought, my eyes found a pair of gleaming black leather boots barring my way. Expecting to negotiate entry with a guard, I looked up with a ready smile. What I saw instead were the pale, sneering eyes of Captain Robert Hamilton. I took a step backwards, trying to control my desire to turn and run.

'Well, well, well,' said Hamilton as he reached out and grabbed my shirt. 'What have we here? A wanted man. A vicious murderer—of children and their mother, no less.' The officer tutted and shook his head in an exaggerated manner as if scolding a small child for stealing an apple. He turned to the sniggering sepoys standing alongside him. 'This wretch has caused us much inconvenience, hasn't he, lads? Forced to quell a small riot of local rabble at this very spot who declared that *satu orang putih*—' Hamilton jabbed me in the chest with a forefinger, pushing me backwards, '—this *particular* white man, had cruelly murdered an entire Malay family.'

Hamilton continued his advance, stabbing my chest with his finger with each step. I struggled to maintain my balance, with no choice but to back away. 'What kind of monster does that?' Hamilton pulled at my shirt again, drawing me closer as he whispered in my ear, 'I would never have thought you had it in you, Jim. Four less pissants for us to manage. Bravo!'

Then, for the benefit of his audience, of which some six or so sepoys had now gathered, Hamilton released me and called out, 'I think we should let the Malays dispense their own, natural justice, don't you, men? Refuse this blackguard entry and let the natives deal with him.' The EIC officer paused for effect, then said ominously, 'In whichever way they choose.'

My eyes widened in horror as I heard a chorus of assent.

Then, more quietly, Hamilton added, 'It shouldn't take too long before we find you in a ditch with your throat cut. Or maybe your body will never be found and good riddance. Save us the expense of a grave.'

Enraged by the officer's attitude I shouted, hoping someone more friendly would hear me, 'You have no jurisdiction over me, Captain Hamilton. I am a private citizen, not a military man.' I stopped and swallowed, dismayed by how high pitched my voice sounded. 'I demand to see Superintendent Light. You have to let me into the fort.'

Hamilton's cruelly handsome face bulged with menace. I looked away in fear mixed with disgust as his spittle sprayed my face. 'I warned you once before not to challenge me, you little shit.' With a thrust of his arm he pushed me and I lost my footing, expecting any moment to land in the ditch. To my surprise I was immediately righted. A meaty arm wrapped itself around my shoulders as I stood, shocked, looking down on to a heavily tattooed arm that secured me upright. A voice from behind said, 'Mr Lloyd is under my protection, and we will be going inside to meet with Captain Light. So, get your men out of my bloody road or face the consequences, *Bobby*.'

I almost swooned with relief to hear the distinctive voice of James Scott who kept an arm around my shoulders as we advanced towards the company captain. The two men faced off against each other. I heard Scott say under his breath, 'Just give me an excuse, Hamilton.' Looking down I could see the Scotsman's right hand flex into a fist. 'Any excuse at all and I'll take great pleasure in knocking you and yer cronies into next weekend.'

'James! You are returned. Good timing. The *Crown* is preparing to leave Penang.' Every one of us looked up in astonishment as Commodore Cornwallis began to cross the bridge.

Hamilton's mouth fixed into a startled O. He and his men parted like the Red Sea as Scott and I walked towards the commander. Assuming Hamilton continued to watch us, I clenched my right hand into a fist with my thumb between my fore and middle fingers and held it behind my back. While I did not have the ability to best Hamilton in a fight, I could insult him with the hand gesture known as the 'fig of Spain'. One day, I vowed, I would get the better of that bastard.

'Commodore, I—' But what could I say to Cornwallis, and should I even bother? Save my story for when we reached the EIC's penal colony in the Andamans where the *Crown* would undoubtedly deposit me before I was shipped off to Calcutta to stand trial.

William Cornwallis held out his hand to me. 'I bid you farewell, James.'

'Farewell?' Was I not to leave as his prisoner?

'Indeed. Still, I won't keep you as I understand there is an explanation for some recent unfortunate event that you must share with Captain Light. All the very best to you, young man.' With a final nod to Captain Scott, Commodore William Cornwallis strode off.

Moments later Scott and I stepped out of the harsh sunlight into a gloomy, humid room. Penang's superintendent sat behind a desk piled with papers: jacketless, necktie loosened and sleeves rolled to his elbows. He looked up as we entered, his face glistening as if fevered, with blood-shot eyes rimmed by dark circles. His clothes seemed to hang off him, like a beggar long deprived of food. Light's entire demeanour belied his name; I thought him a man dogged by dark thoughts. Guilt dripped off me, knowing I had given him a new nightmare. We had needed the local Malays on our side not turned against us. They hated us now, thanks to me.

With barely a nod in my direction, Light said to his business partner, 'You found him?'

'He arrived on his own,' replied Scott, forcing me into one of the two chairs that faced Light's desk. 'He was at the guardroom having a run-in with that bastard, Hamilton. You have to do something about that overbearing piece of shit, Francis.'

Light sank his head into his hands and used his fingers like a comb through his thinning hair. With a deep sigh he said, 'That's not a priority right now, Scotty, you know that.' Turning to me, he said, 'So, would you care to tell us why such a valuable ally was brutally murdered along with his family in Malay Town, allegedly by you?'

My right leg began to twitch. 'I did not murder my friends, Captain Light,' I began. 'I loved Tuan Ismail's family. I had even begun to—'

'Calm down, Jim,' Light interrupted. 'We are not accusing you.'

'Aye,' added the Scotsman. 'We already know the true perpetrator. Just tell us what you know.'

Once I had completed my story, Light looked at Scott. 'Any luck yet finding Reinaert?'

'You know that's not—' began Scott, but Light cut him off with a look.

'Not now, Scotty,' he said, with a sigh.

While relieved, I sank further into my chair and lowered my gaze. 'But it is still my fault they were murdered.'

James Scott's meaty hands rested on my shoulders. 'That yin's a crafty bugger, Jim. We've all been taken in. More than you even know.'

I looked up at the Scotsman and offered a weak smile. Scott made to say something else, but I spoke first. 'I know the Mussulmen bury their dead quickly. It may be too late—' I began.

'It is, Jim. But even if it were not, you cannot leave the fort,' said Light.

'But I want to pay my respect at their graves.'

James Scott's laugh seemed to bounce off the walls. 'You're jesting, Jim, surely? I hate Hamilton as much as any yin but he was right about one thing; if you step outside of here, you're a dead man. The Malays are looking for vengeance. You were seen in the kampong with their blood all over you, a keris in yer hand. That's all the evidence they need. No trial, just execution.'

'But—' I began, then stopped as Light waved his hand at me.

The superintendent said, 'Scotty's right. Once we get Reinaert's confession you can go free but not before. You'll be taken into custody for your own safety. Not the most comfortable of lodgings but it's the best we can do.'

Scott clapped me on the back just as I was about to speak, temporarily winding me. 'Last I heard the *Fame* was headed north. Her captain—' My two companions glanced at each other in a way I did not comprehend. 'If she's anywhere in the region, I'll find her.' Then James Scott turned on his heels and left.

Knowing Light's contentious relationship with Hamilton and his inability to exert authority over that bully I felt more exposed and vulnerable in the fort than I had when sitting naked in Pieter's hideout. Perhaps sensing this, Light called out and I Boon stepped out of the shadows. Almost the same height and heft as James Scott, his appearance put me at ease.

'Take Jim to the prison and stand guard,' Light instructed him. 'He is not to be out of your sight for a moment, do you hear?' The slave nodded and moved to corral me towards the sunlight.

'How are Martinha and William?' I asked, tentatively.

'They are both well,' Light answered with the distracted air of a man whose mind is already elsewhere.

I did not move, unsure of what to say next. Sorry did not seem sufficient but was all I could think of.

Light waved me off. 'It's all water under the bridge now, Jim. There is plenty of fault to go around. Women have a habit of thinking men are mind-readers. It appears Martinha was not clear with you how much she's always detested Reinaert, indeed any Hollander. Her father had told her so many stories about Dutch atrocities when she was young that she never wished to give any of them the benefit of the doubt. So, there it is. I'll ask her to visit you if she feels up to it.'

'You think she will? I betrayed her trust, and William—'

'My son cried himself to sleep for over a week after he forced I Boon to take him to see you.' Light looked over at the slave and gave him a reproachful look. 'I believe you have been forgiven by Martinha and my son. But now, if you'll excuse me, Jim, there are letters I must sign and urgent matters to attend to; I am trying to avert a war and save my legacy.' Light looked back at his papers.

I did not know how long I had been away in the jungle. 'One last thing, superintendent,' I said. 'What day is it?'

Without looking up he answered, 'Tuesday. The fifteenth of March.'

I Boon nudged me, I thought to direct me out of the room. But I watched in amazement as he slipped something into my waistband. An easily hidden but very sharp and lethal keris. I silently mouthed my thanks.

The fifteenth of March. Commodore Cornwallis was leaving on the Ides of March. The date on which ancient Romans settled their debts. Defenceless again, would the sultan now force Light to settle his?

Something bad was about to happen. Following I Boon, I clutched the hilt of the keris and hoped to God I was wrong.

Chapter 36

Glint of Revenge

My prison cell was such that had I a cat to swing, I would have dashed the poor creature's head upon each wall. But at least I did not have to share the space, unlike the two transportees from Calcutta who occupied the cell next to mine. Convicted murderers, Mujriff Sheida and Mohamed Heiant were herded out of the fort before dawn and returned long after nightfall, having carried out whatever public works the superintendent required. Sometimes, as I peered through the narrow window from which I could see the stockade's crumbling northernmost ramparts, they were engaged in ongoing repairs.

The food at the fort was reasonably plentiful, although the same plain rice, fried fish and vegetables boiled beyond recognition became tedious after a while. It was the occasional additions that appalled me. On the days when one particular sepoy brought me my victuals, I would notice a garnish of yellow froth as if the man or some associate—I would not have put it past Hamilton himself—had cleared his throat directly on to my plate. At other times the dish glistened with a layer of slime. As hungry as I was on those days, which occurred two or three times a week, my stomach heaved at what that mongrel might have done to my food, and I could not eat but placed the plate outside for the dogs to fight over. It was easy enough to recognise my tormentor as this particular sepoy grinned with a mouth like a neglected graveyard full of mouldy, broken headstones. On most occasions that I saw him in the fort grounds, he appeared to grovel around Hamilton like a pet dog. He had certainly been one of the sepoys standing alongside Hamilton when he had tried to bar my entry into the fort, egging his master on. I began to wish Light had shipped me off to Bengal to stand trial for crimes I did not commit than remain here to die of dysentery or starvation.

My murderous neighbours and I whispered to each other through rotting walls so thin that if we had had a mind to, we could easily have broken free. They seemed content to eat the food, enjoy the dry lodgings, and indulge in grisly humour as if trying to outdo one another with tales of the most gruesome kind.

One time they described a type of *penjara* where a person unable to pay a fine for offences they had committed, or were merely accused of, was locked in a cage too low for them to stand up in, not long enough to allow them to stretch their legs, indeed too narrow for movement of any kind. Positioned six inches or so above the ground, these cages contained no provision for sanitation, were exposed to the elements, and in which prisoners were many times left to rot.

'Festering torture-chambers,' as Mujriff described them to me. 'In which those unable to negotiate release lose their minds, their will to live, and look upon death as a welcome relief.'

Then the two condemned men laughed about the 'elaborate sword-dances' that preceded the execution of offenders in Pahang.

I was allowed to wander the fort at will as long as I did not leave its confines. Within a few days of being back in my former place of employment, the difference in the harbour and the straits beyond shocked me. I could only see one disabled ship, the *Bombay Castle,* which listed impotently alongside Light's jaga-jaga. No longer a hubbub of trading activity, the esplanade appeared to be mostly deserted. Since the nineteenth of the month, when Sultan Abdullah's armada had amassed again at the Prai river mouth, hundreds had fled George Town with their families, fearing an invasion. None but the ostriches lording over our fate in Bengal believed that the sultan would fail to attack now that Commodore Cornwallis had left; it was simply a matter of time.

I had no time to waste. Exactly one week after my enforced confinement I turned towards the flagstaff and the grassy knoll that overlooked the sea and saw the two Bengalis repairing the fascine barriers, sitting well apart from a group of inattentive sepoys. I needed to hurry in case an officer came over to ask what I was doing in the company of convicted murderers.

'Will you help me?' I exposed the hilt of my keris that nestled within my shirt. 'Teach me how best to wield this?'

Both men nodded eagerly and grinned.

Where the Indian men had learned the secrets of this ancient Malay weapon they never said, but it was obvious from the start that they were experts in its execution. And what a versatile weapon I found it to be. I learned how to use the keris' *ulu* or wooden handle to strike the first blow. I discovered that while the tip could stab and slash, the *luk* or curved part of the blade was ideal for ripping apart a man's internal organs. Soon I could grip this dark-bladed avenger such that it was invisible right up to the moment it slid into a man's body like a knife in butter. My murderous Indian friends had already shown me how to surprise a man so that he could not react fast enough to defend himself.

After two weeks of such training, supplemented by rigorous daily exercises in my cell, I was eager to put this theory into practice. One day, at the mid-day mealtime I was presented with the ideal opportunity. When I threatened to gouge out the eyes of my sepoy tormentor and showed him how expertly I wielded my weapon, I ate better afterwards than I had in many weeks.

'Now you know how to defend yourself and eat well,' declared Mujriff, laughing at my description of that sepoy's terrified face.

I had led my tutors to believe that these were my only reasons for seeking their expert instruction. What I secretly wanted was to learn how to kill my former Dutch friend.

Chapter 37

Revealed

8 April 1791.
'A gift for you.'
'Martinha!'

She stood as plump as a Christmas turkey at the entrance to my cell, holding up what looked like a tea-cosy with a sturdy wicker handle. Since my cell was no place to invite a lady, certainly not one so heavy with child, I placed my keris with which I was practicing on a high shelf before moving us both outdoors. The nearby arsenal was shaded by a large verdant tree, underneath which someone had crafted a small bench. I directed Martinha towards it.

'William wants you to have this bird as a companion,' she said once we sat down. She balanced the covered cage on my knees.

I looked around. 'He hasn't come with you?'

'Not yet,' she said.

I lifted the cover.

'I Boon says it's a Malabar parakeet. It whistles and dances, and William has been teaching it to talk. Listen!'

I stared at the foot-high pretty bird with its luminous long blue tail, orange beak, and black and turquoise feathered ring around its neck. Martinha chattered on as if nervous and tried to coax the creature to show off its vocal skills. She hoped this new pet would make up for the loneliness of my current existence. All I wanted to do was to open the cage door and set the poor chick free.

'William wants to know what you will call it.'

Had it not been for the risk of upsetting the boy, I would have released the bird as soon as she left, then it wouldn't need a name.

'What day is it?'

'Friday.'

We both laughed, immediately understanding the literary reference.

'Then Friday it is. But don't start calling me Robinson.'

We chattered for a while about nothing of importance. When I thought that our relationship had returned to its former warmth, I said, 'Martinha. Could you not speak to your husband? It is only a matter of time before the Sultan of Queda orders an invasion. We are vastly outnumbered, with only this crumbling fort for our defence. I implore you to persuade him to stop his dissembling and tell the sultan the truth.'

As if a cage door had come crashing down between us, she said coldly, 'It is too late for that.'

Neither of us spoke for some time. Then she said, 'It is no different to what I told you before. Francis has a gift. He is a visionary and saw in advance what this island could become. A gift that Sultan Abdullah does not possess.'

'But he has to see sense otherwise countless people will die.'

'Tell that to the Sultan of Queda.'

My frustration shifted to anger. 'I agree your husband has many gifts, one of which involves fooling people into believing he knows best. But we all see how that has worked out.' I should have left it there, but exasperation drove me on. 'It saddens me that he continues to fool you, too.'

Despite the heat, her voice dripped with icy disdain. 'What do you mean by *that*?'

I ignored her condition. 'Never in any of our conversations have I heard him refer to you as Mrs Light or even 'my wife'. And I have seen a copy of his will in which you are referred to as 'the woman

I have cohabited with since 1772'. I doubt that will change no matter how loyal you remain or how many sons you bear him.'

Immediately contrite, I lowered my head and caught sight of her swollen belly. I knew I should not be speaking to a woman so heavy with child this way. But what was it she had once told me: Friends tell friends the truth?

There was one other truth she needed to hear. 'I intend to remain in Penang until we have found Pieter Reinaert and I have helped bring him to justice—' There was no need to tell her what I really planned to do— 'But no longer. Francis Light will have to save his reputation and legacy in this hell of his own making by himself.'

Martinha was so still and quiet she resembled a seated marble statue. Then she muttered, 'Has Scott not found her yet?'

'Last I heard, his cannons caught the *Fame* starboard close to Kuala Muda and she limped southwards until Scott's men captured her near Jerajah. The ship has been impounded, but Reinaert escaped before they could board. He's believed to be somewhere on this island.'

'I wasn't talking about the ship, but that woman.'

'What woman?'

'Pietronella Rodyck.'

I looked at my companion in puzzlement. 'Who are you talking about?'

A weak smile appeared on her lips. 'I am surprised neither Francis nor James Scott has told you.'

She did not need to say any more; it all made perfect sense: The smell of rusty nails that exuded from Pieter on occasions, likely a month apart. The reason for the oversized black coat and the long rolls of binding cloth in Pieter's hideout. The use for that funnel-like contraption that allowed someone without a cock to stand up and piss. The lack of facial hair—oh, the jokes we had shared at our joint distress concerning our inability to grow beards. The change in Pieter's voice during our intense debates. That strange, magnetic attraction between us that I had feared.

'What I thought was an Adam's apple is really a goitre, isn't it?' For that swelling of the throat would look much the same to an unsuspecting eye. I turned to Martinha. 'Who discovered her true form?'

'James Scott recently uncovered a female passing herself off as a teenage boy on his ship. He called her his 'Hannah Snell imitator'. When Scott turned her off, she laughed and said maybe she would have more luck sailing with Reinaert as at least *she* would understand what forced women like them to take to the seas. Only then did they understand who they had been dealing with.'

I was speechless. So that had been the reason for the captains' conspiratorial looks and lack of forthrightness when I had last been in the company of Light and Scott. Why hadn't I seen it before? It was now so obvious. Even the name Reinaert is the Dutch equivalent of Reynard, the trickster fox of French and German folk tales. I shook my head. Why had she not revealed her true self? Then things might have turned out differently.

Martinha appeared to stiffen throughout my silence. 'I knew that person could not be trusted and was not all as they appeared to be. But I never imagined it to be a woman. Yet you, who have been quite intimate with her from what I hear, allowed that monster to insinuate herself into our community. Four innocents are now dead because of your naivety.'

Whether it was anger or anguish that grasped my throat, I could not say. I tried to breathe but that indelible image of little Othman and the rest of his slaughtered family was like a constant noose around my neck. I did not appreciate being reminded of it.

'I think you had better leave now, madam, before we both say things we may regret.'

Martinha Rozells eased herself off the bench, shrugging off the hand I had extended to help her. 'I would advise you to be less judgemental in future about my husband when you have plenty of sins to account for yourself.'

Determined to have the last word, I said, 'I doubt any of us will *have* a future, madam, if Light remains cavalier about the souls remaining here, for they will perish when the sultan invades with his mercenaries and Lanoons to take his island back.' I had one last parting shot, which I shouted at her departing back. 'Yes, I was complicit in the killing of four innocent people. But that will be nothing compared to the deaths your husband will be responsible for. How sad that you will not berate him or lend a hand in trying to prevent a massacre.'

I sat for some time with my head in my hands, weeping. To cover my shame, I had lashed out at Martinha and driven her away for good.

Grief sucked me in like a whirlpool. I had planned to kill Reinaert to avenge the slaughter of my friends. But to kill a woman, however heinous she was. Could I bring myself to do that?

Chapter 38

Weighty Matters

'What the hell do you think you're doing upsetting Martinha so close to her delivery?' screamed Light when he stormed into my cell barely thirty minutes later. His face was thunderous, and I feared he might strike me. My gaze went automatically to the shelf where I had earlier secreted my keris. I detested the man but shuddered at my involuntary response. The Indian convicts had taught me too well.

I said nothing, just stared at my feet. Two years ago, a different Jim might have answered, 'She started it.' How ironic that all the deception on this island had forced me into becoming a better kind of man. Albeit one who had just harassed an expectant woman!

'Sadly, I am stuck with you as I cannot allow an Englishman to be murdered by the Malays while under my jurisdiction,' Light spat. 'But rest assured, James, as soon as I can arrange it, you will be shipped from this island back to bloody India.'

I kept out of everyone's way for the next two days and continued practicing with my keris. By Sunday, the tenth of April, I had calmed down enough and wanted to apologise to Light for distressing his wife. As I ventured passed the bankshall, I heard raised voices inside. Standing close to the door, but far enough away that no one inside could see me, I could make out Light, James Scott, Captains Glass and Hamilton, and Lieutenants Raban and Mylne. All of them were jacketless, with their shirt sleeves rolled up.

Light was waving a piece of parchment above his head. 'This letter from the native chiefs is nothing short of a declaration of war, despite all their flowery language. 'Our friend', indeed!'

Scott removed the document from Light's shaking hand and, scanning it, began to read aloud in a manner that only exaggerated the Malay habit of writing extremely long, unpunctuated sentences: '*Likewise if our friend will not come with us and do homage to the King, the King is not content that our friend should remain any longer on Poolo Pinang therefore our friend will get away about his business quietly for Poolo Pinang is the property of the King of Queda from time immemorial moreover if our friend attempts to stay by force God who knows all things will place the evil upon his head, we are free from blame.*'[7]

'How much is he asking for now?' inquired John Glass.

Scott answered, Light having already sunk into his chair staring off into nowhere. 'Five thousand dollars more and an agreement to pay ten thousand per annum for the years that have passed.'

'It cannot be done,' murmured Light. 'All the specie on this island has been exhausted since the native merchants would not visit us while we were under threat of attack. I have even had to pay the military men from sales of Honourable Company opium.'

'Something else Bengal won't be happy about,' added Scott.

The room remained hushed until John Glass piped up again. 'So, gentlemen, what is to be done?'

'Send over more opium,' answered Light wearily.

I became aware of a pain in one of my palms where I had been pressing my fingernails too deep into my skin. Good God man, I wanted to shout, learn a lesson; that will only delay the inevitable.

I glanced over at Robert Hamilton, who was shifting from foot to foot. 'I think we should prepare ourselves for war,' he said. 'We have a few days at least to get our men ready. The fort can be strengthened if we work on the bulwarks and use the design to our advantage. I suggest supplementing the cannons on the easterly walls and—'

'There are no spare guns to place along the sea-coast,' Captain Glass reminded him.

'But you could purchase three nine-pounder iron guns and borrow four six-pounders from Captain Billamore,' interjected Scott to Light.

'We can face this enemy on our turf and win,' declared Hamilton, sounding as excited as a child told to expect a special birthday present.

'No!' The word was out of my mouth before I could stop it. I stepped out of the shadows into the room of military men.

'What the hell do you want?' Light called across the room when he saw me.

'To save this island and your legacy, Captain Light,' I answered, strangely becalmed. 'It is madness to allow an armada of at least two hundred and fifty armed vessels and ten thousand men or more to land on our shores. You have a garrison of four hundred. This fort is crumbling around us. A few choice shots, and it will be shattered by cannon fire and all your guns with it. You must take the fight to them.'

Had James Scott dropped the letter from Sultan Abdullah's *wakils*, we would have heard it hit the wooden floor. Then Hamilton, who apparently had not noticed how much closer I had moved towards him, laughed uproariously. 'What kind of madcap military manouevre is that? And who are you to suggest—'

With the stealth I had been practising for weeks I now stood behind him, the crook of my arm pressing into his throat, but not too tightly. 'You think that is enough to overpower *me*?' he scoffed, looking incredulously at men he believed to be his friends.

'Certainly not,' I replied, blood pumping. When he saw the keris I held in my other hand, he appeared as transfixed as a bird frozen in place by an advancing cobra. I whispered in Hamilton's ear. 'I might first cut out your liver,' I said, prodding the tip into his abdomen and watched as a speck of blood stained his otherwise spotless shirt. With lightning speed, I shifted the point to the back of his neck. 'Or cut here, which I assure you means you will never need those fancy boots again.' With a final flourish I waved the deadly weapon in front of his face, almost nipping the tip of his nose. 'The beauty of a curved and wavy blade is that it is not the dagger going in that causes the most damage, but what happens to the internal organs when the attacker draws it out.'

'Enough!' shouted Light. 'Leave Hamilton be.'

With a gentle push that sent the terrified man flying, I heard sniggers. In soundless unison, the other men edged away from the former schoolyard bully. I surmised Hamilton was not popular, and I had earned the others' respect. I could barely keep the smirk off my face.

I strode next to the superintendent and addressed the gathering. 'Gentlemen, please hear me out. I assure you my suggestion has considerable historical precedent in situations where one army is vastly outnumbered by its foe.'

I reminded them of leaders who had vanquished similarly horrendous odds: King Leonides of the three hundred Spartans holding out against Xerxes' one million Persians; Henry V's nine thousand Englishmen who defeated thirty-six thousand French at the Battle of Agincourt; General George Washington's continental ragamuffins outwitting the better armed Redcoat army. All because they had each adopted an unconventional, unexpected approach.

'Mystify, mislead, and surprise the enemy.' We all turned to stare at James Scott. 'A lesson from the Chinese general, Sun Tzu. Right, Jim?'

I nodded in assent.

As the sun began to set, the final plan emerged like a butterfly from a chrysalis, bolstered by suggestions from the officers with the exception of the glowering Hamilton who continued to lick his imaginary wounds.

'That's settled then,' announced Light. 'John—' he turned to Captain Glass, 'Instruct your men to be ready to sail the early hours of the twelfth.'

John Glass nodded and strode off, grabbing Hamilton's sleeve like a father about to drag a naughty child home. The two Lieutenants dutifully followed.

'What of you, Jim?' Light said to me. 'Despite your impressive show of prowess with that keris I don't see you in the midst of this fight.'

'I have a battle of my own planned,' I said. 'Also inspired by Sun Tzu's advice.' I directed my next question to Scott. 'Do you believe Pieter is— Is *she* still on this island?'

'Aye,' answered Scott. 'But so far, no one has been able to find her. She could be anywhere in the interior, which means she's lost for good. But for the moment she can't escape. The Malays are on the lookout and the *Fame* is too buggered to go anywhere.'

I looked over at Light. 'I know where she's hiding, having visited there twice. I want to be the one who brings her in.'

Both of my companions hesitated as if unsure whether I really meant to do this or help Pietronella Rodyck escape.

'Justice. For Nakhoda Kechil and his family,' I said, and that was enough. They must have seen the determination in my eyes. 'And you now know what I am capable of. If she resists, I will not hesitate to kill her.'

'Aye and good riddance to that traitorous she-devil,' declared Scott.

'You say the Malays now know she murdered the Ismails?' I asked.

'Yes, but I wouldn't place too much store on that,' said Light. 'Until we have her body, dead or alive, they're still intent on killing you.'

'Then I need a favour. Tomorrow morning, before your efforts here become too far advanced.'

'You are back in my good graces,' Light said with a grin. 'Anything.'

Chapter 39

Darkest before Dawn

Battu Lanchon. Monday, 11 April 1791.

We see what we want to see, what we choose to believe, until stubborn truth forces even the determinedly blind to accept the truth. I had been spying on Pietronella Rodyck from deep within the tangled vegetation of the jungle for most of the day, aghast at how I could have fooled myself for so long. I saw her long, loose tresses lie damp against her shoulders as she freshened up in the barrel of rainwater behind her hideout. No binding cloth flattened the soft mounds of her breasts, no black overcoat concealed the hands-span waist or the spread of her hips. It pained me to think this woman was someone Pieter had never wanted me to meet.

As nightfall descended, I peered at the pocket watch Light had given Scott to loan me during our initial journey by bullock cart. I had lain in the back covered by empty sacks and half-rotting produce so that the Malays, seeing only the burly Scotsman and I Boon, would leave the vehicle be. Light had wanted me to know the exact time in order to give myself the greatest chance of survival. I was long past deceiving myself that Mejuffer Rodyck would spare my life once she knew my intentions. I did not need to be reminded not to underestimate her.

Nine more hours to wait.

She stood on the upper platform silhouetted by the light of the gibbous moon. Petting that misshapen macaque of hers and puffing at her opium pipe in readiness, I imagined, for sleep. All I could think of were the words, 'if only', that sought to drive me towards the rocks of despair. Then, as if my wistfulness had taken shape and risen like a plume of smoke, Pietronella Rodyck turned and appeared to stare directly at me. She held her gaze for too long, I feared, not to have seen me as she stood as stiff as a marble statue. I had successfully quelled the gasp in my throat but could do nothing about my heart trying to punch its way through my ribcage. The thump, thump, thump so thunderous I could not imagine how she did not hear it. Then she cocked her head to one side like a bird. With a shrug of her shoulders, as if telling herself that what she sensed was just her imagination, the woman I had never been given the chance to know disappeared inside the hut.

I must have slept, despite the cacophony of frogs, cicadas, crickets, and other nocturnal creatures chorusing around me. With a start, I jerked awake, the fragrant, fetid air once again assaulting my nostrils. I rubbed at my stiff neck then checked Light's watch. The waxing moon would provide sufficient light for our purpose but not so full as to give away the surprise of our twilight attack at Prai. But it was not yet time.

I heard a rustling in the bushes, somewhere off to my right. Not from some animal but accompanied by the sly tiptoe of human footsteps. I did not have long to wait for their owners to appear; two figures scampered up the stilts like monkeys, needing no ladder to reach Pietronella's door. Then a cry of alarm; the sound of tussling; the dull bang of tin bouncing on wood; an inhuman screech and Raksasa Kechil flung out by an unseen hand.

Lanoons by the look of them, as they emerged into the moonlight, for I had learned to tell the difference in their attire between these particular pirates and the Bugis. One of them held Pietronella by the scruff of her neck, his keris under her throat as his compatriot lowered the ladder into place. With some difficulty, since my former Dutch friend struggled the whole time, they deposited her roughly on to the ground. I glanced nearby to see what else I might arm myself with and noticed a thick, knobbly stick not unlike those the locals called a

'Penang lawyer', with which people settled minor disputes. Very slowly, and silently, I picked it up while chastising myself for my hubris at only being armed with one dagger.

But did I *need* to intervene? Being sold into slavery by these pirates was likely better than what she could expect from a Bengal judiciary. Why risk my life trying to overcome this vicious duo when I could let the Lanoons deal with Pietronella Rodyck, who must have betrayed them too? But then they began to molest her. Having seen it so plainly, I could not bear the thought of her being so defiled. One of them had her pinned hard against the trunk of a tree as he groped under his tunic to free his erect cock, the second man urging him on.

Even then, as the first man began groping Pietronella with his free hand, I could not move. What could I expect to achieve against these cutthroats? Make myself known to them and a quick death was the best I could hope for. I could almost smell the sweet stench of fear as I shook off the vision of these fiends slicing open my stomach, forcing me to watch my guts spill out, hot and steamy like the contents of a pie, laughing all the while at my extended agony. Then ravishing their prey afterwards anyway. All of which raced through my mind as I stepped out from my hiding place and began to advance towards them.

'Hey! Let her go.'

The blackguards looked first at me then back at their captive as if unsure which of us to give precedence to. Rooted to the spot, my false courage having left me, I became hypnotised by the glint of their knives in the moonlight. *Please God, let me at least live to see the dawn.*

Pietronella smiled, the meaning no more obvious than it had ever been, given the slant of that disfigured mouth. As those fiends released her and made a move towards me, I watched them drop like felled bamboo. She moved so swiftly, the next thing I saw was one of them stare at me in stunned surprise. She had sliced the back of his knees. The other gurgled, grasping at the side of his neck in a vain attempt to stem the blood that spurted through his fingers with each fading heartbeat.

As nimble as a dancer, Pietronella approached the man now kneeling, tendons severed by her slender keris. Calmly, she removed the flintlock from the pirate's belt and blasted away the left side of the man's head. She threw the spent pistol to the ground and walked over to where the second assassin's unused weapon lay. She picked it up. Without her neckerchief, what I had mistaken for an Adam's apple seemed even more swollen, but she had never looked more beautiful or enticing to me.

'Did you come to save me?' she said with a sneer. Then, nodding towards the slain assassins added, 'As you can see, I did not need your help.' She stood in the moonlight, a single breast exposed like the orb of a finely sculpted Greek goddess. With no sense of embarrassment, she tucked it back inside her nightshirt but left the garment loose and free.

'I beg to differ,' I said as she approached, kicking the pirate whose throat she had cut to confirm he was well and truly dead. 'At least I distracted your would-be attackers before they could—'

My voice trailed off as Pietronella stared below my waist and retorted, 'Their minds no different to yours, I see.'

To hide my blushes, I glanced at Light's pocket watch.

'Is there somewhere else you need to be?'

'No,' I answered truthfully. 'We should talk.'

How she achieved it I could not have said, but as I stood in that steamy jungle with Pietronella's breath further warming my face I found that I no longer had possession of either my dagger or the stick. She had robbed me of any means of defence. Then she whispered, seductively, 'Let's run away together.'

Chapter 40

Fall

Tuesday, 12 April. 5.47 a.m.

As she stood back to study my reaction to her enticement, Pietronella voiced something else. But her words were drowned out by the satanic carrions now gathered above us, hopping impatiently on nearby branches. Their cacophonous shrieks communicated their desire to begin this early morning feast.

I looked across the strait to where Captain Glass' gunboats were surely on their way to the mouth of the Prai river, the fact of which Pietronella Rodyck was not aware. I pointed to where the moon was reflected like a heavy-lidded silver eye on the narrow strip of sea. 'Might we move away from here and leave the crows to fight over eyeballs and innards?'

Her gaze never left me. Pietronella scooped up the broken macaque into the crook of her left arm and used the dead pirate's pistol to indicate that we should move sideways down the rise, like a pair of crabs.

'That's far enough,' she said, once we were on flatter ground. I noticed that the flintlock was no longer aimed at me but lay caressed in her palm, the muzzle pointed down towards the ground. 'Dig!' she commanded.

I looked at her in horror. Was she going to force me to dig my own grave before shooting me?

'Not for you, fool,' she said, at my stunned gaze.

I looked back to where the two dead Lanoons lay like discarded marionettes, soon to be a meal for jungle beasts.

'And certainly not for them.' She caressed Raksasa's tiny face left frozen in a macabre grin then placed him gently on the ground.

'For the monkey?' I said, bemused.

'Raksasa was like a child to me,' Pietronella spat. 'Dig while we talk.'

I kicked the sod with my foot. 'With what? My hands? Give me my dagger so I can cut away the top vegetation at least.'

Her laugh was like the crack of cannonball fire. 'Oh, Jim. Now you see I am a woman, don't treat me like a fool. Get on your hands and knees. You need only scratch a little way. I intend to burn Raksasa, not bury him. I'll take his ashes with me to spread on the ocean, for I will be leaving here soon enough, once the Malays are victorious. Sultan Abdullah remains grateful to me.'

But was he? If it was not Queda's ruler who had sent the Lanoons to kill Pieter Reinaert, who had? Then again, who knew how many enemies he—she—had amassed. I sank to my knees like a penitent and began scratching at the surface with my fingernails. The ground, sodden by the rains, easily broke apart.

'It was you who murdered those two Siamese shortly before I arrived here, wasn't it? And likely killed the Chinese girl thought to have committed suicide,' I said as I dug into the dank soil. 'But why?'

My captor shrugged. 'Can't you guess? It had long been my hope that by causing sufficient chaos and unrest in this settlement it would be easier for my countrymen to take over Penang. By undermining Light's hold on this island my intention was that we Dutch would reclaim our glory days and rule over the whole region once more.' She looked wistful as she stroked the fur of the dead monkey. 'Sadly, those old men back in Holland lack the courage of my ancestor. So, I turned to Sultan Abdullah and offered my services to him. As you well know, the raja was most eager to see you English gone from his country.'

Neither of us said anything for some minutes, as I pondered what she had just told me, while making a pretence of digging further into the ground. Then she said, 'How did you know it was me who dealt with the Ismails?'

'You left your keris behind. In a pool of blood,' I spat back, not daring to look at her in case she saw the tears pricking my eyes at the mention of their name.

I heard Pietronella chuckle. 'A foolish mistake,' she said.

'How so?'

'The old woman proved to be more powerful than her menfolk. She grabbed my wrist even after I had sliced her throat open. Surprised by her strength, I dropped the blade. Then I heard scratching at the door and thought I had been discovered. It turned out to be some mangy dog but by then dawn was breaking. I left in a hurry and only some distance beyond Malay Town did I discover that I had left my keris behind. But then, who would know it belonged to me?'

'I did,' I mumbled, to which Pietronella responded, 'Yes. I had forgotten about that. As I said, a foolish mistake.'

She sighed, then added, 'So, what do you say to my earlier suggestion? Should we run away together, Jim Lloyd? After all, you can no longer use my former pretence of manhood as an excuse to subdue your obvious lust any longer.'

The air around me was ripe with sweat and fear and the stench of rotting vegetation. I could not seem to grasp a coherent thought. Every sense in my body heightened, and I longed for some kind of release. My desire for her was like a sickness that threatened to overwhelm me. I looked over at Pietronella who wore such a defiant, wounded expression that I almost succumbed to running away with her. I would have, had the need for justice for Tuan Ismail—for Awang, Othman, and their mother—not prevailed.

The look on my face must have told her everything.

She scoffed. 'Ah! You harbour some noble notion of taking me back to George Town and from there to India to face your *justice*?'

Again, she gleaned the answer from my expression. 'Sorry to disappoint you, Jim,' she sneered, 'but that will never happen. I love my freedom too much to ever accept being a slave. If I were even to escape the hangman's noose.'

Lifting my hands from the earth as if in prayer, I said, 'Why did you not show me who you truly were? I thought—'

'Oh, but I tried,' she interrupted. 'Do you not remember the day I brought you here and what I said as you were about to leave?'

I did but wanted to extend the conversation for as long as possible. 'No,' I said.

'That if you stayed the night, you might see things differently. I thought I could trust you then. But you were too scared to risk finding out what was on offer.'

'I misunderstood your meaning,' I murmured.

'Yes, well. Then you accused me of keeping Light's letters for nefarious means.'

'Like blackmail?' It was foolish of me to risk antagonising her but I couldn't help myself.

'Well, the proceeds from such indiscretions never stopped you from taking money for yourself.'

I thought of the wealth I had amassed, buried near the kampong, marked with signs that only I and Awang, now slain, had known about.

I had nothing more to say on that subject and so, with a disdainful look, resumed my half-hearted scratching at the soil. *Mystify, mislead, and surprise your enemy.* I just needed a little more time; I had to wait for the sign.

'I'm sure you can expect lenience in Bengal. As a woman,' I said.

Pietronella laughed again, sounding genuinely amused. 'Come now, Jim, you know that women are executed no different to men,' she said. 'Unless, of course, they're pregnant.'

She reached over and began stroking the dead monkey. 'But I could never have children. Raksasa was the closest thing—'

'Couldn't or wouldn't?' I interrupted.

She sank down on the ground opposite me, raising the pistol so that it was aimed at my head. I had no doubt she was an excellent shot. I sensed her need to talk, and I needed to fill the remaining minutes, assuming all had gone to plan. I asked without judgment, 'What happened to you? Why this masquerade?'

'Look at me, Jim. As a woman, can you imagine how my life would have been with a face like this? My own parents couldn't love me, with my twisted mouth and this monstrous bulge on my neck.' She paused, as if reliving the cruelty of her childhood and added, 'Then after—' but said nothing more.

'After what?' I asked. As I carved out that shallow crater with my hands my fingertips had rested on something hard and sharp. I prised out a large flat rock and placed it on the ground. Pietronella looked at it suspiciously. 'A headstone for Raksasa, perhaps?' I said, then asked, 'What did you mean by 'then after'?'

She sighed. 'As a child I went through a time of much loathing. For myself as much as anyone else. I would run away, frequenting places where no young girl should be found, taunting death to come and find me. I knew my parents hoped that it would.'

I sat back on my haunches and rubbed the dirt from my hands. 'Go on.'

'I had just turned ten—it was my birthday, I remember, although nothing so frivolous was ever celebrated in our household. I must have wandered into some dark alley plotting another impotent escape. I think there were four or five of them, the details have become hazy over the years, although I've willed myself to remember rather than try to forget. When they were done, they left me insensible and bleeding. The doctor said I had been much damaged. *Inside* as much as out. To which my father exclaimed I was surely fit for nothing but prostitution. I could perform my devilish urges—for had I not taunted those men to do what they did?–without worrying about birthing bastards.'

I leaned towards her, my heart aching with pity.

'Stay where you are,' she said quietly, raising the firearm again. 'It must have been then that I realised how life is weighted to the advantage of men. Bruised and battered, telling the first seafarer I ran into that my father had beaten me, I dressed and acted such that I was taken on as a cabin boy.' She sighed as she placed the dead monkey into the indentation I had made in the ground. 'The rest is exactly as I told you previously.'

We sat in silence for many minutes. I was sorely tempted to reach for Light's pocket watch but dare not. What was delaying them? All I had between me and my Maker were words, for I could not believe I meant anything to Pietronella Rodyck or ever had.

'I did—do—have feelings for you, Jim. Sensations I thought I could never feel. I think you felt the same?'

'Yes,' I croaked, mystified at how she always appeared to read my thoughts. 'But why didn't you reveal your true self to me earlier?'

She looked confused and it took her a while to put whatever she was thinking into words. 'My companions have long been suspicion and hatred, the only way I could survive this cruel world.' Her voice sounded sad, lonely. 'Trust must be coaxed, like a shy, reluctant lover. Until I met you I had no need to do so, relying on my wits. But even then—' Her voice trailed off and she sat, impassively, gazing at the horizon where soon enough a golden orb would begin its ascent.

I stared at her, hungrily. Twilight seemed to play tricks with her face. At certain moments I saw my friend Pieter: confident, defiant, manly. Then, at others, she was Pietronella: vulnerable, wretched, yearning to be understood. I opened my mouth to tell her that I would protect her. I could not in all conscience have us run away together but I would sail with her to Bengal and speak up in her defence.

But then, over her right shoulder I saw plumes of white smoke rise in the distance at the mouth of the river Prai. Then the blast of cannonballs crashing into the Malay's makeshift forts on the mainland. Pietronella turned towards the sound of the battle that we had taken to the enemy rather than risk them invading this island, since they vastly outnumbered us forty to one. Captain Glass' troops had begun their pre-dawn assault that we hoped would confuse the unsuspecting armada, thus giving us the advantage of surprise.

An advantage I needed to grasp, too.

Pietronella looked confused by the noise coming from the opposite coast, her mouth open like a fish caught on a line. Without thinking I lunged, careening into her just as she turned back to face me so that the top of my head struck her chin, throwing her backwards and both of us on to the yielding undergrowth. Even with my softer landing atop her body I was winded, as was she.

I had heard the soft thud of the flintlock after it had gone flying out of her hand. But somewhere on her person she likely still had one or two daggers. Pietronella would kill me to save herself, I had no doubt of that, unless I could subdue her. Was I strong enough, mentally or physically, for the task? I forced myself to control my thoughts, to imagine little Othman as I had seen him last, lying in his pool of blood. No child deserved to die that way. I needed to make up for my naivety and take this murderess to face trial. I owed my Malay friends that at least.

We began to grapple once again and the earth turned, just as it had when a school bully had placed me in an empty barrel as a child and rolled me down a hill. I could hear Pietronella's heartbeat ricochet in my right ear, like the drums of an advancing army. In a nervous frenzy, as we rolled over and over one another, I kept patting the ground, moving my left hand this way and that until I felt something rough scrape my fingertips, just out of reach.

We came to a halt, with me squatting on top of her. I looked down at her chest and, defying everything my grandfather had told me to never do when playing with girls, I thrust a fist down as hard as I could just above her ribcage. I heard her exhale deeply and felt her body sag. I seemed inured to what should have been pain in my knuckles. But in the next moment, her head rose and she bit my cheek so viciously that I loosened my grip in shock. She toppled me over and with a knee to my groin pinned me down like a mounted butterfly.

All around, I could smell nothing but decay. Would my body become part of this desolate place? Would this be my white man's grave?

'It was my idea,' I gasped, struggling to take air into my lungs, 'to take the fight to the Malays rather than risk an invasion, given the parlous state of our fort and defencelessness of the town. I persuaded the officers that our only hope was to do the unexpected, to take an unconventional approach.' I did not know why I was telling her this other than to keep the conversation going until I could find what I sightlessly sought.

'I'm impressed,' she said, with a glint in her eyes, and then I knew why I had said what I did. I had not changed as much as I thought but was still looking for approval. My body sagged, not from her weight but with disappointment in myself. When would I stop being that little boy desiring approbation?

I forced myself back into the present. 'Give up, Pietronella. Come back with me to George Town. I promise I'll do everything I can to see you are given a fair trial.'

My assailant looked down at me with a strange, conflicted expression, her hand reaching—I thought—to where she had hidden her keris. Then her eyes narrowed with contempt. Perhaps she doubted how a force of a few hundred could prevail against thousands of ferocious Malays. At least her hand had stopped moving, although mine had not.

'Four hundred well-trained sepoys led by disciplined British officers against a mob of mercenaries and rag-tag pirates for whom this is not a fight they care about,' I panted, my breath blowing Pietronella's soft, sun-streaked hair across her face. 'British heroes with a fine commander in Captain John Glass who have just pressed a strategic advantage: the element of surprise.'

When I looked into her eyes, I recognised what I had never fully understood before— something that could no longer be disguised: The desire that each of us harbours, even if seemingly sunk like a Spanish galleon on the ocean floor, to love and be loved. With determination, I shook my right arm free and raised my hand to caress her cheek, feeling the smooth skin we had laughed over so many times. Then I lifted my head and parted my lips, and she lowered her face on to mine. How long we kissed I could not have said; the world had given way to utter bliss. Our caress was long, languid, tender. It was the kiss of two ill-fated lovers. As my heart struggled to burst from my chest, all I could think of was how different our story could have been had we each made different choices.

When we came up for air, I gazed into those glorious indigo orbs and knew her demons would never be exorcised. With a sideways strike, as hard as I could muster, I crashed the rock I had earlier grasped with my left hand into her skull. Then, my eyes blinded by tears, I hit her again to be sure.

Convinced that I had killed her, I wept over her bleeding body, salty tears and sweat stinging my swollen, torn cheek. Pietronella's mark, the scar I would carry with me forever. No more than I deserved.

I tried to stand up, but my knees buckled, just as a sound like a screaming banshee filled my ears. I fell back on the ground, winded once again. My eyes flickered in surprise, and I thought I saw two black boots advance towards me. Then, as if a phalanx of witches had blotted out the moon, everything turned dark.

Chapter 41

None So Blind

Letter from Captain Francis Light to Edward Hay, Secretary to Government, Calcutta. 19 April 1791.[8]

'It being now apparent that the Malay force was bent on accomplishing our destruction, I communicated all the intelligence I had received to Captain Glass who, taking the circumstances of our situation into consideration, joined with me in the opinion that it was necessary for the security of the Settlement to attack the enemy immediately. Accordingly, having fitted out four gunboats with the *Dolphin*, *Princess Augusta*, and *Valiant*, a vessel belonging to the King of Acheen, to attack the prahus, Captain Glass embarked with three companies of sepoys in boats at 4 a.m. on the 12th instant. Having landed undiscovered on the opposite shore, he surprised at dawn of day the fort upon the point and dispersed with little loss the large force that had been collected for its defence. Then our men proceeded to the second fort, for the enemy made some show of resistance. But the sepoys, having mounted the ramparts, soon put them to flight. Both these forts were immediately burnt.

'At daylight, the gunboats advanced to attack the fleet of prahus amounting to at least two hundred, under the command of Lieutenants Raban and Mylne, and for a considerable space of time, they bore heavy fire from the whole fleet. At length our vessels, which were retarded for want of wind, were towed in and the enemy's fire silenced by noon, when both the troops and gunboats returned, the enemy's forces having previously retired out of sight. On the night of the 12th the Lanoon prahus absconded.

'On the 14th, the prahus again appeared at the mouth of the Prai river in great numbers, and hearing that the prahus were seen by fishermen off the south end of this island, I desired Captain Glass to prepare for a second attack. Having refitted the gunboats and mounted an eighteen-pounder on a large punt, the boats and vessels attacked the prahus a second time the morning of the 16th and, after a short while made them retreat with great loss, pursuing them to the distance of four miles. Two companies of sepoys were landed in the morning on Prai Point, but the shores being quite deserted, they met with no opposition.

'I have the honour to transmit a list of the four company men killed and the twenty-one wounded in these two attacks. Our loss, considering the number of the enemy and the heavy cannonade they kept up on the 12th instant, is very small. Troops on land and sea showed the greatest steadiness; the vessels that were able to approach near enough to the prahus kept up a well-directed fire, and the commanders of the country vessels in the harbour with their own services, their boats and people, assisted the public service.

'I beg leave to inform you that I have in my possession the King of Queda's order to his officers to attack this settlement. In this paper, the word 'attack' being erased and the word 'godown' has been inserted in its place and the paper then sent over by his officers as a justification for their conduct, but the deception is too gross. I enclose a translation.

'A messenger is this day arrived from the King of Queda with a letter blaming the bad conduct of his officers at Prai and denying any intention of attacking this settlement. He requests that he may still be allowed ten thousand Spanish Dollars per annum and everything forgot. To this, I have not yet returned an answer, although I am of a mind to offer to pay the Sultan six thousand Spanish Dollars a year so long as the English should continue in possession of Penang, subject to ratification by the Honourable Company, of course. In the meantime, the King of Queda's prahus remains blocked up by our vessels in the Prai river. I request a supply of gunpowder and cannon in case of a further attack.'

***

I handed Light's copy of his letter back to James Scott without comment. What was there to say? The leopard had not changed his spots. And why should I care, since once I was well enough I would sail away, to where I yet did not know.

I had been surprised to find myself in Martinha's bungalow when I first awoke. The mistress, having recently borne a son, had left to convalesce at Light's Suffolk estate. Whether from the concussion caused by the stray cannon ball that had knocked me out at Battu Lanchon, or just a deep desire to sleep, I had dozed in and out of consciousness for almost a week. A dream state in which I was free to visit those exotic islands: The Celebes; the Moluccas; Timor; Flores, that I had once wished to see but now never would.

I supposed I had been considered a hero of sorts who deserved more luxury than my cell at the fort. At least that is what I surmised until I discovered from the hushed chatter of Light's slaves that my prisoner was in chains at Fort Cornwallis. Light obviously wished to keep us separate. He and Scott had maintained the ruse that this was Pieter Reinaert, preventing any of the sepoys harbouring lewd ideas when dealing with our traitorous captive.

'So, you did not trust me to capture and bring back the Dutchman,' I said to Scott, as I propped myself up on one elbow on my bed, he already having settled himself in the room's only chair. Despite what I had seen at the hideout, I still had the habit of thinking of Pieter as a man.

The Scotsman had the good grace to admit it. Yes, he had allowed me to gain a certain distance after I left the bullock cart, then he secretly followed me. He had seen everything, he said, ready to step into the breach if needed. I blushed at my remembrance of that kiss.

'I Boon carried the traitor back to where we left the cart. I had the bad luck to haul your prone body over my back.'

'I expected you to take part in the battle.'

Scott scoffed. 'Laddie, I am far too old for that.' Then, 'I came by to see how yer feeling. I see the surgeon stitched you up well enough.'

I touched my cheek.

'Anxious to be away from here,' I said, trying to keep the rancour out of my voice. 'What news about Pieter— Pietronella. Is she still being held at the fort? I trust she has not been sent to Bengal without me.'

The man turned his head and appeared to stare beyond the shutters.

My bowels shuddered. 'Did I kill her? Did she die of her wounds?'

He shook his head then turned to look at me. 'She merely had a nasty gash on her forehead after coming to.'

'So, what is it you are not saying?'

The Scotsman sighed and said, 'She's gone, Jim.'

I sprung up from the bed. 'What do you mean, *gone?* Gone where? To Bengal?'

'No.'

'Has she escaped?' The thought left me feeling both elated and dismayed.

'We think someone stole her away in the night.'

'You *think?* Who? Friends or enemies?'

'Possibly the Siamese. No one seems to know. Or wishes to say.'

I shook my head in disbelief. I had lived for weeks in that very cell with the local Malays baying for my blood. How was it that someone had managed to free her under the sepoys' noses when I had been secure?

Scott shrugged. 'She may have been taken by the families of those two Siamese she'd slain some while back. They'll be imposing their own natural justice very soon if she's not dead already.'

I thundered, 'This is outrageous. Why wasn't she better protected? I—'

Scott sprang up from the chair and grabbed my arm with a vice-like grip. It hurt, and I tried to shake him free. I had lost my keris and needed to replace it. The man held on like a barnacle and pulled me close. 'I wouldn't make a fuss, Jim, if you know what's good for you. Let's just say she's getting or has already got what she deserves. And it might not go down too well, given the raw feelings still rampant in this settlement, if you start showing sympathy for that traitorous Dutch cow.'

He pushed me gently as he let go of my arm, and I made a performance of straightening myself, although my entire body felt like sagging into a heap.

'A Bengal judiciary would have shown her lenience,' I said. 'She had the most terrible of childhoods. Cruel, unloving parents. Attacked and left barren by a gang of vicious men.'

Scott began to laugh then, seeing my stricken face, made as if to cough.

'What?' I countered, stepping so close to him that our faces were only inches apart.

He patted my arm and I backed away. 'Barren you say? Jim, Pietronella Rodyck has borne three children at the last count, according to my intelligence. One shipped back to Holland with the wife of a VOC officer, the other two given to older women with no offspring of their own in Batavia.'

'No,' I cried. 'That can't be true. She told me—'

'For God's sake, Jim, can you still not see the truth? She'd tell you the sky was green if it suited her purpose. That woman thrived on lies as much as breathing. I received a brief account of her affairs from several people who have long known she was a woman but thought nothing of her calling herself Pieter Reinaert and dressing as she did as long as she made them money. I assure you she's given birth on at least three occasions and is not barren. Or *was* not, I should say.'

I winced, thinking back to the various tales I had heard Pieter tell William and those unsavoury cronies of his, about how his mouth had come to be misshapen. Had anything he—she—said, including at our last encounter, been true?

'What about being related to Jan Pieterszoon Coen?'

Scott shrugged again. 'Who can say? Coen died without leaving any heirs as his two daughters died in infancy. But his wife's sister, Lijbeth Ment, married one of Coen's trusted colleagues and had a son named Pieter. Maybe your traitorous friend was descended from that line. Pietronella Rodyck might have been the spawn of Satan, just not directly from that Dutch devil, Coen.'

The Scotsman looked towards the door, as if anxious to be on his way. 'Good to see yer feeling better, Jim,' he said, as if nothing untoward had passed between us. 'I only came to say farewell as I'm headed to Palembang on the morrow. Who knows when, or if, we'll see each other again?' He held out his hand and I shook it. Then he passed me a letter. 'My second cousin once removed, named Walter, fancies himself becoming a biographer and a poet. He may still be in Kelso—'

'The name you've given your bungalow on Light's Suffolk estate?' I said.

'Aye, I've always had a fondness for the Scottish Borders. Wattie may be back in Edinburgh with his parents by now, of course. The lad is lame, as a result of polio, but a fine young man, by all accounts. Must be close to twenty years old, around your age. Here is a letter of introduction. Look him up if you're ever in Scotland as you may find things in common with young Walter Scott.' Then James Scott left the room, although not yet my life.

My dreams that night were of goal cages, with Pietronella restrained within such a horror. Was she still in Penang, taken to Queda, or on her way to Siam to be impaled or stamped to death by an elephant? Perhaps her captors would be merciful and have her beheaded. But I doubted it; she would be made to suffer. Man, woman or child—*she'd had children, had lied to me even about that*—people here only imposed rough justice.

Sickened, I determined to leave this island and everything connected to it as soon as I could. But first, I needed to make my peace with Martinha.

Chapter 42

See the Light

Thursday, 5 May 1791.

I waylaid I Boon as he drove the bullock cart past the fort. Upon hearing he was off to Light's Suffolk estate to pick up his master and return him to George Town, I insisted he take me with him.

Light's country home looked exactly as Miss Davis had described it before she left for Macau with Mrs Beal: A bamboo, attap-roofed pavilion poised some six feet above the ground, open underneath to keep it cool and secure from jungle beasts, with windows on all sides. I had been told that the superintendent often held dinners and dances here for EIC officers and visiting guests. None of which I had been invited to in the two years since the night of the fire.

I almost bumped into Light in the doorway, who looked to be leaving the moment I arrived. 'I see you are well recovered, Jim. Is Martinha expecting you?'

'I thought I would make a chance visit,' I said, aware of two very different sets of wails coming from separate parts of the house. A woman's and a baby's.

Light paused as if deciding whether to let me in then said, 'Keep Martinha company while I'm away. Indeed, stay for dinner. I'll see you later.' And with that, he strode past me and left with I Boon.

As I entered the house, I saw Martinha standing in a doorway noticeably upset, with red-rimmed eyes and nostrils, sniffing into a kerchief. I said the first thing that came into my head, not wishing to embarrass her. 'I wanted to congratulate you in person and see the baby before I leave Penang.' Thinking this might be the cause of her distress, I said, 'Is the child healthy?'

Somewhere in the far reaches of the home, the infant's cries were reduced to whimpering.

'Yes. He is a robust little fellow. At the moment, a wet nurse is comforting him. Perhaps you can see him quickly once he has quietened down or is asleep.'

'What name did you give him?'

'Francis. Although my husband insists on the nickname Lanoon, in honour of his recent victory.'

This was a subject I did not wish to enter into with her. Light's ironically named 'Treaty of Peace, Friendship and Alliance', that a subdued Sultan of Queda had signed on the first of May, forced that ruler to accept the paltry sum of six thousand dollars per annum as long as the English remained in Penang. No mention was made of the protection of his country from invaders. I wondered if the Malay ruler had yet discovered the English deceit, that military help had never been forthcoming despite Light's assurances and Macpherson's long-ago ambiguous promise about protection. Perhaps Abdullah still held out hopes of future assistance, given the wording of the new treaty's final paragraph that stated, 'Queda and Penang shall be as one.' Since the EIC would undoubtedly secure its investment I hoped this implied that the English would provide Queda with equal protection against its detested enemy, Siam, should that be needed in the future. But I doubted it.

Even more egregious was the fact that Lord Cornwallis had approved a payment of ten thousand dollars to the Queda king, but Light had offered no more than six thousand. When I had challenged him, he said, 'Six thousand dollars is enough, at least for the time being. Increasing the sum to ten thousand will make me look magnanimous later.'

At the time, I had wondered how kind posterity would be to the duplicitous Francis Light. But I had no wish to aggrieve his wife further, who seemed upset enough. If husband and wife had an argument, I did not wish to be in the middle of it.

'Come,' she said, with a wan smile. 'Take some refreshment with me.'

As we drank our tea and nibbled cake, Martinha asked, 'What are your plans for the future, Jim?'

I admitted I did not know. Having no means of establishing my independence I would either have to crawl back to Calcutta and plead for my old position or sail to England and throw myself on the mercy of my father. Neither course appealed.

'Then the rumours I have heard seem even stranger,' she said.

'What rumours?'

'That you have recently been very generous with your money, giving it away as if you had all the wealth in the world.'

Once recovered, I had gone back to the Malay kampong and dug up the bags of silver Pieter had given me. I sought out the relatives of Haji Mohammad Salleh—Nakhoda Kechil's deceased older brother—in Batu Uban and turned over most of my stash to pay for improvements to their mosque. Then I took some of what remained to Nachiappan the moneylender, to boost the funds he was able to lend those foolish enough to gamble away their land and properties. Stealing into the cell of my friends Mujriff Sheida and Mohamed Heiant, I left them a little to bribe the sepoys for better food or to send back to their families in India. I wanted nothing to do with funds earned by extortion and murderous deeds. But not wishing to raise the spectre of Pieter/Pietronella again, I merely told Martinha that it was money I could not keep in good conscience.

The two of us played congkak for hours, and it almost felt like old times. I admired the baby when the wet nurse brought him into the room and unwrapped the bundle to reveal a tiny puce face framed by a shock of black hair. I was much more interested in his brother, whom Martinha had not mentioned.

'How is William?' I ventured.

Martinha broke down into sobs again.

I let her be. When she regained some of her composure, she said, 'Little Francis will never know his big brother.'

'Your husband is insistent that the boy be sent to England to be raised by the Doughtys in Suffolk when he turns seven?'

Her assent was barely loud enough to hear.

'I am so sorry, Martinha, but it is likely best for the boy in the end.'

She looked up at me, eyes sparkling with tears but something else. As if the thought had just occurred to her she said, 'Would you stay in Penang until William's seventh birthday, James? Please? It would give a frantic mother much greater confidence in his safe arrival, not just to London but on to Doughty's place if you were by his side.' She added with a smile, 'A responsible adult to look after the boy's welfare during that long and arduous voyage. He has such little experience of the world beyond what you have taught him.'

My response was instantaneous. 'Martinha, I cannot. Once I can arrange passage to India, I intend to leave.'

We both looked up as two sets of footsteps entered the house: Light followed by William. How the boy had grown in the seven months or so since I had last seen him. But there was another change that troubled me greatly. A reticence, a sadness. I wondered how he had been spending his time since we had last met.

'Stay for early dinner, Jim, no excuses,' declared Light, pecking his wife on the cheek.

William stood in the doorway, looking solemn. I wondered how he felt about his little brother now that all the attention in their household had undoubtedly shifted to Lanoon. Martinha's nod was barely perceptible but when she gave the signal, William walked over to me and held out his hand. I took it and pulled him towards me into a hug. 'No need to stand on ceremony between us, surely?' I said as I ruffled his black curly hair.

Martinha said, 'I will check with Esan but expect we will eat in about an hour.' Then she left the room.

'Good,' announced Light. Turning to me he said, 'That will give I Boon sufficient time to rest before making the journey back to George Town. He'll see you safely to your lodgings after dinner, Jim.' He exited in another direction.

Left alone with William, I asked, 'Is this an interesting place? Where might we explore to build up an appetite before we eat?'

'Nowhere really,' he said sulkily.

I held him at arm's length and in a mock scold said, 'Obviously you haven't tried hard enough to find them, young man. Follow me. Let's carve ourselves a new adventure.'

The beam on the boy's face almost broke my heart.

After the meal, with Martinha gone to rest with the baby and William taken by Esan to bathe, Light and I sat alone sipping port.

'Martinha has asked me to stay a further year to accompany William to Suffolk and place him safely in the hands of Mr Doughty and his wife,' I said.

Light nodded, too quickly for this suggestion to have been a surprise. 'I know that would put her mind at rest. It is indeed a long and arduous journey and the boy is very young with no broad experience of life.'

'Almost the exact words Martinha used,' I smiled wryly. I had been wrong about them; the two were well-suited to one another. 'I'll do it on one condition.' Then I told Francis Light what he and Scott had to do for *me* over the next year.

While William and I had explored the Suffolk estate I recalled the advice William Roxburgh had given me about the 'middle way'. The trick being, of course, to recognise when such an opportunity presented itself. I wanted to make amends with Martinha as well as help young William regain his former buoyant, confident self in readiness for the great changes he would experience in England. There was nothing to fear from obscurity when you are loved and live within people's hearts and memories. What was a year to me, in order to prepare for such a heaven?

Chapter 43

Insightful

The deck of the Valentine, George Town harbour. Thursday, 14 June 1792.
'We're off to England. We're off to England.'

I glanced down at Friday perched in the new traveling cage that my convict friends had fashioned out of rattan and muttered to the bird, 'We are indeed.'

Earlier that day, I had visited the graves of the nakhoda's family and remained in solitude, praying and reflecting, for several hours. Then I went to say goodbye to those I had come to love and admire in Penang: Malay, Chinese, and Indian.

As William's dark head tore through the harbour's assembly like a human battering ram, I scanned the crowds hauling all manner of Eastern commodities: bales of Indian piece goods; koyans of rice; tin; bird's nests; pepper; forest resins; gold. The panorama looked little different to how it had when I first arrived here three and a half years ago.

I spotted Light, looking world weary. How bowed he had become by the consequences of his deceptions. I had a strong premonition the man did not have long to live: a year, perhaps two at most. My greater concern was for his wife. What would happen to Martinha without Light or me to protect her?

'Uncle Jim!' William bounded up the gangway and excitedly reached for Friday's cage. He held it aloft as if to show the bird the frenzied scene below. While waiting for Light and Martinha to catch up, I considered the diversity around us: men of all shades from the ebony-skinned Moors, nutmeg-hued Malays, honey-coloured Arabs, and pale-skinned Europeans and Chinese. There were red-haired Scots and white-headed Danes; merchants that had sailed in on grand, long-distance ships headed for Macau, and those who ventured in prahus that traversed regional seas. Everyone coming together peacefully for a single purpose: trade.

Martinha reached us first and kissed me on the cheek. Little Lanoon was at home with his sister, Sarah, she explained before thrusting a package into my hand. 'A gift from Francis and myself with our deepest thanks. Something to remember us by. Don't open it until you're over the horizon,' she said, adding with a smile, 'And don't drop it, it's very fragile.'

She crouched down to speak some parting words to her son, obviously distressed. Then Light puffed his way towards us. I used him as the excuse to turn away from the scene that had me, too, almost in tears.

'Here are two letters for George Doughty,' Light said after our initial greeting. I glanced down at the envelopes addressed to the High Sheriff of Suffolk at Theberton Hall. 'One bears instructions concerning William's education and its financing. The other is my letter of introduction for you. George is highly respected and very well connected. He will help you find other pupils to tutor or raise money for you to set up your own school, whichever you prefer.'

Light and I had talked often of my plans, now that the money he and James Scott had helped me earn from lucrative trades over the past year swelled my bank account in Madras. I had explained my love of teaching to him, something I had first discovered while tutoring William, Awang, and Othman. How I had no intention of shutting my pupils away from the real world with proscribed books, interacting only with those from their own class, race, and imagined superiority. I would teach them not to be fearful of challenging the prejudices of authoritarian rulers, of which some of the worst were schoolmasters.

I intended to help young boys become open-minded, curious individuals so that they could maturely reflect on and navigate through life in all its complexity and confusion. How to discern truth from propaganda, and how to take into account the viewpoints of people whose voices were often ignored or silenced and, without broader life experience, they might never come to know.

I accepted the missives with thanks and placed them in my jacket pocket. 'I have a gift for you,' I said, extracting a small box. 'For the pocket watch I lost. You know when.' I let my voice drift, not wishing to mention Pietronella's name. Somewhere near her tree hideout lay Light's original timepiece; I had never found it.

As I handed over the chain, our eyes met briefly. 'Have faith that William will make you proud. Through him, at the very least, the name Light will never be forgotten.'

'Thank you,' said Light. 'Be sure to tell Doughty to continue to plough his fields, for farming is a thousand times preferable to governing.'

I nodded, understanding the personal hell in which the man had opted to reign.

The elder and younger Lights spoke for many minutes, the boy barely holding back his tears. I knew what it was like to no longer have a mother or father you could count on. Laura had written me several letters during the past year, one of which informed me that Father had told her family he was amending his will in favour of his eldest brother's son, and they might wish to bear that in mind when considering their daughter's future. Cousin Leonard was the kind of compliant, uninspiring nincompoop my father obviously preferred to run his business. Like William, I was now a sort of an orphan too.

Captain Wall strode over to tell us that the ship's hands had completed their preparations; it was almost time to weigh anchor. After uttering our final farewells, I grasped William's hand, holding the package Martinha had given me with the other. His parents remained on the esplanade to wave us off.

As we watched Penang become more Lilliputian, I heard William sniff as if he had a cold. Periodically he would raise his right hand to swipe it across his face. I remained strangely dry-eyed but grasped the boy's shoulder in a gesture of support. While grateful for my education on that island it was what lay ahead of us that inflamed my passions most.

Later, as I tried to settle down for our first night on board, William kept badgering me to, 'Open it, open it!'

'You are beginning to sound as annoyingly repetitious as Friday,' I said, rising and cuffing him gently around the ear. 'Go on, bring it then.'

The boy eagerly did so and, in the candlelight, I pulled at the string and carefully peeled off the packaging of the Lights' gift.

'What is it?'

Holding it up to the candlelight I said, 'It's a toasting glass. Some years ago, I wrote a story about your father and his school friend, James Lynn, and what had inspired them to scratch their names on a school window where they were pupils in Suffolk. When you are older I will show it to you.' But William was less interested in that future promise than what I held in my hand.

'There's writing on it,' William pointed. 'What does it say?'

I held the glass up to the light and turned it gently to read aloud what had been finely inscribed there. Wisdom that Tuan Nakhoda Ismail had once impressed upon me and would forever guide my life:

When a man is dead his reputation lingers on among later generations.

Chapter 44

Leading Light

Midsomer Norton, Somerset, England. Saturday, 21 May 1842.

Dear Colonel William Light:

It is with great sadness that I write to inform you that my dear husband, James Lloyd, died the evening of the 16th instant. His funeral took place two days ago and was very well attended by friends, family, and former pupils.

In the week preceding his death which occurred, mercifully, after only a brief illness, James wished to relive the years in which he first met your father, and his subsequent adventures on the island of Penang. He somehow found the strength to communicate his Eastern experiences directly to me, but this was such a lengthy and emotional tale that he ran out of time in which to dictate a final letter to you. I hope this contribution will suffice.

I have enclosed two items, which I trust will reach you safely in your new colony of south Australia. The first is my husband's most prized possession: the toasting glass your mother and father gave him on his last day in Penang. I know you are already familiar with its existence not least the inscription, the meaning of which James so dearly took to heart.

The second is a short story he had penned as a young man—not unlike those written by his sadly missed friend, Sir Walter Scott—about your father's childhood desire to make his mark upon the world.

My husband was distressed to learn of the disgraceful way your father's executors, James Scott and William Fairlie, cheated your mother of her inheritance having sold your father's Penang Suffolk estate to a company official under her nose. We heard she sued them for breach of trust and misappropriation in the courts and won her case, but that the award was overturned on appeal. How very sad for a lady my husband held in the highest esteem.

James was also dismayed when news arrived that the Siamese—as Sultan Abdullah had long feared—had overrun Queda in November of 1821, whereupon their savagery was such that the sultan and many thousands of refugees were forced to flee to Penang, their lands and means of livelihood having been decimated. The intelligence we received suggested that not only did the British fail to protect Queda in any way but that they aided the invaders. What horrors men will perpetuate and sanction when they value transactions ahead of relationships. A choice my dear husband abhorred.

James found it laughable that the British government claimed that the tributary dependence of Queda on Siam, as implied by the tradition of bunga mas, relieved them of their duty to return that country to its rightful owner when they had so clearly recognised Queda as an independent state in 1786 and 1791. A shameful state of affairs that continues to this day, as far as we are aware.

But let me not dwell on unhappy thoughts, even though the loss of my dear departed husband is still raw.

James always spoke of you fondly. Indeed, of the hundreds of young students he helped to launch into the world, he thought of you more like a son. (A fact he was fond of telling our own two boys so often that in past years I fear they harboured a mild resentment towards you.) I will admit to my own jealousy, having heard of the many and varied talents you have displayed throughout your career: from your acquisition of several languages to the excellent water colour paintings that grace your books, *Sicilian Scenery* and *Views of Pompeii,* copies of which we were delighted to receive. Also, the illustrious company you kept during your naval and army careers, including King George IV; Lord Wellington; Sir George Napier, and the Pasha of Egypt. There was even some speculation that you met Napoleon Bonaparte whose sword you are reputed to have demanded he surrender on behalf of Lord Keith while serving on the *Bellerophon*. Perhaps you would let us know if that story is indeed true.

James was especially delighted when you notified him of your appointment as Surveyor-General of South Australia. Not least when learning that *you* determined the location of the new settlement named Adelaide despite considerable interference and opposition from the Governor and other colonists. My husband was amused to hear that in rebuffing one pompous settler who claimed you had ruined him by not ratifying his earlier, ill-advised land grab, you had told that gentleman he could publish his grievances about you in all the newspapers in England but would be taking a great deal of trouble and expense to prove himself an ass!

My husband regarded your sagacity to be rare among those who hold high ranks, but only to be expected from such a broadly experienced and knowledgeable officer and gentleman. Indeed, he expressed hope that one day we might see your life story memorialised in print.

Please call on us should you ever find yourself again in England. You and I have never met, but all here consider you family. As I learned over the years from my dearly departed, some friendships are more influential and enduring than ties of blood.

Yours very respectfully,
Laura Lloyd (Mrs)

Enclosure

A Tale of Young Francis Light

Woodbridge Free School, Suffolk. Autumn 1752.

Francis Light spits out the fingernail he has just ripped off and stares through the mullioned window in the school's upstairs corridor, watching pupils and masters swarm like nomadic ants across the quad on their way to Matins. He knows he has but three-quarters of an hour to complete the task his friend James Lynn has convinced him cannot be undertaken without a diamond. Something neither of these twelve-year olds own. But there is no sign of James yet. Even if he is not on his way to morning prayers, his friend might be hiding. Too embarrassed to show his face if he has failed to liberate the promised diamond from his mother's jewellery box.

To distract himself, Francis digs into a jacket pocket for his prized copy of Mr Samuel Johnson's *The Merry Thought: or, The Glass-Window and Bog House Miscellany*, in which the man who went by the pseudonym Hurlo Thrumbo had collected musings from those scratched on the windows of taverns, parlours, and even the panes of fine London houses. For amusement and to calm his irritation Francis presses the pamphlet between his palms to flatten it, then searches for the bawdiest verse he can find:

Damn Molley Havens for her Pride
She'll suffer none but Lords to ride:
But why the Devil should I care,
Since I can find another Mare?

The boy throws back his head and laughs, appreciating the writer's *double entendre* of that final word, 'Mare'. Then, with a sudden bolt of inspiration, he drops the pamphlet on the floor and rummages through his pockets. There, nestled in among a cache of conkers, he grasps his lucky charm.

Some weeks earlier, while Francis was gazing out at the ships anchored at Woodbridge harbour, dreaming of his future as a merchant trader, a sailor smoking nearby had called out to him. 'Hey, boy! You ever seen jade?' Francis only understood the word to mean a mare or fallen woman and thought the man was asking for directions to the local whorehouse. Pointing towards a nearby Inn, a favourite haunt of women known locally as being of 'ill repute', Francis saw the man grin as he took off his shoe. Poking within its toe, the sailor extracted a circular object the size of a guinea coin and the colour of water at low tide, flat on one side and carved with what the man described as a fortune horse on the other. Francis did not know if the sailor, who had told him tales of a faraway land called China, meant to leave the grey-green stone behind when he had gone to relieve himself. But he did not seem in any hurry to return and that exotic treasure had lain there like a siren, heightening Francis's desire to own it. That piece of jade has been hiding in his breeches ever since.

Francis wonders if his lucky charm might serve a different purpose now. Otherwise, if James has not secured the diamond he insisted they needed for this task, he might have to sneak into William Negus' bedroom while the old man and his wife Margaret are at church. Although his mother, Mary Light, has warned him time and again not to go up to the big house too often on account of him being Mr Negus' bastard.

The longcase clock in the downstairs hallway chimes the quarter hour. Behind him a stair creaks. Francis spins around, open-mouthed, ready with an excuse for not being where he should be. But it is only James with hair and clothes askew, as if he has just tried to retrieve a ball from inside a hedge.

'Almost got caught,' James pants, then holds out both hands, palms up, like a scoundrel clamped in the stocks. Empty. 'Sorry, Francis—no diamond.'

'We don't need it.' Francis kneels in front of a low pane of glass, as if about to pray. He begins to abrade the glass window with the jade.

'Why're we doing this again?'

'Shush. Let me work in peace,' Francis whispers to his friend. With mounting delight, he sees that the swirls and lines will soon be recognisable. This isn't vandalism but an accomplishment, something important. Emulating those prominent politicians and men of letters of the Kit-Kat Club in London who scrape the walls of conveniences and on the sides of fine crystal goblets not just to be amusing or amorous, but to be *remembered*.

Minutes later, with a final flourish, Francis sits back on his haunches and beams with satisfaction at his work. He reverently hands over the jade and James begins to abrade the glass in order to add his name—J. Lynn—in the space above that of F. Light. As James works, Francis recites some of his favourite verses from Mr Johnson's collection, too absorbed to hear the downstairs clock chime once again. But when James grabs his arm, looking as crouched and wide-eyed as a grotesque on the church roof, the talisman suspended in mid-air between his fingers, Francis hears the low noise of excited voices too.

'We're goin' to get caught,' whispers his friend, nervously.

Animated by a lightning bolt of urgency, Francis lifts his eyes away from the pamphlet and peers through the window. Outside, boys and schoolmasters spill out of the church, their chattering faint but growing. 'Are you done?'

James hands back the stone. He blows white dust from his fingertips and rubs his nose as if to stifle a sneeze. 'Yes.' Then he looks up, an unspoken question emblazoned across his face.

Francis begins to examine the jade for damage. 'Go! I'll be right behind you.'

With mumbled thanks, James bounds down the stairs.

The noise from outside has increased in intensity. Somewhere below him a door bursts open and boys agitated from sitting too long in church run like demons along the corridors. Determined to bask in this moment for as long as possible despite the risk of getting caught, Francis traces a finger across the etchings. At both their names expressed in the glass. His first mark on the world, but not his last.

While admiring his handiwork, another revelation takes hold. He could have executed this daring achievement without his friend's help. For what had James done, *really*, to bring it about? Francis had come up with the idea to use the jade talisman instead of a diamond to scratch the glass. *He* had inspired their actions, ones similarly taken by the kind of prominent men Francis intends not only to know as equals in years to come, but who will one day speak of him in awe. In a few years' time, he will be out on the open seas like the adventurer Sir Francis Drake, whose fighting ships were built in Woodbridge harbour. A hero whose deeds and glory, despite his being dead a century and a half already, have never been forgotten and never will.

With a sense that if he raises his arms aloft he could touch the ceiling, twelve-year-old Francis Light turns around and, with a triumphant burst of energy, vaults down the stairs, laughing inwardly at the easy lie he will tell about why he did not attend church. Rejoicing in the fact that his name—first here at Woodbridge and soon the wider world—will never be erased.

SIGNATURES OF FRANCIS LIGHT (lower)
AND JAMES LYNN (upper)
ON WOODBRIDGE FREE SCHOOL WINDOW

THE END

Acknowledgements

The 'Hero's Journey' became as true for me as a novelist as it was for my protagonist, Jim Lloyd. This novel would not exist had it not been for my good friend, Keith Hockton, co-founder of Penang-based Entrepot Publishing. As the 'Herald' and catalyst for my own 'inciting incident', it was Keith who, shortly after I arrived in Penang, outlined how tenuous Francis Light's hold on Penang had been in the early years of the East India Company's possession.

While I was comfortable digging into the research, with decades of experience as a journalist and non-fiction author, my past experience was not enough to make me a novelist. I needed to find great 'Mentors'. Kimberly Kessler helped me apply the principles developed by Shawn Coyne of Story Grid to produce a good first draft. Then author, screenwriter, editor, and story development consultant extraordinaire, Jeff Lyons, guided me as I pulled it all apart for a major rewrite. Thanks to both for their expertise and wisdom.

I was embarking on a long and perilous journey (almost four years in total), and knew that I needed 'Allies' to help me: My deepest thanks to Jennifer Rouse who suggested we take an early road-trip to Alor Star for a visit to the Kedah Royal Museum, located at the site of former palaces of Kedah sultans dating back to 1735; N.A.R.K.N.N. Nachiappan who helped explain the history of the Chettiars during one of Penang's wonderful cultural tours (and now has a character named after him). I am indebted to the many Malay historians and other experts who so generously shared their knowledge and resources. These include the staff of the National Library of Singapore where I spent many happy pre-pandemic weekends conducting research; Ooi Keat Gin, Honorary Professor, School of Humanities, Universiti Sains Malaysia and Honorary Advisor, the International Journal of Asia Pacific Studies; Dr. Shaikh Mohd Saifuddeen bin Shaikh Mohd Salleh, Senior Fellow/Director at the Institute of Islamic Understanding Malaysia; and Professor Dato' Dr Ahmad Murad Merican Noor Mohamad, professor at the International Institute of Islamic Thought and Civilisation, IIUM KL campus.

I have been very fortunate to benefit from the insights, guidance, and eagle-eyes of superb early readers. My deepest thanks and appreciation go to Anushia Kandasamy; Daniel Rosien; Patricia Jamieson; and Pauline Mortensen for their candid feedback. With special recognition to Helen Guy and Michael Toussaint who went above and beyond for not only reading one draft, but the extensive rewrite I made after it. Sincere thanks also to amazing author and editor Azlina Ahmad who saved me much future embarrassment by pointing out the most dastardly of errors: the ones I didn't know I didn't know.

Every writer should become intimate with their 'Shadow', whose evil whisperings can stymie even the most determined of writers. Luckily I was brought up by parents—Jimmy and Joyce Alexander, *sedih meninggal dunia*—who not only imbued me with great curiosity and a love of words, but the characteristics necessary to overcome many 'tests and enemies' and retain my passion for lengthy projects such as this one. I miss you, Mum and Dad.

Last, but by no means least, my deepest thanks go to Nora Nazarene Abu Bakar, Associate Publisher, and her team at Penguin Random House SEA—with a special shout-out to my wonderful editor, Thatchaayanie Renganathan—who helped this debut novelist 'return with the elixir'. To be published by such an internationally respected brand is beyond any reward I could have wished for.

Terima kasih, semua!

Glossary

Bankshall:	Derived from Malay word *bangsal* meaning barn or shed.
Betul:	Malay word for 'That's right.'
Burra-khana:	Hindi word for a feast or banquet.
Conkers:	Horse-chestnuts, strung together for childhood game.
East India Company (EIC):	Also known as The Honourable Company and John Company.
Glacis:	A downward slope around a fortification.
Gudang:	Malay word for warehouse, corrupted as 'godown' by Europeans.
Gundek:	Malay word for concubine or courtesan attached to the palace harem
Istana:	Malay word for a palace.
Jaga-jaga:	Lookout or guard boat.
Jawi script:	Derived from Arabic script, in which court correspondence, official texts and agreements were originally written at the time.
Junk Ceylon:	Modern day Phuket, Thailand. A corruption of Ulang Salang or Tanjung Thalang.
Koyan(s):	Malay unit to weigh grains.
Lanun:	Malay word for pirate, mispronounced as Lanoon.
Makkah:	Mecca.
Mati:	Dead or died in Malay

Maund(s):	Indian unit of weight.
Mejuffer:	Dutch word for Miss.
Mengkuang mat:	Colourful floor-covering made from screwpine leaves.
Mussulmen:	One of various 18th century terms used by the English for Muslims.
Nabob:	Word used in colonial India, derived from the Urdu *Nawab*, to describe someone returning to Europe from India with a large fortune.
Nibong:	Palm tree that provides timber, with leaves used for roof thatches and basket-weaving.
Penjara:	Malay word for jail or prison.
Perkenier:	Dutch plantation owner.
Prahu:	Malay word for a sailing boat, also war vessel.
Puloo/ Poolo/Pulo:	Various spellings used in 18th century for 'island' (now Pulau in Malay).
Rakyat:	Malay word for the people or citizenry.
Rumah:	Malay word for house or home.
Sambal:	Hot chili paste made with ingredients including garlic, lemongrass, fish sauce, and tamarind.
Seruling:	A small bamboo flute.
Siam:	Former name of Thailand.
Snow:	Small sailing ship.
Specie:	Currency or coinage (as opposed to bank notes).
Towkay:	A business owner or boss.
VOC:	The Vereenigde Oost-Indische Compagnie or Dutch East India Company.
Wakil:	Official representative, delegate, or agent.

Endnotes

[1] Samuel Johnson, '"Of the Duty of a Journalist": Contributions to the Universal Chronicle and the Public Ledger (1758-60)', in The Works of Samuel Johnson, Vol. 20 (Yale University Press, 2019), p. 406

[2] Alexander Dalrymple, *Oriental Repertory: Published at the Charge of the East India Company. (United Kingdom: W. Ballintine, 1808) p. 586.*

[3] *The Burney Papers Vol. 2.* (United Kingdom: Gregg International, 1971) p. 171

[4] E. H. S. Simmonds, "Francis Light and The Ladies of Thalang" in *Journal of the Malaysian Branch of the Royal Asiatic Society*, Vol. 38, No. 2 (208), (Malaysian Branch of the Royal Asiatic Society)December, 1965

[5] E. H. S. Simmonds, "Francis Light and The Ladies of Thalang" in *Journal of the Malaysian Branch of the Royal Asiatic Society*, Vol. 38, No. 2 (208), (Malaysian Branch of the Royal Asiatic Society)December, 1965

[6] E. H. S. Simmonds, "Francis Light and The Ladies of Thalang" in *Journal of the Malaysian Branch of the Royal Asiatic Society*, Vol. 38, No. 2 (208), (Malaysian Branch of the Royal Asiatic Society)December, 1965

[7] Marcus Langdon, *Penang: The Fourth Presidency of India 1805-1830*, Volume 2, pages 26-27

[8] Harold Parker Clodd, *Malaya's First British Pioneer: The Life of Francis Light (London: Luzac, 1948)*